Bannock

Inner City (Polygon, 1987)

Bannock

A Novel

Ian McGinness

Polygon
EDINBURGH

© Ian McGinness 1990
Polygon
22 George Square, Edinburgh

Set in Linotron Sabon and Bauer Bodoni
by Koinonia, Bury
Printed and bound in
Great Britain by
Redwood Press Ltd, Melksham, Wiltshire

British Library Cataloguing in
Publication Data
McGinness, Ian
    Bannock
    I. Title
    823'.914 [F]

ISBN 0 7486 6060 7

The publishers acknowledges subsidy
from the Scottish Arts Council towards
the publication of this volume

Waking Up In A Strange Town

My suitcases and I were travelling by public transport because my wife had stolen our car. 'It's just as much mine as it is yours,' Joyce had said, just before the keys disappeared into her jacket pocket to form the kind of bulge which demanded to be patted.

This appropriation had annoyed me but I didn't do anything about it. My motto at this time might have been, 'Anything For A Quiet Life'. My aim was to avoid stress, even at the cost of self esteem. I had an ego the size of a gnat's ball.

The Sunday bus from the city was a slow affair but I was in no hurry to arrive. There were only a few other passengers: a man asleep on a female shoulder. A middle-aged mother with a retarded son. Two old ladies with tight perms. A uniformed soldier. And me: sleepless and hungover, my possessions squeezed under the seat in front and balanced in the luggage rack above my head.

When the bus left me alone on the station platform I looked around at nothing and felt the silence of someone else's town. No one saw me as I shuffled through the ticket office, no one passed me as I walked along the streets towards my boarding house. There seemed to be no movement and none of the usual sounds I was accustomed to in the city. The creak of my shoes, the rub of the bags on my trouser leg, my breathing: all of these seemed louder, more significant than should have been the case. I watched my shop window reflection approach without recognition. We met then passed, heading in different directions.

Through backstreets, following the map in my head, I reached my lodgings in Tummle Row. The storm shutters were open but the glass inner doors were closed and locked. A light shone through the frosting but no one answered the silent bell or my knock on the letterbox. Not even a dog barked. It was the end of the world.

I left my cases behind a low wall and hoisted my umbrella against the soft rain which drifted through the glow from the

1

sodium lights. My shirt was wet against my chest but the night was warm. As I walked, I flexed my stiff fingers and felt the tightness ease in my shoulders.

The streets were still empty but from somewhere in the distance, over the rooftops, I could hear an engine revving slowly. Further on, I heard voices: raised high then trailing off, then bursting out again. Those human sounds became louder as I walked, and the sky seemed to lighten.

There was a thump, then the sound of running feet, then what sounded like an exhortation and a roar. I walked on. Louder. More lights, the street opening out: the town square, cornered with floodlit statues. Figures, frozen, looking sky-wards. More shouts, feet running once more, coming closer, then a whoosh and a smack as an irregular object landed in a puddle and bounced around my legs. A group of large men in what seemed to be medieval dress came running towards me; others leapt around in the background and made trumpeting noises with their fists and lips. Nearer. Straight for me. The towel-wrapped, red-stained ball rolled towards the gutter. The men, closer. I smelled the embrocation, felt their heat as they passed. The ball was held: a tackle, down on the hard, wet pavement. A man got to his feet; the ball in the air again, the chase moving to the other side of the square.

About fifty players seemed to be participating in the confused game. Others, dressed in similar fashion staggered around the perimeter of play, obviously drunk. The ball headed my way again and I pressed close to the protective bulk of one of the statues.

Then, a series of impacts on the stretched nylon above my head: a manic, geiger-counter burst against the shouts and the soft, hissing background of the drizzling night. It made me jump. Out of my pants, out of my shoes, out of my pink, crinkly-wet skin suit. But then, everything did at the time. Make me jump, I mean. I was stressed; under strain: jumpy. Scared shitless of everything from a spider stitch to the sound of a farting cat.

I skipped over those puddles like a dancing star and from a safe distance looked up and saw the source of the stream against the clouded moon. A man sat in the vast lap of the statue above me, adopting the same looming shape in the dark.

2

The only difference was the white mouse which protruded from the smaller figure's trousers, and the voice, which seemed to emerge from under the verdigrised topcoat or from some bronze bellybutton, but in fact came from the mouth in the shadows.

'Enjoying the game?' He raised his arm to point to the spectacle in the square and leaned forward into the glow of a spotlight. 'Hm?' He looked down at me expectantly, his eyes wide apart in a drink-reddened face. The arm moved upwards and back. A hand rubbed a flat, broken nose then squeezed rain from blue-black hair which stood up from his forehead in an electric, manic sweep. I looked at the game, then back at him, and nodded:

'Very interesting.' The ball appeared to be lost in a gigantic, swirling scrum.

'We're an interesting people. This is just one of our many historical festivals. Swattin' The Turk. I must tell you its origins when I sober up. I'm an expert in things like that.' The living statue obviously had perfect control over his sphincter muscles because he began to piss again. Not just a trickle but the kind of gushing stream only a beer drinker would recognise. At its end, he leaned towards the centre of the square once, twice, then launched himself into the air to land with the luck of a man who has been drinking all day. 'Wait for me!'

Where Am I?

In Bannock. A stone-built town of six thousand. In the valley of the River Irk. 'The Silvery Burn'. Which flows fast and then slow, seventy miles before it is absorbed by the sea.

It is a town with a history: everywhere you go there are statues and plaques, and the homes where famous men and women were born. Street names refer not to trees and flowers but to people and events from the past. This means that every time a person who lives in Bannock receives a letter or a bill or

3

a circular, there, on the envelope, below the name, is a reminder of how things once were.

Bannock, like a hundred thousand other collections of buildings, is the friendliest place on the planet. The town has a motto which emphasises the point. That motto reads: 'Hail, Laddie, An' Feckle In The Nook'. Roughly translated, this means: 'Lay your head on the comforting, homely lap that is our pride, our modest joy. There you may sleep until your name is engraved in stone with ours, until the Irkdale grass grows over the soft, crumbling surface of your memorial.'

It's a comforting thought.

I lived in Bannock for a short while. I went there because there seemed no better place to go. I wasn't thinking clearly at the time. I wanted to escape from everything and thought a two hour bus trip would do the trick. As you can imagine, I was wrong.

During the course of my first week in the town, I found out who the pissing statue was. This wasn't terribly difficult as I saw lots of people every day as a matter of routine. I was actually introduced to many of them by Mr Macroom, my immediate superior in the Bannock branch of the Royal Northern Bank:

'Hello, Mrs Trumpeter. May I introduce Mr Weems, my new assistant manager?' 'My' assistant manager: I had been sold into bondage.

'Good morning, minister. Can I introduce you to the latest member of my team?' 'Member of my team': suddenly, I was a wing-threequarter; the latest spin bowler. Play up, Bannock!

'Mr Bogle, could I interrupt you for a second to meet the latest member of our happy crew?' 'Happy crew': chained to an oar; keelhauled; weevilled biscuits.

All those names, all of those faces. Very few of them stuck, because my grey matter was dissolving in its own juices. My thoughts were not concentrated on the world of Bannock banking, not concentrating on anything, but were radiating in a thousand directions: flashing past Bogle's chequebook stubs; singeing the minister's pink deposit slips. But I smiled anyway, because it was expected. And I nodded and tried to joke while absorbing nothing.

Brain input was retained for a maximum of ten seconds. There was too much competition for space. 'Depressive Anxiety' my city doctor called it, as he wrote out a prescription for those beautiful, yellow and green capsules that I flushed down the pan the following day.

I regretted my actions almost immediately.

The happy-pills looked like little lifeboats as they bobbed in the blue sea of the toilet bowl.

I Needed A Lifeboat

I sure did.

But I wanted it to be manned. I wanted to see smiling faces on board, feel comforting arms around me as they dragged me from the waves.

Later, when I read a brain book, I saw the water as my own history: a tide over which I had no control, in which I was drowning. Or being drowned: slowly and sadistically.

The book was called *The Psychopathology Of Everyday Life*. It had been written at the beginning of this century by a man called Sigmund Freud.

I found the book in the home of Stanislaw Kowalik, a man who, despite his name, had been born and raised in Bannock. Stan became a friend during my stay there. He made friends easily. His wife told me that this was because Stan had a great desire to be loved. By everyone. (She viewed her hubby with great insight. Maybe she was a brain doctor in her spare time.)

We didn't stay friends for long. Stan burned people off without noticing. He didn't even remember them when he flicked flecks of their ash from the shoulder of his suit.

Anyway that's all in the past; or rather, in the future as far as this short anamnesis is concerned.

An Adoption Agency

'George, welcome to Bannock.' And so, with a watery smile, Macroom had greeted my arrival on day one of my self-imposed sentence. 'I'm afraid the red carpet is away at the cleaners. Ha, ha.' The expression switched, like a sequence change on a neon sign. 'But seriously, George, I do welcome you, to the bank, to your new job with all its added responsibilities, and, perhaps most of all, to our community; to the town.' Change to smile mode. 'Or as we 'Bannock Bunters' say, 'Hail, laddie, an' feckle in the nook'.'

I was barely receptive to normal conversation. Macroom's words must have produced a bemused look on my face.

'You look puzzled, George.' I was now treated to a whimsical, yet fatherly expression. (One dad is enough for any man, thank you very much indeed.) I felt physically ill but tried to rearrange my features in a neutral sort of a way. 'I think I'm going to have to take you under my wing.' (Feathers with body odour; a moulting, corvine oxter. Clear the decks, I'm going to boak.) 'We can't have you living in the grand old town of Bannock and not know anything of the local dialect and history.' Sick grin from me. 'Once you settle down I'll lead you gently into our ways.'

'That's very kind of you, Mr Macroom.' The shame of it all.

'After all.' Neon switch three: business as usual. 'A man in your position should have a full knowledge of the people he is dealing with. And I'm not going to be here in this office for ever. Who knows where a bright young man might end up. If he fits in.' Macroom stood up to show that the short interview was over. I stood up too, and knocked a fat file on to the carpet.

'It might be an idea to look over some of this material, George, if you can find the time in the midst of all your upheaval.' I looked up from my position on the floor to see Macroom, seated once more, tunnelling behind his desk top. He emerged with a wad of pamphlets which he dumped two inches from my eyes. 'I happen to be a member of the Local History Society: publications secretary, as a matter of fact. And these,' Macroom pointed to the mouldy pile before me, 'are some of our little efforts. I looked them out for you last night.'

'Thanks very much, Mr Macroom. That's very kind of you.' How could I do it?

'Not at all. Take them with my compliments. They might help you to understand some of our little ways.' Macroom laughed his tight-mouthed laugh and leaned over the desk to pat some of the dust from his gift. 'Perhaps we can discuss them one day. Or you might even decide to join our small group. We are fortunate to live in an area so rich in history.' Macroom rose to his feet once more and looked me in the eye as I replaced the file before him. 'We ignore the past at our peril, George.' He stretched his hand towards me, grasped my damp palm in his, and held on to it tightly, intimately. 'But let me just say, we have, from time to time, opportunities to put behind us episodes from the past which perhaps we might rather forget. These opportunities are precious. They should not be squandered. This fine country air can allow a man to breath again. Expand your chest. Fill those lungs.' Macroom gave me a demonstration, still holding tight my sweating hand. 'Isn't it wonderful to be alive?'

Sweat

Not only my palm was damp. My whole back was running with sweat. I couldn't cope any more with pressure, even of the mildest kind. Sometimes, my pants were so wet, a casual observer might have suspected an incontinence problem. My armpits were swamps, my deodorant bill enormous: roll-ons, sprays, aerosols – I needed to be encased in plastic. Despite cotton socks, maniaical scrubbing and special inserts in my shoes, my feet were beginning to smell, so much so that I began to worry that they were rotting: putrefying like fish on a quay; fallen bananas; a dead rat under the floorboards. Sometimes, I could smell food I had consumed as juices exuded through my pores. One day I would walk around like a mobile tandoori, an onion bhaji with legs, a perambulating pakora. On another, colleagues walked in my chilli slipstream as I moved through the bank in a Tex-Mex haze. At meetings I had to continually dab sweat from my face with a handkerchief or else be salt-blinded. It would drip from my nose, from my chin, soak my eyebrows and hair, stain my shirt collar as it trickled down my spine to collect in pools among the hair which grew in the small of my back. I had to watch which clothes I wore, had to discard favourite pieces from my wardrobe. When I wore my cream summer suit I looked like an Alabaman slave overseer, a Florida Keys rummy, a brothel keeper from Manaus on the Upper Amazon. With every movement, dark, damp, patches spread from seam to seam, threatening to merge into one vast, osmotic ocean. Sometimes I could almost hear the whirr of the overhead fan and the buzz of mosquitoes in my ear.

A Mosquito In My Ear

'God, you're disgusting.'

Nice, eh? 'Disgusting'. That's how Joyce saw me the morning she informed me she was moving to the spare room. All I was doing at the time was eating a lightly boiled egg, dipping bread into the yolk, popping the agreeably soggy slice into my gob. I looked up from my paper in some surprise to see her back going through the door into the living room. I was silent. Ten seconds later she reappeared.

'I'm fed up looking at your egg-stained face over the breakfast table, do you hear?' I did. 'And another thing...'

Here comes another thing. 'I've spent my last night squelching in that swamp we sleep in.' I was plagued with night sweats at the time. 'It's like lying beside a frog.' The prince: trapped, bewitched; no one understood.

It was no use arguing with Joyce when she was in that sort of mood. Anyway, what was I to argue about? Most breakfast times, my face was egg stained: what was the problem? I could wash it off. The bed was damp. I was wet almost constantly; my skin wept at night. What then? Plead for forgiveness? I am very, very sorry. I will never have an eggy face again, as long as I live, so help me god. For understanding? My nocturnal sweatings are a symptom of an underlying malaise. Hug me and say you love me.

What about losing my temper? Unfortunately, it wasn't in my nature. Not that it would have done any good. Joyce wanted an argument. I did not. She was looking for a set-piece battle which would end in her packing her bags and marching out, or whose climax would involve my possessions flying through an upstairs window into the street. I always tried to avoid unpleasantness. I was frightened of losing what I didn't really want. A drop of sweat fell from my nose to the table. I dabbed another soldier into the congealing goo of my boiled egg.

'God, does nothing get through to you these days?' Very little did, does, in any real sense, any sense beyond the neurotic. Sorry.

'When you get back from work, I'll have moved into the blue room.' Even in this moment of crisis, she remembered the name she had once given to our spare bedroom. Take Monsieur Le Duc to the Chambre Bleu. We lived in the Palace of Versaille. 'It will be my room. That means not your room. I don't want to see you in there. I need to escape.'

I wanted to help her, I really did. If it had been within my power, if it would have facilitated her flight. Just to please her, to win favour, I would have dug a tunnel, scraped mortar from the brickwork with a sharpened spoon handle, stuffed a dummy with sawdust to fool the Kommandant at roll call. Can I book you on the next flight to Rio? The Express to Trieste? Secure a seat at the Captain's table? No, not any of these things. Just remove your yellow-spot face and keep your clammy hands to yourself. I am out of bounds in the west wing. Incommunicado. I want to be alone.

'Alone'. Actually, this was not the case at all. In fact, Joyce wanted lots and lots of company. For much of the time, our house was full of people whose names I did not know. Joyce wanted me to be alone, not her. Confined to my room ('The Master Bedroom') in case I frightened or offended anyone. *The Incredible Sweating Egg*.

A few weeks later, on my return from work, I found the living room full of talk, coffee cups and crumbs. Half a dozen of Joyce's female friends had come over for a chat, bringing little gifts like cream cakes, or tiny wooden ducks, or the most beautiful pebbles they had found on the loch shore. (By this time I hated even inanimate objects.) They had brought with them their pre-school children, dressed variously as Bolivian peasants, or rainbow clogdancers, or engaging, middle-class ragamuffins.

As I entered the room silence fell. Breaking it, my wife gestured towards me in a grand manner:

'Ladies and gentlemen, may I present the lodger.'

Everyone laughed, including the kids, who followed the example of their mothers. It was great to see everyone enjoying themselves so thoroughly. To see everyone having such a wonderful time.

Poles

'Hello, Mrs Tummle, this is Mr Weems, my new...'

Yes, Bannock is a friendly place. After a few days, half the town knew me by name, nodded to me in the street, discussed what I had bought for my tea from Fiorentini's fish and chip shop.

On the Friday of my first working week, the man who had pissed on my head came into the bank. He did not seem to remember me. My features merged in with the calendar on the wall and the pots of geraniums on the counter.

10

He entered with a group of noisy companions, male and female, all of whom looked as if they had drank a good bucket. They seemed to be speaking a foreign language. Was it unadulterated Bannock patois, or had alcohol damaged their capacity for speech? I couldn't understand a word but felt I wanted to be part of the show. Instead, I was stranded on the other side of the counter: suited, sober, silent; trapped inside an eggshell.

Disturbed by the noise, Macroom emerged from his little mousehole and peered around, whiskers twitching. He began to say something then appeared to reconsider, turned tail, silently pulled the door shut behind him.

I watched them all furtively as they blew through the bank on a gust of energy. I saw the broken-nosed man fan himself with a newly acquired wad of notes. I saw him leer at Kathy, the teller, and carelessly, proprietorially drape his arm round the shoulder of an attractive woman who radiated gin and sex. When they left, I could hear the ticking of the battery clock which hung above my desk.

I felt resentful when they had gone. I was envious of those who appeared socially at ease, yet they filled me with suspicion, as if they had won this particular facility through a pact with the devil in which they had sacrificed integrity, sensitivity, intelligence. My role models were the corpses of Grover Cleveland and Lord Baden-Powell; the mummified remains of Clement Atlee. People who enjoyed themselves without inhibition made me feel morally superior, while at the same time I secretly longed to join them. Why had they left me behind? The man who had pissed on my head did not even have the decency to recognise me. Could they not have thought of me for a moment? Was I completely invisible?

I arranged my face in a sneer which developed into a nervous tic and asked Kathy who the revellers had been. She laughed:

'Oh, them? They're Stan Kowalik's Poles. It looks as if they enjoyed themselves at lunch.'

'Stan's Poles?'

'Stan's the one with the broken nose and all the money. Hair standing up like a buck goat.' I nodded:

'We've met.'

'So, you'll know Stan's Polish. Or at least his dad was.

11

Stan's actually Bannock born and bred. But then, if you've talked to him you'll probably know that anyway.'

'Well, we didn't have the chance to do much in the way of discussion.'

'The others are real Poles, if you see what I mean. They come over from time to time on business. Stan always takes them out for a big blow-out. He's quite a lad, although some people think he's a bit....' At this, Kathy made a circling movement with an index finger, pointing towards her right temple to indicate that some people thought that 'Stan' was screwy, nuts, coco-pops: a wild, whacky character. What kind of person would constitute a threat to the stability of Bannock? What kind of person would be too hot for the townspeople to handle? A twitching corpse in a mortuary. Suddenly, I felt a sense of solidarity with the Pole. Maybe we could be outsiders together and spend our spare time laughing at everyone else.

Holy Christ, the urge to kill. A wave passed over me: panic as I contemplated my fate in that town which had as much relevance to me as Ulan Bator. Anger towards all of the innocent people whom I blamed for my predicament. I wanted to replace that index finger with a brace and bit, to bite into Kathy's skull, to expose the damp sawdust that lay inside. Then split Macroom with an axe, add his bones to the pile. Then tackle each customer with a hammer and chisel: just one tap, neatly down the middle like an Easter egg. A long line: the whole population of the town. Crack, crack, crack with a hardwood mallet until I was knee-deep in chocolate splinters, eggshell, coconut shards, and deflated innards.

But then, what right did I have? I should have been first in line for trepanation. Stand back: see the gas escape from the hole. My anger was useless. It was used up in dreams. I was frightened to focus it correctly in case I might be injured.

When I told my city doctor I was leaving for Bannock, he told me a depressive carries his burden with him like a hunchback's hump. Regardless of geographical location, I would be a prisoner of my medical history. Drowning, as the lifeboats floated out to sea.

12

Nice

After work, I invited Kathy for a drink to celebrate the end of my first week. My homicidal urges had subsided. I needed company.

She hesitated briefly then, perhaps seeing my desperation, agreed: 'That'll be nice,' she said. Kathy thought a lot of things were nice. And most people. Almost everything in the world. She was very, very lucky. I asked where we should go. She suggested the lounge bar of The Old Mill. 'It's very nice there,' she said. See what I mean? 'But only one, mind, my man's waiting at home looking after the kids. I'll have to get home to let him out to his bowling.'

'Oh, he's a bowler, is he?' I asked. 'That's nice.' Stop it.

'Mad keen he is. He'll take you along one night if you fancy.'

'Oh, that'd be....' By this time we had reached the pub and turned in.

Kathy sat with a Dry Martini and lemonade, I with a pint of lager and a whisky. The whisky disappeared quickly. I had to restrain myself from throwing back the pint in a couple of gulps. I wondered if Kathy would buy a round too. Would she think I was an alcoholic if I bought another before she had finished? In those days, I was very concerned with what people thought of me, assuming that everyone's views counted, except my own. My confidence had gone. It had been sandpapered off.

'Another, Kathy?'

'No, thanks.' She eyed my empty glasses. 'You must be very thirsty.' It's this Amazonian heat.

'What a week,' I said as I came back with my refills, hoping this would be viewed as an excuse for my excessive drinking. Kathy gripped my arm, causing me to slop on the table. She whispered:

'Up at the bar.' I looked round, bewildered. 'Don't look round.' I slopped again. 'That woman who just came in. Don't look round.' I froze, crouched, knees bent, hands holding my glasses out towards the table. 'That's Stan's wife.' I couldn't see.

'Remember Stan?' I remembered, nodded. 'From the bank?' Nodded again. 'He's probably not been home yet. She'll be out searching for him. Probably better if she didn't find him.'

I sneaked a look, saw a brown pigtail wave over a waxed jacket and muddied wellingtons, caught a soft profile as she turned, swept the lounge, over, through me, like Stan.

'Stan could be a hundred miles from here now. Poor soul.'

'Poor soul?' By this time the woman had gone. 'Which one?'

'I suppose that depends on how you look at things.'

'How come?' Why did I care? It was just conversation. It filled in time. Filled up space. What was it to me?

'Well...' Kathy leaned forward and began to tell me of the lives and times of Mr and Mrs Stan Kowalik. She provided lots and lots of local background information. Everything was accurate in every detail. Bannock was full of historians. It made me feel lucky to be part of it all.

How Lucky Can You Get?

That night, at my boarding house, long after I had said goodbye to Kathy but not long after I had left the pub, I started writing. This was something I often did, and still do, when drunk. With often startling results. So startling I often cannot understand a word the next, furry-mouthed morning.

Feeling depressed and alone in a strange town, I decided to try to cheer myself up by making a list of good points in my life which might be grounds for optimism. This is it. It is valuable source material for this short history. It is an original document.

1. Health – reasonable.

2. Finances – not too bad, especially with new job, no ties.

3. Job – not too demanding or stressful. Possibility of further promotion.

4. Environment – beautiful. Lots of tourists come here to admire the scenery.

5. Interests – playing the guitar, squash, tennis, chess. Music, literature, cinema, travel, writing.

6. Friends – since splitting up with my wife, I have discovered who my real friends are.

7. Family – since splitting up with my wife, I have grown closer to my family.

8. No impediment to sexual fulfilment.

9. No history of criminality or deviance.

10. I am alive. Lots of people are dead.

The exercise helped. I went to bed feeling happier than in a long time. I had pleasant dreams. The effect even lasted through to next morning. When I awoke, I reread the list and, instead of putting it in the bin with the rest of my drunken drivel, I pinned it to the wall with a pin from a shirt box.
After a moment's thought, I took it down again and added a title. The title was: 'Cheer Up! It's Not The End Of The World!'

Back When I Thought It Was The End Of The World

When Joyce finally left me, or rather, when she squeezed me out, I thought it was the end of the world and I did not want to go on with my life any more.
However, I did not kill myself. I went to Bannock.
And in Bannock, I found out that doctors are sometimes right. I found out that, as had been predicted, I carried my depression with me like the hump of a hunchback.

Sometimes I would forget it was there but always it waited for me. I saw its shadow on the pavement, or caught a glimpse in a shop window. I did not want to be reminded of it and sometimes I thought if I dug up the concrete or smashed the glass it would disappear. But that did not work.

When I woke up some mornings the hump had spread over the pillow and folded itself over my face, suffocating me.

Another List

At the end of a nasty evening back in the city, after another one sided row with Joyce, I suggested that, as a form of therapy, we should each sit down and construct a list of what we perceived to be the other's faults. Joyce didn't see the point. She said things had gone too far for Mickey Mouse solutions. But after much persuading she agreed.

We sat down at opposite ends of the kitchen table, each with a pen and a sheet of headed bank notepaper. At first she looked at me, not at the page, but then she smirked and began to write, slowly at first, then more quickly. She smirked a lot, and once laughed out loud. She muffled her laughter with her hand and apologised. I added to my list.

When we had both finished, we silently exchanged papers. This is what she wrote about me:

1. You are a mess. You seem to take no interest in your appearance. Your clothes are always stained with food and beer and God knows what else. Your hair looks like the pelt of a frightened skunk.

2. Your eating habits are revolting. This, in turn, contributes to problem number one, i.e. egg and gravy stains, etc.

3. You drink too much. This makes you snore and dribble in bed.

16

4. You are rude to my friends. Why? Do they make you feel inadequate?

5. You ignore my ambitions. You know I begin my university course in a few months but you will not discuss the future and how we can manage without my money coming into the house. Basically, you don't care.

6. I am fed up hearing about what you are going to do in the future. About giving up your job and travelling the world, etc, etc, etc. Why don't you get up off your backside and do something for a change instead of just sitting there boring everyone with your fantasies.

7. Even when you are not fantasising you are still a bore. You are full of self pity. I am tired of hearing how the world has given you a bad deal. Snap yourself out of it for God's sake before you send both of us round the twist.

8. I have had enough of your delusions about being a misunderstood artist. What gives you the idea that you have any talent whatsoever? Surely not the rubbish you write when you are drunk, the stuff that you wake me up to read. And what happened to your painting phase? What about all the money you poured down the drain on oils and watercolours and paper and canvas. Where did it all lead to? I'll tell you, it led to a pile of junk lying in the garage and to you boasting in the pub about how once you used to be someone else.

9. You have no real ambition. You will stay in that little job at the bank for the rest of your life, whining about it every day. At least I had the guts to do something about it.

10. I have had enough of this house with its tiny rooms and paper thin walls. We are surrounded by idiots which is, I suppose, the reason you don't want to move. What about the flat we were going to buy in the city? I suppose that was too much of a challenge for you.

11. You sweat all of the time. But I suppose you can't help it, can you.

12. You are always making out lists. Now you've got me doing it too. Does that make you happy? Does that make you feel as if we have grown closer together?

13. I don't want to go on with this any longer.

You Don't Want To Go On With This Any Longer? I Don't Want To Go On With This Any Longer.

On the afternoon of my third Sunday in Bannock, I went out to the pub but ended up walking in the park along the banks of the River Irk. But I didn't stay long. Too many people.

I wasn't feeling too good. There was an ants' nest inside my head and I just wanted to reach the refuge of my room in the boarding house where no one would bother me. There was a bottle of whisky in the wardrobe and I could close my eyes on the bed with a full glass beside me.

At the door I bumped into my landlady as she backed out on to the street with her shopping bag in her hand.

'Hello, Mr Weems. And how are you today?'

'Just fine, Mrs Tochle, just fine. And you?' Mrs Tochle was a difficult woman to edge past. She stood in front of me, small, grey, round; immoveable.

'Well, there's no use complaining, Mr Weems. As they say around here: 'Wha's tae gliever, haw's tae siever.''

I considered a nod of the head and a smile to be the most suitable response to this, and attempted to squeeze by into the hall. A hand detained me: 'No luck with the house hunting yet, Mr Weems?' I shook my head:

'Not so far, Mrs Tochle. But it's early days yet.'

'Well, you know you're very welcome here as long as you want to stay. As they say....'

'Thanks, Mrs Tochle, very kind of you.' I needed that

18

drink. I needed to breath Tochle-free if not Bannock-free air.

'Just one thing, Mr Weems.' She moved closer. I heard her emphysematous wheeze. 'You know I don't mind you drinking and smoking in your room.' Well thank's very much. 'And even eating your fish suppers there.' Welcome to Liberty Hall. 'But I must ask you to refrain from pinning anything to the walls.' What? 'That's very expensive embossed paper you know.' My list. 'My late husband put it up. He was quite a handyman in his d...' You've been reading my list.

After droning a few more platitudes, Mrs Tochle shuffled off with her string bag. I thought of her unpinning that sheet of paper from the wall and felt humiliated. It was as if she had ticked me off for reading *The Beano* instead of doing my homework. I also felt guilty, as if she had been discussing strange stains she had discovered on my pyjama bottoms.

When I reached my room I saw the list in the centre of my neatly made bed, with the pin lying on top. 'Cheer Up!' the title read, 'It's Not The End Of The World!'

When I Believed That, Without Even Thinking

I haven't always been like this. Despite having what my doctor describes as 'a depressive personality', I have been happy at many times in my life. Here are some happy episodes from my early childhood:

When I helped pack the cases for my family's annual summer holiday.

When it rained at the seaside and I could stay in the boarding house reading comics instead of being forced down to the beach.

When I saved up stamps and spent hours looking at them, sorting them out and rearranging them in envelopes and albums.

When I played in goal for my primary school football team.

When my mother told me I would not be having any brothers or sisters.

When I won a spelling test.

When my father won me a goldfish at the shows and we bought a bowl for it on the way home.

When I took home a good report card from school and my parents praised me for my efforts.

When I began a small garden round the back of our house and grew tall, varicoloured lupins from tiny seeds.

When my painting of a clown won third prize in a newspaper art competition.

When I first read Enid Blyton books and began a little library on the shelf above my bed.

When for Christmas I was given a torch which could shine red and green at the press of a button.

When I banked money at the Post Office and had my own account book.

When I was given bacon and egg sandwiches for my tea every Saturday.

When my father bought a car.

When my mother bought a colour television set.

When I caught a fish.

When I was allowed to stay up after midnight for the first time ever.

When I found a penknife in the woods in the park.

When I was told that people go to heaven when they die.

When I wore a kilt at my cousin's wedding.

When my mother made ice lollies in our new fridge.

When I was told that when I grew up I would get married, have children, and live happily ever after.

Living Happily Ever After

Once upon a time there was a Pole called Janusz Kowalik. In 1939, he served as a soldier on the eastern frontier of his country. There, in the September of that year, he carried out what he saw as his patriotic and religious duty by resisting invading Soviet forces. Later, Janusz joined the underground Armia Krajowa, or 'Home Army', and helped to fight the Germans until victory was achieved. In late 1945, when most of Europe was at peace, Janusz's war continued against the People's Army, the armed wing of the Polish Workers' Party. Six years without rest. Six years without a home. Some people thought he was a hero.

In 1946 he left Poland, sick of war, tired of fighting, searching for peace and a new life. At that time, whole chunks of Europe were moving or being moved. Boundaries changed, countries disappeared, whole populations woke up to discover that their nationality had changed overnight. The roads were packed with people who carried their whole lives on their backs. Janusz Kowalik was one of them.

After a long, difficult journey, he reached the British Zone of occupied Germany. There, in a camp for displaced persons, he found work as an interpreter. He was well suited to this job for, although not well educated, he had an aptitude for languages. In addition to Polish, he had a good working knowledge of German, Czech and Slovak. Soon, he could speak English too.

Later, as a reward for his services, the authorities allowed Janusz Kowalik entry into Britain. This was not a purely altruistic decision. At the time, there was a shortage of labour in certain key industries. The Pole could help out.

Janusz had been a miner before serving as a soldier. When he arrived in his new country, he became a miner again, but not for long. He found he could not stand the darkness any

21

more. He did not want to spend his new life burrowing through geological history. Instead, he felt a great desire to live in the countryside, where the air was pure, where he could see the upper world in the sunshine and in the rain.

He moved to Bannock.

This was not a purely chance decision. There already was a small Polish community in the town; like Janusz, debris from the war. Although they did not know him, they welcomed their fellow countryman. They toasted his arrival. All of them had been soldiers too, or airmen. They had spent most of the war as aliens, in military camps in a strange land. When the fighting ended, they had decided to stay rather than to return to a country they no longer recognised as their own.

To begin with, Janusz worked on farms in the area. He was suited to the work because years of hard, physical labour had made him very strong. He was only five feet three inches tall but his body was so wide he seemed like a block of granite. He had huge hands for such a small man, and fingers so thick they seemed to crowd each other out. No one could equal him in lifting bags of corn and potatoes. His party piece was bending then breaking six inch nails in his hands. He could do this in five seconds.

The last farm Janusz worked on was Blackwater Mains which belonged to a Bannock Bunter called George Logan. Mr Logan's youngest daughter, Kathy, was later to work behind the counter in a bank in the town.

Janusz was very happy there and was treated like one of the family. The Logans, none of whom had ever travelled more than thirty miles from Bannock, were fascinated by Janusz's stories about Poland before the war, about the mines, about the fighting, about the camps and the cattle trucks, about the struggle for life on the roads of Central Europe.

Then Janusz told Mr Logan he was leaving. He wished to give a month's notice. He had met a local girl at a dance in the Polish Club and they were to be married. Using the money he had saved and some he had borrowed from a friend, Janusz and his wife-to-be were going to buy a business in the town. They would live in a flat above what Janusz called 'the antique shop' but which was, in fact, a repository for second-hand clothing, furniture, domestic appliances and gimcrack. Janusz was going to spend the rest of his life sifting through the detritus of life in Bannock.

The Logans were invited to the wedding ceremony and the reception afterwards in the Polish club. Kathy's father, unused to strong spirit, became outrageously drunk on green, scented vodka and had to be taken home early in a taxi.

Mr and Mrs Kowalik spent their wedding night in the bridal suite of the Hydro and returned home the following day to pull up the shutters and open for business.

Janusz, then thirty-six, was seventeen years older than his new wife. He was of a different religion, spoke five languages to her one, had been blue-scarred down a pit before she was born. But they seemed happy, in a quiet, undemonstrative sort of a way. They worked very hard, opening the shop six days a week, from eight in the morning until seven at night. In addition to this, Janusz spent long hours in his workroom, glueing legs back on chairs, cleaning up old brasswear, sponging the stains off cheap suits.

Nine months after the wedding, in the bedroom of the flat above the shop, a son was born to the Kowalik family. They called him Stanislaw, after Janusz's brother who had disappeared in the war. Just after he was born, Mrs Kowalik held the baby, young Stan, up to his proud father:

'Look, Jan,' she said, with the sweat still standing out on her face. 'A little Polish Bannock Bunter.'

The Bannock Bunters

The Bannock Bunters by T. J.Macroom. The single sheet smelled of mushrooms and earth floors. I held it at full arms length as I lay on my rented bed. 'The fifth in an occasional series of monographs published by the Bannock Historical Society.' It dropped from my fingers to my chest. I tilted my glass to my lips and swallowed a large amount of whisky mixed with tepid tap water. It did not revive me.

I made an effort. My sinews stretched, my toes curled towards the blanket box. But as I read, I dozed. Some words entered. Most escaped. It would have to do. The blanks could be filled in later. I had never found History a straightforward subject for study. I just had to make the best of things.

'Imagine, as through the misty morn
comes the sound of an approaching
army, off to fight, perhaps die for king
_____cavalry horses make the
very_____rattle and jolt along
the poor country tracks. The infantry
raise_____
in wonder at the armour, at the
pikemen, at the_____
and destruction.
'But wait._____Where are the
banners, the flags, the bright_____
canvas only half finished,_____
_____robbed of its richest colours.
Call for the Bannock Bunters!
'Yes, Bannock, that little town which
_____, astride the border between
two warring____oasis of____island
of_____sea_____
_____that all came in their turn:
kings and queens, heroes_____
_____master craftsmen of
the_____Ancient   Guild   of
Broontailers and Bunters, _____
symbols of war and peace, of
unity_____.
_____the
finest banners and flags to be found in
the known_____
____barely a country on the globe
_____known, not as

24

"Bannockites" or "Bannockonians" but as "Bunters", after one half of the craft which_____.

'The bunters were in fact those crafts-men who made the flags and banners: an exclusively male_____. The broontailers, sadly in decline in this era of_____men who made the poles and ropes which held the material in position. Both, bunters and broontailers, joined together in a guild in 1351 to protect their trade and to_____.

'The first Master of the Guild was Thomas Bogle, a broontailer of _____ironically, in modern usage, he would not now be considered to be a true "Bannock Bunter", since this term is restricted to those who were born within a one mile radius of the baptisimal font in the old kirk. _____known as "God's Welk", a "welk" being a wooden disc used by bunters to push needles through the unyielding cloth of _____.

_____bunter and a broontailer on alternate years. _____line of over six_____history of the Guild can be seen as the history of Bannock, as generation succeeds_____,as father_____accumulate on the roll of honour: Tummle, Thwaw, Bruce, Jeffrey, Winkie, Nichol, Weir, Pumphry. The list_____role not only _____ but

_____,of the____.

_____not restricted to those in the crafts_____
men of worth and good reputation in the town, _____further afield_____good service. Honorary _____Fourteenth Duke of Leuchars; Sir Frederick_____
George;_____; Field Marshall, Sir Arthur Draym, M.C.; Winston _____
_____Edinburgh;_____Royal Highness, King An Wan Lee of Malabbar.

_____also organises the famous Bannock festivities on behalf of ordinary_____: "The Rollin' o' The Ring", "The Bawbee Fair", "The Reem Oot", "The Fetchin' o' the Lads", "Swattin' the Turk". _____, part of a tradition which would not have survived without____of _____

_____
_____!

_____lies ahead for the_____
future is uncertain, but_____hope. For example, the recent commercial arrangement with

A Polish Bunter

Once upon a time, in the town of Bannock, a little baby boy was born to Janusz and Margaret Kowalik. They named him Stanislaw, after Mr Kowalik's brother who had disappeared in the war. Mrs Kowalik called him 'Stanny' because Stanislaw seemed a grown-up name for such a little baby.

Stanny became a Bunter because he had been born within one mile of the baptisimal font in the old kirk. His mother was very proud of this fact, as was his father, although for different reasons. Mrs Kowalik was proud because her family had lived around Bannock for generations and she valued the traditions of the town. Mr Kowalik was proud because, although people had always been friendly towards him, he had felt a stranger because the community was so closely woven together. Now, Stanny was a part of the Bunter fabric, and this gave his father a new confidence in his own standing. With his newly extended family around him, he felt he belonged. This was important for a man with Janusz's history. He had not felt as if he belonged anywhere for a very long time.

Shortly after Stanny's birth, the local priest called round to the Kowaliks' house. His parish covered a large area but embraced few people, mostly Polish and Irish immigrants. He was pleased to see the new arrival. In the years to come he, and hopefully other little Kowaliks, would bolster the roll of the small Catholic primary school in the town.

Janusz was very embarrassed by the visit. He had to tell Father Dwyer that Stanny was not going to be brought up in the faith. The Kowaliks had discussed the matter at great length and had decided that Stanny would attend church with his mother and her family. Stanislaw Kowalik was going to be a Protestant.

This had not been an easy decision for Janusz to take as he was a committed Catholic and as such felt bound to raise his children in the one, true church. He did not need Father Dwyer to remind him of this. He knew the Church's instruction on the matter. It was on practical rather than theological grounds that he felt compelled to fall in with his wife's wishes and release the boy to her.

Janusz did not want the child to suffer any disadvantages in later life. In particular, he did not want Stanny to stand out, to be different from all the other little Bunters in the town. As Mrs Kowalik put it, having a Polish name was bad enough. Being Catholic, they both agreed, would set him apart from most of his contemporaries. Janusz wanted Stanny to fit in; to merge in with the background.

It wasn't that Stanny would be persecuted: Bannock was not that kind of a place. It had been untouched by thumb-screws and the rack; it had no history of pogroms, no walled ghetto; no Bunter had been witness to auto-da-fe, had sniffed heretic toasting in the market square. No. It was just that, having emerged from the rapids, Janusz wanted to paddle further into the backwater, to beach his canoe in the shallows, feel the river mud squelch between his toes. Silt up.

At ten, Stanny was bilingual. He had picked up a second language by listening to his father speak in Polish with his friends in the shop and at the club. Janusz was secretly pleased with his son's unanticipated gift but warned him against unguarded chatter at home as his mother didn't like hearing what she couldn't understand. When Mrs Kowalik heard Polish she refered to it as 'gibberish' or 'mumbo-jumbo'. Janusz meekly accepted the language ban in the house and her disapproval of his friends. 'Anything For A Quiet Life,' he would say, and fill his pipe, or hide himself in his workroom.

At school, Stanny was very successful. He was a bright kid. He finished first in each of his classes, all the way up to Primary Seven. He was an extrovert and liked to exert control over people and things, although he never became visibly upset if he couldn't get his own way. He was sometimes teased because of his name and called 'Bean Pole' or 'Ice Pole' or 'North Pole'. This didn't really bother Stanny because he was a balanced, well adjusted child who could cope easily with that sort of thing.

When he went to the High School, Stanny grew up very quickly, in all sorts of ways. His mother complained because it seemed impossible to keep him in shoes and trousers. He was 'shooting up like a weed', she said. Janusz was proud to walk beside his son, at thirteen, taller than his father. The Kowaliks had produced no other children. Janusz was disappointed but accepted this as with everything else. He focused all his attention on his only boy. Stanny was a special child.

The young man decided he didn't want to be called 'Stanny' any more. Probably he associated this name with the childhood he was leaving behind. 'Stan' sounded more mature. His mother couldn't get used to this and they had minor arguments over it. Maybe she was frightened he was growing away from her.

At the High School, Stan was an all-rounder. He was successful at sports and academic work seemed to come easily to him. Certificates and prizes piled up without much effort; without him appearing to notice.

Stan soon found he was atttractive to girls. He wasn't particularly good looking: a broad, Slavic face; a nose smashed on the rugby field; stiff, uncontrollable hair cut too short at the back and sides. But he could look into their eyes and smile; make them giggle nervously, and maybe shiver. With his height and premature stubble and confident manner, he was usually taken to be older than he was. He sometimes walked out with girls three or four years his senior. One of the first, Heather, drove a Morris Minor, a present for her seventeenth birthday. On the second night they went out together they parked at the top of Mossy Glen, and Stan had sexual intercourse with Heather on the back seat as the windows misted and ran. He loved it. It gave life a whole new meaning. Stan decided he would like to do it as often as possible. He was fourteen years of age.

When I Was Fourteen

When I was fourteen, I was heavily in to stamp collecting.

Like most people, I have mixed feelings now, looking back at it all: my 'formative years'; puberty; adolescence; spots; adenoids. A lot of it has disappeared: wiped clean from my memory banks. My wife blamed this on the action of alcohol on my brain cells. By now my brain must be the size of a prune. I am walking around with an empty head. A little man is standing on top of my spinal cord, looking up into the vaulted chamber above. His voice echoes: 'Where has everything gone?'

All in all, I was pretty happy as a child. In my case, childhood extended up to eighteen and beyond. I was a late developer. Apart from the usual agonies of growing up, I seem to remember being quite content for most of the time. And always happiest when collecting something. Or making lists. Here is a list of things I have collected at various stages of my life:

Used matches.

Loose change.

Bus tickets.

Stamps.

Coins.

Postcards.

Postmarks.

Comics.

Matchbooks.

Pens.

Dinky cars.

Football programmes.

Model aircraft.

Cigarette cards.

Marbles.

Miniature toy soldiers.

Bottle labels.

Butterflies.

Birds' eggs.

Miniature whisky bottles.

Typhoo Tea cards.

Ball bearings.

Cap badges.

Headed notepaper.

Pencil rubbers

and

Empty beer cans.

Sounds exciting, doesn't it?

Stanislaw Kowalik and I are approximately the same age, so at round about the time he was screwing Heather Muir in the back of her Morris Minor, I was covering my tongue in the gum from stamp hinges, or sticking my finger on the pin of a Black Watch cap badge.

It's a funny old life, isn't it?

No It Isn't

A few days after I wrote it, I decided to change one of my 'original documents'. To revise history in the light of contemporary experience. Bannock was getting me down. I realised it had been a mistake to move there. I felt trapped. My wife had left me. I was drinking too much. I was escaping more and more into a fantasy world in order to avoid unpleasant reality.

I looked at the document. 'Cheer Up!' it said, 'It's Not The End Of The World!' I decided it was time I faced facts. Reassess my life. Set the account straight. Grapple with the real world. Come to terms with my problems, whack them down like a cane slash through a nettle.

1. DELUSION: Health – reasonable.

   REALITY: Health – constant sweating, sore guts, diarrhoea – alcohol related?

2. DELUSION: Finances – not too bad, especially with new job, no ties.

   REALITY: Finances – spending money like drunken sailor.

3. DELUSION: Job – not too demanding or stressful. Possibility of further promotion.

   REALITY: Job – awe inspiringly, crushingly boring. Possibility of further promotion only through extensive brown-nosing.

4. DELUSION: Environment – beautiful. Lots of tourists come here to admire the scenery.

   REALITY: Environment – no use to a blind man.

5. DELUSION: Interests – playing the guitar, squash, tennis, chess. Music, literature, cinema, travel, writing.

   REALITY: Interests – drinking, moaning, worrying, whining, fantasising and general complaining. Last time I played the guitar –

32

1971. Last time I played tennis – 1976.

6. DELUSION: Friends – since splitting up with my wife, I have discovered who my real friends are.

   REALITY: Friends – since splitting up with my wife, I have discovered who my real friends are: I haven't got any.

7. DELUSION: Family – since splitting up with my wife, I have grown closer to my family.

   REALITY: Family – since splitting up with my wife I have grown closer to my family: that is one of the reasons I ran away to Bannock.

8. DELUSION: No impediment to sexual fulfilment.

   REALITY: No opportunity for sexual fulfilment.

9. DELUSION: No history of criminality or deviance.

   REALITY: Too cowardly to try anything.

10. DELUSION: Being alive.

    REALITY: I am dead as a hamster's fart.

The exercise helped. I went to bed feeling happier than in a long time. I had pleasant dreams. The effect even lasted through to next morning. When I awoke, I reread the list and, instead of putting it in the bin with the rest of my drunken drivel, I pinned it to the wall with a pin from a shirt box.

After a moment's thought, I took it down again and added a title. The title was: 'Facing Reality Is The Only Way! Do Not Live In The Past! Grasp The Nettle Of The Future!'

33

Facing Reality Is Not So Easy

I spoke to Stan Kowalik again during my fourth week in Bannock. Our meeting came towards the end of a dreadful day which began at breakfast time in the boarding house, as I sat in the dining room at what had become known as 'Mr Weems' Table'.

The room contained the usual mix of people: a couple of American tourists, studying a map over their coffee; a man in a wig who looked like a salesman; Wilton, a Jehovah's Witness, who came down to Bannock two days a week to lecture in computer studies at the Technical College.

I dutifully greeted my fellow inmates as I squeezed between them.

'Good morning.'
'Morning.'
'Good morning.'
'Morning.'
'Nice morning.'
'Beautiful morning.'

Then silence, broken only by the crunch of cornflakes and the rustle of the Americans' map.

A tiny glass of fruit juice awaited my arrival. Mrs Tochle always prepared the breakfast tables the night before the feast so this morning, as on many other mornings, there was a thin surface layer of dust on the plates. A small fly bobbed in the milk jug. The toast sat in the rack: as always, four small triangles. I had asked for more on my first morning and Mrs Tochle had shrieked: 'Never let it be said that I'm starving my guests. This is Bannock, not Bangladesh.' She then returned with one more triangle in a separate rack, and deposited it grandly before me. I never asked again.

That morning, Mrs Tochle dropped my breakfast on the table and departed with a sniff. No choice of food offered. No cheery hello. I had sinned.

A curling sausage sneered at me from the plate, daring me to eat it. Underneath was a fried egg, seemingly totally encased in a transparent, plastic suit. I attempted the fried bread but the slice exploded as my fork speared into it. A piece flew across the plate, ricocheted against a gnarled rasher, and was sent spinning towards the sugar bowl. Half a fried tomato rocked in the slipstream, anchored in a blob of grease. I reached for the toast.

'Good morning.'

'Morning.'

'Beautiful day.'

'Wonderful.'

More guests had entered the dining room. An elderly couple, dressed for the holidays.

'Morning.'

'Morning.'

I joined in the chorus.

Later, as I left for work, Mrs Tochle detained me at the coatstand in the hallway. In her right hand, she held a pin.

'Mr Weems, I believe I have brought up the question of pins in the wallpaper once before. I can't have it, Mr Weems, I really cannot have it.'

My self esteem and confidence were at such a low ebb that I was frightened of this little, round lady. I began to sweat and mumbled apologies as I edged towards the door. The two Americans swished past in waterproof coats, trying to avert their eyes from my humiliation. I looked down at the floor, as if I was searching for where my nappy-leak had wet the carpet. Mrs Tochle gained strength from my weakness.

'My dear, late husband laboured mightily in that room, Mr Weems. I cannot believe any decent person could deliberately disfigure his work.' A memory brought tears to her eyes. 'That embossed paper cost six pounds a roll. Wanton destruction, that's all it is. Wanton destruction.' I was the Ghengis Khan of Bannock.

Tochle. Bannock. Fried. Bread. Macroom. Bank. Rubber. Eggs. Feckle. Nook. Good. Morning. Hail. Laddie. Americans. Wonderful. Morning. Toast. Morning.

'Morning.'

'Morning.'

'Lovely morning.'

I turned the keys in the locks of the bank door and let myself, Kathy and young Winkie inside.

'I bet we could all think of something better to do on a

35

morning like this, eh, Mr Weems?'

Winkie said this to me every day. Given a twenty-four hour start, one million pounds in used notes, and a naked, full breasted woman, Winkie probably could not think of any thing better to do on ninety-nine occasions out of a hundred. My personal tragedy was that I couldn't either.

Toast at breakfast had not satisfied my appetite. I looked in a drawer at my desk for a leftover sandwich from yesterday's lunch and found the white bread lightly speckled with what looked like black pepper.

'Kathy. I've got a mouse in my desk.'

'Don't worry, George. It'll be away back to its hole now, sleeping it off.'

'But it's eaten my sandwich.'

'Poor mouse. Those sandwiches gave me indigestion yesterday.'

We'll have to get rid of it.'

'Listen at the skirting board for its belly rumbling.'

Macroom appeared round about ten o'clock carrying a pile of files and papers. The top cover read 'Bannock Historical Society Minutes'. I told him about the mouse.

'I'm far too busy to concern myself over rodents,' he replied. 'Take some money from petty cash and send Winkie for a mouse trap or poison or something. You have to learn to take on responsibility, George. It's part of the job.' He disappeared into his office only to reappear a second later. 'I'll be occupied for most of the day, George. Please don't disturb me unless it's extremely urgent.' He tittered. 'If the mouse decides to rob the bank, for example.' He vanished.

Tochle. Bannock. Winkie. Toast. Fried. Bread. Feckle. Mouse. Macroom. Better. Morning.

'Good morning.'

'Morning.'

'Nice morning.'

'I'd like a mouse trap, please.'

I had decided to go shopping myself. I needed the challenge. The owner of the hardware store spread a selection of mechanisms on the counter before me.

'Mice in the bank is it?' I grunted as I fingered the merchandise. ' You get them in a lot of these old buildings.'

36

And the Nobel prize in zoology goes to.... 'I just hope they're no' eating my money.' He laughed. I laughed. Why not?

Mouse. Bannock. Trap. Robbery. Droppings. Feckle. Toast. Macroom. Morning. Winkie.

'Did you get it?'

I nodded at Winkie in reply, and waved the brown bag containing my purchase.

He turned to Kathy: 'The Great White Hunter.'

I had the feeling Winkie was taking the piss. That would have been the final humiliation. I treated him to a warning look and he returned to counting small change.

The trap I had selected was the cheapest available but it appeared the most effective. It looked as a mouse trap should, that is like a prop from a 'Tom and Jerry' cartoon. I pulled back the spring loaded action and baited the trap with a piece of bread. It lay like a Colt 45 at the back of my desk drawer.

Bannock. Mouse. Trap. Juice. Squash. Toast. Bread. Bank. Bait. Morning. Afternoon. Winkie. Feckle. Nook. Better. Things. Do. Macroom. Tochle. Gliever. Kathy. Wife. Mosquito. List. Guild. Flags. Evening. Bunters. Bannock. Bannock. Drink. Drinks.

'What'll it be?'

'Pint of lager and a whisky, please.'

Another day over. All of the barmen in The Old Mill knew me by this time. They smiled when I came in the door. They reached for glasses, for the tap, for the optics, as I spoke my order. It was good to feel such a sense of belonging.

As I waited for my drinks I heard the sound of laughter coming from the furthest corner of the lounge. I squinted into the mirrored backdrop behind the gantry and saw fairground images of a group of men and women rocking around a table full of empty glasses. They quietened and listened to another anecdote from a raconteur with a broken nose.

'There you go, George.' The barman knew my name. I was pleased. 'That'll be one eighty.' I handed over the money. My lips skimmed the foam off the top of my pint, delaying the moment of satisfaction.

'Not a bad day, eh?' A conversation.

'Well, we don't see much of it in here, George.' A joke. I laughed.

I turned from the bar as the story ended. Heads tipped back, glasses tinkled, knees and thighs squeezed together in momentary intimacy. A woman choked on her drink and two men slapped her back. I sat down on a seat at the opposite end of the room from Stan's happy, laughing, exclusive group.

Beside me, wedged against the wall, was a painted cartwheel. Above was a selection of harness for horses, dominated by a huge collar for a Clydesdale. Around the lounge was a selection of banners and flags produced by Bunters gone by. I was sitting in a Bannock time capsule.

The crossword was easy that day. I soon had most of it finished and turned to the sports pages, the features, the small ads; read then reread. Gravity seemed to pull me towards the floor, my eyes to the table.

But after a few drinks, I began to relax. I unbowed my head, waved and nodded to a few of the bank's customers who called in on their way home from work. A couple more halfs and I was happier still. I could feel the tension leave my facial muscles and shoulders. Things didn't seem quite so bad.

Another pint produced a state of euphoria. My head filled with delusion and fantasy. Alcohol induced chemical changes in my brain told me I was happy. Let's look on the bright side.

I felt young, full of energy, in command. I was off the leash. Many a man would envy me. New town, new faces, new opportunities.

The young woman who banked the takings from Bannock Craftwear came in. I smiled at her. She smiled back.

I had to look to the future. Start to control my life, not let fate dump what it liked on me.

A barman, clearing the table of glasses, laughed at one of my quips.

I had to be positive, be assertive, not live life like an ant under an elephant's arse.

I sat there for a long time, getting more and more excited. I wanted to talk, to share my good feelings. An old man sat down beside me. I greeted him with a cheery hello. He knew me, had seen me at the bank, around the town.

'George Weems.'

'Charlie Trummle.' We shook hands. The cuffs of his

jacket were worn and frayed. After a few more rounds of slurred social chitchat, I suggested a drink. He agreed.

When I brought the glasses back to the table, I asked him if he was a Bunter. He slurped Pale Ale then laughed, but without humour. I could see his tongue through the space which should have been occupied by his two front teeth:

'Oh, I'm a Bunter all right. Born in God's Welk.' He laughed again then put his hand on my arm. 'Don't believe all the talk you hear around this place.' He looked round the bar but I knew he was seeing beyond the walls. 'They all live in the past, especially Macroom and the rest of those old duffers.'

'So you know Mr Macroom?'

'Silly auld bastard.' We both laughed and clinked glasses. I'll drink to that.

'And Winkie?'

'Silly young bastard. But his father's worse. And his grandfather before him. Don't get on the wrong side of that family.' Gurgle, gurgle, gurgle.

'And Mrs Tochle?'

'Silly auld bitch.' That calls for another one.

'Take my advice, son,' Charlie went on. 'Unless you want to end up like all these folk, get out now, before it's too late. Bannock is hell. Believe me, I know.'

'Come on now, Charlie. It can't be as bad as that.' Listen to me. Mr Optimism. Let's compose a song. Put on a show! You do the music, I'll do the lyrics:

Don't waste tiiime a mopin' and a pinin'!

'Cos ev'ry cloud's got a won-der-ful silver linin!

When you're bluuue, a wailin' and a cryin'!

Smile on through: it's some-other-bum that's dyin'!

Same again? How about another? Do you want a wee half to go along with that? Room for another pint? Yes. Yes. Yes. Yes. I was so happy, I didn't even notice I was buying all the drink. Who cares? Let's play millionaires. What a great pub. What a laugh. This old boy is a real character.

I weaved up to the bar for yet another round. The Old Mill was now crowded. All the seats were taken and groups stood crushed together around the room. The place was alive with conversation. A few people nodded and smiled at me as I pushed between them.

39

'Same again, Peter.' By this time I knew the first names of everyone.

'Celebrating tonight, George?'

'Why not?' My knees buckled slightly as I felt in my pocket for more money. Peter looked up as he pulled the pints:

'I see you've met Charlie.'

'Great old spud.' Peter laughed:

'Oh, Charlie's a character all right.'

I recognised a bank customer to my right and nudged him with my elbow: 'How are you doing?' He smiled back. I turned to my left and recognised a woman, seemingly alone, staring sadly at the gantry. 'Cheer up!' I said to her. 'It's not the end of the world!' She turned to me, looked into my bleary eyes:

'How the hell would you know?'

Now, I know I was drunk but I can remember what happened next very clearly. I swear I can. I mean, why would I bother to lie about it at this stage? I know I shouldn't have done even what I did but – no excuses. I put my arm round her shoulders and pulled her towards me – to console her, for god's sake. I was happy. I knew what it felt like to be sad. I would have been delighted if someone had taken the time to hug me.

I put my arm around her and it sort of fell off, slipped on her waxed jacket and, and...dropped. I did not touch any other part of her anatomy. Remember, the bar was crowded; someone else may have rubbed against her, deliberately or accidentally. It wasn't me. I'm not a groper and I never have been. There's no need to defend myself anyway: my innocence has now been established. I don't have to resort to that to get my balls afire. I didn't do it.

She screamed.

The whole bar stopped.

Everyone looked at the woman. Her ponytail shook. Without looking, she pointed a finger at me and spoke in a loud, quavering voice:

'This man has just touched me.' And again: 'This man has just stroked my bottom.'

Everyone looked from the woman towards me, George Weems: the toucher; the stroker. Peter had two pints in his hands, suspended three inches from the bar. I looked to the side. The bank customer was staring at me, mouth open. Sweat was pouring from every pore in my body. I staggered round and could see only a hundred featureless blobs. I struggled to focus and saw the two Americans, still dressed in their waterproofs, sitting at a table with their map spread before them. I couldn't speak. From the corner of my eye I saw a figure approach, shove his way through the still crowd. It was Stan. At that moment I remembered who the woman was. Mrs Stan. I waited for the blow.

'I'll deal with this, Peter.'

'If you say so, Stan.'

He grabbed me by the arm and guided me quickly to the door. With his other hand he gripped his wife above the elbow and dragged her behind. As the door swung shut, noise broke out once more in 'The Old Mill'. I realised miserably that all the conversation would be about me. George Weems. From the bank. The pervert.

We stood outside for a second of silence. It was broken by laughter. From Mrs Stan. She laughed as if this was the funniest thing that had ever happened to her in her life.

'Shut up.' Stan tried to silence her but the joke was too much to bear. 'Briony, will you shut up.' He raised a hand as if to strike her. The door to the pub opened and closed once more behind us.

'Now, now, Stan.' It was old Charlie. Stan turned to him:

'Look after this man until I get her home, will you, Charlie.'

'Surely.'

'Into the car.' Stan shoved his wife in the direction of the car park. She was still giggling.

A light drizzle fell on us. I was standing, hopelessly drunk, waiting for the assault. At this point I almost hoped for death. Stan turned to me, almost as an afterthought: 'Go on with Charlie,' he told me. 'He'll look after you. I'll explain later. Sorry about this.' He left, prodding Briony ahead of him with a finger.

Charlie led me along the street, across the square, past the statue from whose lap Stan had pissed on my umbrella. I followed helplessly. All I wanted now was for someone to show me a quiet corner, somewhere safe where I could sleep, where I could escape from this shambles. We went into an alley, turned a corner, climbed some stairs and came to a solid wooden door. Charlie looked in his pocket and brought out a key. As he was turning it in the lock, he turned to look at me as I shivered in the rain:

Remember what I told you?' I stood, stooped and crushed. Gravity was again at maximum force. The door opened and Charlie guided me inside. 'Get out now, before it's too late.'

Another Reason For Flight

The Bannock Festivals by E.B.Thwaw

The third in an occasional series of monographs published by the Bannock Historical Society.

_____to any student of history, standing as it does in what was the 'Borders Cockpit', where _____

_____

_____best seen in the festivals which occur in the_____deep significance for local _____

_____ as the fame of Bannock spreads.

THE ROLLIN' O' THE RING
The Rollin' O' The Ring takes place on the 21st_____

_____

_____the River Irk.

_____date in 1215 when, in Fogorig House _____

_____. The Fair Maid Of The Loch _____Red Strachan supported The Maid in her struggles against her half-brother, Andrew Rankine ('Surly Andy') and had become the focus of rebellion____

_____

_____and confiscation of lands,

43

_____good fortune did she evade capture. Rankin's agents seemed to know her every move. No avenue _____ _____ inevitable fate on the block, and with her demise would come the end_____

As The Maid and her followers gathered round the great table in the hall of Fogorig House that night in 1215, word came_____: Red _____bonfire on Hogspike Hill. _____had been sent to the enemy. Was there a traitor in the camp? If so, it could only be a member of _____beyond suspicion. _____ _____to be identified____ _____fate took _____two villagers from Bannock, Mary Dunlin and Robert Winkie. Mary and Robert were cousins, _____ _____sixteen, and by all accounts_____shining black hair. _____lust of one John Heddington, a member of the Fair Maid's escorting _____ force his attentions on _____ tore her attacker's clothing, clawed _____chain from around_____ _____. Attached to the chain was a ring which_____under the gap between the flags and the door which separated Heddington's room from the corridor beyond. In this corridor was Robert Winkie, alerted by_____protect his cousin's honour,_____ring roll_____ _____seal

_____Andrew Rankine.

_____speedily dispatched,
but not before _____

_____false trail _____evade
capture _____
returned to rid _____

_____free_____tyranny.
The Maid conferred upon young
Robert the title 'Ring Bearer' and on
her victory handed over to_____
_____estate at Middledyke.
Winkies prospered: _____twelve
_____every corner
_____Dunlin
joined_____tragically
early age of_____.
_____The Rollin' O' The Ring
commemmorates the unmasking of
the traitor by these two young people
from Bannock. Each year, a huge cer-
emonial ring _____

_____

_____
_____sets afire cylindrical
torches attached to the rim. These
torches are twelve in number, and rep-
resent the Bannock men who later fell
at the Battle of Slawning Mound,
where the Maid finally crushed_____

_____
_____Flaming, smoking, the hoop
is then_____
In attendance are four other_____
_____'Winkie Boys' to restrain

_____
_____shout, 'Oot, John Heddington!

45

Oot, Surly_____

_____not the whole spectacle,
because another townsman_____
_____not empty, for
a brave Bannock man stands_____
_____ cartwheels over the
cobblestones as the_____
_____'The Sinning Wretch',
who has also been elected at the Ring
Supper, and who represents the twin
evils of Rankin and Heddington.
_____set alight and Surly Andy
and Heddington are burned in _____
_____cleansing himself and_____
_____wee sma'
hours____

SWATTIN' THE TURK
Imagine the Bunters' surprise when,
returning from the Crusades, John
Leep of Bannock brought with him the
severed

Plans

Once upon a time, a father and a son grew close as close can be.

From the first week of the boy's life, Janusz had taken Stannie with him everywhere. He changed his nappies, bottle fed him at night while his wife lay asleep. While he worked in the shop, the baby slept in a cot by his side, much admired by the customers. The easiest way to beat down the price of a table lamp or a chest of drawers was to tell Janusz what a beautiful son he had.

Mrs Kowalik loved her son too, but not to the exclusion of everything else. She came from a large family, had three brothers and four sisters. Whenever she popped in to visit her mother, the place was always seething with children. After a while, young Stannie just became one of the crowd.

Sometimes, when Janusz visited his mother-in-law, he would tire of the noise in the whinstone terraced house. When together in Bleachfield Street, everyone in his wife's family spoke loudly and quickly, as if time was rationed. The waves of words would become more and more indistinct; the temperature in the small rooms would increase as the Sunday roast cooked and huge pots of potatoes boiled. Listening to a conversation, Janusz would miss a word, then a sentence, then the whole complex verbal structure would collapse, sweeping him away in an avalanche of syllables, glottal stops, and fragmented syntax.

On these occasions, Janusz would slip unnoticed from the house and wheel the boy in his pram, or later guide him on his first steps along the pavement towards the park. There, on a bench or in the shade of a tree, father would speak to son in Polish, and a soothing calm would descend.

At the club, Janusz's friends called Stannie 'the little Protestant'. Their teasing was always gentle because they loved the boy too. Many of them had never married and they huddled together in those attic rooms for warmth and companionship. Stannie was a link between them and the still strange world they lived in. The boy gave them a new interest in the future: in nurseries and schools; in toys and birthdays. Everything they thought they had left behind. Everything they thought they would never be part of. As they aged, Stannie would grow. As they declined, Stannie would progress. Life no longer ended in death.

Most children are lucky if they have one birthday party a year. Stannie had two. Celebrations above the shop or in the house on Bleachfield Street would be followed some hours or some days later by toasts and the presentation of small gifts in the club. As more beer and spirits were consumed, songs would be sung. One year they dressed Stannie in army cap and medals. On the boy's second birthday, Tadeusz Szydlak baptised him as a Catholic over the sink behind the bar. The day became a feature on the calendar for Janusz's close friends.

Janusz had received only a bare education but he was proud of his son's academic achievements. He showed off Stannie's report cards in the club, and when the boy finished primary school his Dux medal was placed as the centrepiece on the largest table in the bar for one glorious night of celebration. For once, Janusz was allowed to take the boy out at night. He gave him a glass of beer and a small measure of vodka and almost exploded with joy when his son proposed a short toast in Polish to all those men with their hard, broken faces.

It was around this time that Stannie told his mother and father that he wanted to be known as 'Stan'. He felt he was growing up, and needed some outward sign to show this. Young Stan already looked a couple of years older than his age and this, together with his mature bearing, made Janusz treat him more and more as an equal. The boy liked this change in their relationship but never forgot to show the respect due to his father.

They began to speak of all kinds of things, sometimes in English, sometimes in Polish. Stan grew more and more interested in the war and in his father's life before Bannock. Sometimes they would talk together for hours. They would sit in the empty shop or in a corner of the club and the world of Bunterdom would pass by unseen, unheard. To his father the boy was a son, a workmate, a friend, a lost brother, a fallen comrade. Janusz felt he had been given the chance to live his life again.

The more Stan learned, the more he wanted to know. He borrowed books from the library to fill in the gaps in his father's knowledge and took part in discussions with the men

48

in the club. While other boys built model aircraft and collected stamps, the little Protestant read of Cardinal Wyszynski and the Concordat. Instead of football and fishing, Stan talked of Pilsudski and Sikorski. Geography was the Bug and the Vistula. Ships were built on the Baltic, coal was from Silesia. History was 1863 and November 1918; the Polish Commonwealth, Somosierra, Lwow and the Oder-Neisse line.

The men began to listen to Stan's point of view although, of course, they could never accept it unless it happened to coincide with their own. After all, a boy is just a boy. And when the spirit fumes cleared, what did he know? What had he seen, what had he done? He meant well, but books are not life. Black and white photographs do not smell of fear and death. You do not hear the sound of women crying when you turn the page. And who had ever heard of a Pole playing rugby?

When Stan finished his final examinations at secondary school, Janusz took him out and they got drunk together. Just the two of them, father and son, in a corner of the club, alone. When friends came to join them, Janusz asked them to go away. He didn't want to be rude but that night was to be private. They had things to talk about and time was short. Stan had fixed himself up with a summer job in the city and after that would be going to university. The city was a long way away.

For years, Janusz had dreamed of his son becoming a doctor. He could imagine Stan's triumphant return to Bannock. A practice in one of the old, detached villas across the river. Emergency call for Dr Kowalik. Headed notepaper. Off duty, he could drive his old dad round in a big, fancy car. They would pull up outside the club and offer a lift to Kociolek and Michnik. That would show those jumped-up bastards. And then Michnik would say, 'Could you have a look at my back, doctor. It's an old war wound.' 'War wound my arse,' Janusz would say. 'You've been jumping too many of those chambermaids at that crummy flophouse of yours, you old goat.' Then they would all laugh and the hotel-keeper would invite them back for a drink. 'Sorry, Wlodziemierz, but we're too busy.' Fuck you, Michnik.

But it wasn't to be. Stan wouldn't listen to reason. He said he wanted to be a teacher in the High School. A teacher. Janusz thought of all the pasty-faced, short-arsed no-hopers from back home. Sadlowski with the vodka nose who had been caught embezzling school funds. Szczepanski, who felt up little girls on the sly until Joseph Brus gave him a thrashing in front of his own pupils. He groaned at the thought of his son joining that brigade. Better to go down the mines.

It was no use. Stan's mind was made up. He said he felt the urge to explain things to people, to set the record straight, to explode myths. He wanted to study History at university, then explain it to others. It was a dangerous business, History. Handled incorrectly, it could lead to the deaths of more people than had ever died digging coal in Silesia. He had a vocation. That sort of thing couldn't be ignored.

Janusz couldn't argue with that. Vocations came from God. At least Stan planned to come back after completing his education, unlike many of the other young people from Bannock. Teachers weren't paid very much but maybe there would be enough for a just a small saloon.

My Life In A Nutshell

How did I end up as I did? It was inevitable, really. I had been in training for years.

Minutes after I was born, my mother looked at me in her arms and said to the nurses: 'He's a sad looking baby.' Did I have an inkling even then of what life had in store for me? I looked for the breast but my mother's tiny nipples were inverted, pressed inward. Instead I received a bottle and guzzled it down in double quick time. 'He's a hungry boy,' the midwife said. All my life, I have associated happiness with a full belly.

I was christened 'George', named after my father's elder brother who had disappeared in the war. Unlike Stanislaw Kowalik's uncle, the original George Weems did not disappear under mysterious circumstances. Everyone had known what had happened to Uncle George. It had even been reported in the local paper. The man after whom I was named had vanished on the 16th September 1941 while he was patrolling the streets on A.R.P duty. He, along with his good friend Charlie Syme had vaporised when a German land mine exploded in their vicinity.

My namesake, a master butcher by trade, had joined the A.R.P. when turned down at the army medical because of perforated eardrums. This was a great disappointment to him as he had wanted to fight for his country. His mother, my granny, had been secretly pleased at this rejection because she wanted her two sons to survive the war in one piece. At his funeral, Uncle George's coffin had been filled with little piles of rubble and unidentifiable fragments of bone and flesh found at the scene of the explosion. Quite probably, some bits of Charlie Syme were mixed in there too. It couldn't be helped. Everyone had tried their best.

My father, Bill Weems, was luckier than his brother. He had passed the army medical and had been drafted into a tank regiment. He served in the desert campaign in North Africa, took part in the invasion of Italy, and was in one of the first Allied units to cross the Rhine. He was involved in a lot of fighting but was never injured. While hospitalised in Palermo with amoebic dysentery, the tank he should have been driving was hit by a shell from a German 'Tiger'. Everyone inside was fried. My father wrote to the families of all those who had died. He had known those men for years. In one of the letters he asked the question: 'Why did I survive when all the others perished?' He felt guilty. He thought that he should have been dead too. He felt as if he had cheated all of his friends, like a lover who had refused to leap over the cliff after his partner.

My mother has some photographs of my father taken during the war. In one of them, he is sitting on top of a tank with the members of the crew who were to die in Sicily. All of them are tanned and smiling, dressed in baggy khaki shorts. They seem very thin: the ribs show on their bodies; knees and elbows create a geometric puzzle of interlocking, bony angles. In the background is sand and sky. On the tank is written the words: 'The Tartan Terrors'.

In another snap, my father is hugging a Soviet soldier. The Russian is wearing an enormous greatcoat and has a rifle slung across his back. His face is obscured by that of my father. Dad has pushed his goggles on top of his beret, and he has two large circles round his eyes, the only white visible on a smoke-blackened face. Maybe the Russian is one of the ones Stan's dad fought in Poland.

A third photograph is taken in a studio and it shows my father in full uniform, wearing his campaign medals. His hair has been newly shorn and oiled. He looks very serious and mature. He should have been smiling because it was taken at the end of the war, after the killing was over. He had come through a lot for a young man of twenty three, and it showed on his face. In the photograph, he looks older than I do now. There doesn't seem to be a great deal of similarity between us, although we both share the same, worried eyes.

On demobilisation, my father went back to work in the family butcher shop. He lived quietly at home with his mother and most nights sat in his chair beside the fire, thinking about the war, wondering why he had lived while others had died. He started keeping a diary. It was full of references, not to the present, but to the past. It was as if everything that had happened after the war did not count. He should have been in the tank, part of the burnt offering, should have gone up in smoke like the rest of the Tartan Terrors.

My father conducted the earliest part of his courtship of my mother in the butcher shop in Corsock Street. He wooed Flora Beaton with extra rashers of bacon, under-the-counter stewing steak, contraband lamb chops. He joked he was trying to fatten her up. During their romance and their engagement, my father filled his diary with entries on the Desert War, the sound of a German 88, the merits of the Sherman tank, the fear and happiness of life in a 'tin can'. On the day of their marriage, he took the time to write the following: 'Sicily must be nice at this time of year.'

About six years after the wedding, I was born. Later, I got the impression from one of my aunts that it had taken mum and dad a long time to find out how to make babies. Perhaps I was the result of their first success.

After my birth, my mother became very ill. It had been a difficult delivery. I had caused a lot of damage in my attempts to enter the outside world through that narrow pelvis. I was to be the first and last to pass that way. My mother had what my aunts and my granny referred to as 'woman's trouble', which meant I would not have any brothers or sisters. When I asked about it all, I was told that god had decided I would be the only little Weems and that I had to make sure I would live up to this responsibility.

After I was born, my father stopped keeping his diary and took up photography. He became very enthusiastic about his new hobby and thoroughly documented the trivia of our everyday lives. In the Weems family albums are snaps of the shop and the butcher's van, of my grandparents, of our flat, of my mother with her sisters, of our many cats, of the motorbike and sidecar which roared like a Spitfire at full throttle.

There is also the usual selection of photographs of me as a baby and as a young child: I am in my pram, shaded from the sun by a frilly canopy. I am naked on the beach, driving a motorboat made of sand. I am in uniform, ready for my first day at school. I am holding a Halloween lantern made from a hollowed-out turnip. I am playing golf on the links with a cut-down set of clubs. I am wearing a Christmas crown made of paper as I bite into a roast potato.

Underneath each photograph, in my father's scrawling handwriting, is written date and location, and sometimes a little funny remark. For example, below a snap of my mother preparing some food at the cooker is the caption: 'The Witches' Scene From Macbeth'. Accompanying a photo of me, aged one, bollock naked in the bath, is the text: 'Preparing For A Night Out On The Town'.

The last photograph in the final volume shows me holding a book, a prize awarded for finishing top of the class in my first year at secondary school. Underneath it says: 'Albert Einstein I Presume'. There are no more entries, no more funny captions, because soon after this my father fell ill and died.

He left behind a lot of material which was supposed to take its place in the albums, but after his death neither my mother nor I had the urge to add to the collection. Most of the pile was composed of colour shots from our holiday which that year, for the first time, had been spent abroad. That summer, my father had surprised everyone by announcing he was taking us on a camping trip to Europe. He said he was fed up with the same old boarding house on the same old sea front. Business had been good that year. Young Tommy could look after the shop. You only live once.

From the moment he told us the news, both my mother and I knew our eventual destination. We said nothing, but when we crossed the Channel we could feel the pull of Italy, of Sicily, of the Tartan Terrors. My father fretted at every campsite, found fault with every town and village. He complained of the weather in Belgium, said he could not drink the beer in Germany. The French were rude, the Swiss stuck up. At Italian traffic lights, he drummed his fingers on the dashboard of our Morris Estate. He had an appointment to keep.

Many of the photographs he brought home from Sicily are of cemeteries. Somewhere in amongst the white crosses were his friends, his comrades, scorched; under the earth.

One morning, I heard him being sick in the toilets at the campsite. My mother called in an Italian doctor. Too much sun. Perhaps over-indulgence in the local wines? Drink only bottled water. Wash all fruit.

My mother had to do most of the driving on the miserable journey north through Europe. Dad lost weight alarmingly, almost before our eyes. He felt very weak and could not eat any solid food.

Back home, even the thought of the butcher's shop seemed to nauseate him. Young Tommy had to carry on. His temporary helper was taken on the books. Dr Ralston told my mother that some continental bugs took a long time to clear up. The sanitation in Italy just was not up to scratch. There was nothing seriously wrong: no cancer, no ulcer. Perhaps his wartime illness had weakened the constitution.

But he became weaker and weaker. He developed pneumonia and had to go into hospital. On the last occasion I saw him, I noticed other visitors and patients on the ward looking at my father, at me, at my mother. They would stare over at us and whisper, then look away when I turned in their direction. I had the feeling they knew more than I did. I sensed what was happening, despite the cheeriness from the doctors and nurses and my aunts. My mother could not communicate with me. She had focused completely on the thin, grey figure on the bed.

My father waved weakly at me as I left the ward and I began to cry. Walking out through the lines of beds, I felt humiliated by the pitying glances from those strangers with their false teeth and dirty fingernails. My father, the Tartan Terror, died the following morning.

54

Another Father And Another Son

Once upon a time there was a young Bannock Bunter called Stanislaw Kowalik. He was a clever boy and did well at the High School, gaining five 'A' passes at Higher level. The subjects he sat were English, German, History, Latin and French.

He didn't like the English Literature he was forced to study. A lot of it seemed peculiarly empty. He preferred his own private reading which consisted of writers like Thomas Mann, Kafka, Conrad, Hasek and Hesse.

Foreign languages came easily to him. Maybe he inherited this from his father, Janusz Kowalik, a Pole who spoke not only his own language but also English, German, Czech and Slovak. Sometimes, in fun, father would insult son in Czech, and in turn be abused in French. In this way, both added to their scatological vocabulary.

One language in which Janusz showed no interest was Latin. Once, Stan began to translate the Mass into English for him but his father told him to stop. He said he wasn't interested. Latin had been good enough for his mother and father and it would be good enough for him. Stan explained that soon he would have no choice, soon the vernacular Mass would be introduced. 'In that case,' said his father, 'I'll stop going. It will mean I no longer have to listen to the Irishman.' The 'Irishman' was Father Dwyer, Bannock's parish priest. The Poles didn't think much of him. They said he had the hands and the head of a labourer.

Of course, Janusz didn't stop going to Mass when the changes came. He, along with the other Poles in Bannock continued to attend Father Dwyer's ten o'clock service, filling one third of the congregation. But instead of the Mass of their youth they heard the tones of Co. Kildare from the altar and strangled Bunter vowels from the pews.

Stan never attended Mass with his father. Instead he went to the Presbyterian service with his mother and her family. But he never felt quite at home there. He disliked the neat, grey suits favoured by the minister, Dr Thwaw, preferring even the shabby, shiny, black cloth worn by Father Dwyer on his occasional visits to the Kowalik house. The priest's pastoral visits were short, embarrassing affairs. Mrs Kowalik would disappear into the kitchen and make loud noises at the sink. Janusz would sit with Father Dwyer and make polite conversation while Stan sat in one corner, a silent accusation.

Religion made Stan uncomfortable. With Father Dwyer, with the Catholic Poles, he felt like an outsider, a member of the family who had taken the wrong path and of whom no one could bring themselves to talk. The priest rarely spoke to Stan directly, instead addressed his remarks through Janusz. 'How did the son get on in his exams?' he would ask, while the object of his question sat only feet from him. 'How is the young lad's nose now?' He seemed to have an aversion to Stan's very name. 'And the young fella, does he follow the football?' The boy felt he should be doing something positive to earn Father Dwyer's favour, but he did not know what that something should be.

Dr Thwaw was always exaggeratedly polite to him, asking after his health, his progress at school. But sometimes, Stan sensed the minister's eyes upon him, as if he was being examined for signs of regression. He felt as if he was constantly on probation. He always had to be on his best behaviour. If he transgressed, he would be sent back from whence he came. The body of the kirk reacted to him as an invasive presence. As his religious paranoia developed, he saw spaces being cleared in front of him in the church hall as if he had an infectious disease.

Over the years, sensations merged, interweaved into a damp Sunday blanket. Dr Thwaw's pipesmoker's breath; the incense smell of his father's best suit; heel-clicks on the tiled floor of the church; white gloves and silky, clip-on ties; the ponderous intonation of the words 'God' and 'Christ', 'Saviour' and 'Sin'. Life was sunshine and light until slippered shuffling and the creaking of the oak wardrobe in his bedroom announced the dawning of the day of rest.

Once, when he was nine years old, he went on a Sunday School outing to a neighbouring congregation in Eckmouth.

As it was raining, all the children were herded into the local Scout Hall where lemonade and biscuits and cakes were laid out on trestle tables. After a feed, games were organised, balloons were blown up, funny hats were issued.

Even back then, strangers could be attracted to Stannie's obvious confidence and love of life. A little girl with curly, blonde hair came up to Stannie and handed him her balloon. 'It's leaking,' she told him. 'It's no good. Would you like to burst it for me?' Stannie smilingly accepted. He placed the red balloon on the floor and jumped on top of it but since it wasn't fully inflated it merely bulged at both ends. He stood on its middle and squeezed the swelling rubber, digging in his nails until the balloon exploded with a satisfying bang.

He glanced up, searching for the approving face of the pretty little girl, but instead saw Dr Thwaw and the neighbouring minister studying him with pitying looks on their faces. They did not scold him for his crime but turned away shaking their heads. Stannie burned. He knew it was useless to explain. He ran from the hall in tears and waited on the bus for the rest of the group to arrive at the end of the party.

Some weeks later, Dr Thwaw visited Stannie's class at school and gave them a little talk on respect for other people and their property. Although the minister never once looked directly at him, Stannie knew the remarks were meant for him. He burned again and felt all the class knew of his disgrace, suspected that their parents had warned them about playing with the little Polish boy who had burst the balloon.

When, at the end of his lecture, Dr Thwaw asked the class if they would all try to be better boys and girls in future, Stannie shouted 'Yes!' louder than everyone else, and waved his arms in the air trying to attract the minister's attention. He wanted some positive sign of understanding, of forgiveness, of absolution, but the grey suit turned its back on him for some last minute words with the teacher of Primary Five.

Stan grew to resent the guilt induced in him by both minister and priest. Up in Mossy Glen, in the back of Heather Muir's Morris Minor, he decided that fornication and religion did not lie well together in a healthy brain. Something had to go. It was not a difficult choice to make.

It was an emotional moment when Stan announced to his

parents that he no longer wished to attend Sunday service. His mother suspected that Janusz and his friends lay behind the decision. She feared Stan would soon pop up in St. Margaret's. In a Presbyterian nightmare she could see him kneeling in front of the altar, rubbing his rosary beads, praying to the statues. She knew where the blame lay. All those rainy afternoons in the Polish club, talking to smelly old men. There would be no more.

Mrs Kowalik eventually forgave her son. How could she hold a grudge against her Stannie? Besides, the boy did not switch sides. He rejected both religions in equal measure, and somehow this satisfied his mother. Her real dread had been of a further conjunction between father and son. Already she was excluded from visits to the club and from an entire language, the 'mumbo-jumbo' of the secret conversations in Polish.

After the initial shock, Stan's rejection of religion was not discussed again. Like most families, the Kowaliks had an unwritten list of topics which they felt uncomfortable talking about. Under certain conditions, dialogues were containable: father and son; mother and son; father and mother. The critical mass was three Kowaliks. The ensuing reaction could produce a fallout of embarrassment, sulks, anger, tears, remorse, guilt.

A few years later, Stan's career choice joined that list. On the surface Janusz accepted his his son's decision; after all, what could a father do in the modern world? But in private he expressed his disappointment to his wife. He had dreamed so long of Stan the doctor. Now it would be Stan the teacher, dressed in a shabby little suit dusted with chalk. He remembered throwing snowballs at Sadlowski back in Tuszyn. The old man, headmaster of the little school, had despised all of his pupils and their parents and was in turn despised by them. He called them peasants, saw himself as a beleaguered outpost of civilisation. Outside of work, he distanced himself from community life. Most evenings he spent alone in his flat, reading English novels and listening to 'good music' on the wind-up gramophone he had brought with him from Warsaw.

One evening after school, Janusz and his friend Andrzej Tymowski had lain in wait for Sadlowski. Their teacher had kept them in late that day because he said their work was unsatisfactory. They lay on the flat roof of the baker's shop where he called every evening. They meant to shout abuse at him and escape across the flour store to the alley behind. As Sadlowski approached, he raised his hat to a lady and her daughter. All three stopped directly below the boys. Janusz could hear them talking about a concert they had attended the previous week. 'Marvellous!' Sadlowski was saying. 'Quite stupendous!'.

From where they lay, the boys could look down directly on top of the teacher's head. He had a bald patch on the crown and the scalp looked grubby through the thinning hair. Janusz turned to Andrzej and put an index finger to his lips. In reply to his friend's questioning eyes he gathered saliva in his mouth and stretched it out on the tip of his tongue, at the same time pointing to the street below. Andrzej grinned and nodded.

The two boys leaned over the gutter and took aim, working their cheeks and tongues to gather two healthy spitballs. Andrzej cut loose and his elastic gob dropped to land on Sadlowski's shoulder, dribble down his chest. As the teacher looked up, Janusz, taking sight through interlocked fingers like a bomb aimer, released his load and caught his target on the forehead.

As they scrambled to safety they shouted. 'Warsaw bastard!' 'Your ma's a whore!' In their haste, it was difficult to think of much more. They went home the long way round. It was worth the extra walk.

If Only I Could Drift Back To Childhood

Among all the horrible certainties of life is the inevitability of waking up the morning after a night on the piss. That is, unless you have died in your sleep. In many instances, death is the more attractive prospect.

I had dreamed bad dreams; I had sweated; I had contorted my body into the most uncomfortable position on the narrow bed. Now consciousness was returning. My eyes were glued together; my sinuses hurt; the inside of my mouth tasted like a badger's arse. But above all, edging through the cracks in the pain and discomfort, swamping the bewilderment at waking up in a strange room, came guilt.

Sometimes, hangover guilt has no real focus: it is just a vague feeling of unease, the mild paranoia induced by a rundown of alcohol in the system. At other times, memories of glazed hilarity from the night before can induce my toes to curl, make my body curl inwards to escape into a blanket womb, suspended in a pool of amniotic sweat. That particular morning was bad. As the memories came back, I wanted to disappear. If a self-destruct button had been available, it would have been pressed.

I had been awakened by music. Muffled, almost inaudible as I came to:

'Mummblemuff, ammffll mufflemuff, behiii mfffle dooe.'

Then as I fought to release my tongue from the roof of my mouth, as my ears unstopped, more distinctly:

'Mummblmuff, ammffll mufflemuff, behind the gree dooe.'

Was the record stuck? The same phrases seemed to be repeating:

'Mummblmuff, ammffll mufflemuff..' The door opened...'BEHIND THE GREEEEN DOOOOAAA!!!' A man came in. He spoke:

'How are you feeling this morning?' ('...BEHIND THE GREEEEN DOOOOAAA!!!')

I mumbled and felt my lips dry and chapped.

'Not too clever, eh?' ('...BEHIND THE GREEEEN DOOOOAAA!!!')

'Any chance of you turning the music down?' Charlie Trummle looked behind his shoulder as if surprised the record was playing:

'Not in the mood for old Frankie, eh?' ('...BEHIND THE GREEEEN DOOOOAAA!!!')

'Not in the mood for very much at all this morning, Charlie.' I rubbed my head, squueezed the temples. Charlie, my new pal (ah, the kinship of the bottle), disappeared and the music ended with a needle-rip. He shouted from the next room:

60

'Cup of tea?'

'Yes, thanks.' I looked at my watch. Thank God. Not late for work.

'Toast?'

'Yes...' I squirmed once more, trying to burrow into the lumpy mattress. Mrs Tochle. My table would be empty that morning. I looked at my watch again: half past eight. Barely time to make it to the bank, no time for any remedial action at the boarding house. I could see my landlady looking at my congealing fry-up. Her mouth would narrow. Later at my bed: pristine. Shake of the head. A libertine as well as a vandal. Then when she heard of my disgrace in The Old Mill: 'Hello. Is that 999. Give me the police.'

I ate my toast dry and gulped down the hot tea. Charlie sat opposite and laughed:

'What are you bothering about?' I had a long list. 'You worrying about being late? Old Macroom going to feel your collar? Tell him to fuck off. Catch the first bus out. Head for the South Seas.' He laughed again. He seemed to have fewer teeth this morning. 'No more Bannock.'

I wanted to follow his advice but knew I couldn't. Anyway, it would only be one more escape from reality. I would still have my knapsack on my back, full of Joyce and my father and my mother and myself.

'No more Bannock.'

'So you said, Charlie.'

'Talking of which, Stan called round late last night to see how you were. You were beyond talking at that stage. Do you remember anything about it? No? Well you'd drank all my whisky by that time right enough. You don't recall shouting out of the window at one o' clock in the morning? You weren't frightened of Macroom then.' My mouth dried up. 'What was it again? 'Fuck you Macroom. Away and screw Mrs Tochle' ('Hello, is that the police...?')

'You don't remember?' I didn't. Charlie laughed, louder this time. He was enjoying himself. 'What about pissing over the roof into the street?' ('Officer, I'd like to report....') I put the remains of my toast back on the plate. 'Don't worry; just kidding.' I was going off Charlie. It was time to go.

'Don't forget, Stan's calling in to see you at one o'clock.

He wants to apologise in person.'
  'Thanks, Charlie.'
  'Don't mention it.'
  'I'll see you again.'
  'You sure will.'
  'Sorry about the whisky.'
  'Forget it.'
  'Cheers.'
  'No problem.'
  'See you later.'
  'Have a nice day.' Ha, ha, ha.

Other Memory Lapses

I value photographs, diaries, all kinds of substantive records, because I have a very poor memory. I have to be constantly reminded of the truth about the past. If I do not have these reminders, I reinvent my own history. This is dangerous, because my doctor told me before I left for Bannock that I must confront and learn to live with reality, that is, with what I am and what I have been. It is not that I have anything to hide; there are no horrible secrets decomposing under the floorboards. It's just that life has never lived up to my expectations. Fiction seems more attractive than autobiography.

I have no one to blame for this but myself. All my life I have been waiting for something to happen. I have allowed tiny events to shape my future. I have been like a small rock at the bottom of a river, rubbed smooth of interest by a thousand million water molecules until I present no resistance. I lie there and the world washes over me. I should have been more in control. I should have tried to influence events. But it was always easier to wait until tomorrow.

I cannot remember ever making a rational decision about the course of my life. As a child, of course, my path was dictated by my parents. As a teenager, after the death of my father, my mother and my aunts influenced me greatly. When I became a man and gained some sort of independence, my twin aims were the avoidance of pain and the seeking out of a world where I would be happy. Unfortunately, I had no idea what happiness entailed, so I rejected every option in the hope that something better would turn up.

Much of my life has been spent in flight. On the run from anything, provoked by everything from fear, to vague unease, to boredom. Flight without a destination, all the while carrying a rucksack full of parents, of wife, of past failures, of groundless hopes. When I land and collect my luggage from the carousel, the whole poisonous mix explodes in my face, tainting me once more, setting me apart, restarting the whole process.

Some Of My Missed Flights

At various times in my life I have wanted to be:

1. A trainer of horses.

2. A pilot.

3. A writer of Science Fiction stories.

4. A farmer.

5. A popular figure with many close friends.

6. A dealer in postage stamps.

7. An artist.

8. A deck hand.

9. A scrap metal merchant.

10. An expert lover of women.

11. A professional football player.

12. A fisherman.

13. A financial czar.

14. A scientist on the Antartic Survey.

15. A famous man in any sphere of life.

16. A long distance lorry driver.

17. A film director.

18. A gold prospector.

19. An auctioneer.

20. A well-respected man in the community.

21. A fur trapper.

22. A marine biologist.

23. A bricklayer.

24. A forester.

25. An expert, to whom people would turn for advice.

26. The owner of a second-hand furniture shop.

27. The perfect family man.

28. A publican.

29. A turf accountant.

30. A connoisseur of fine wines and food.

31. A vet.

32. A pianist.

33. A wit.

34. An ornithologist.

35. A deep-sea diver.

37. A zoo-keeper.

38. A bookseller

and

39. A builder of dams.

Back In The Real World

Going to work with a hangover. In pain. Late. Sweating. How many zillion times before? How many zillion times to come?

Back in the city, queuing for the bus, squeezed in the subway, I would try to forget about my predicament by focusing my hatred and disgust outwards. Sometimes it worked. I would chew my way through the morning paper, wondering why the whole world, apart from me, could be so stupid. Every statement inane; every policy insane. I would look at the old women sucking at their cigarettes, look at the men who stared at the breasts of young girls. Comfortably anonymous, I could feel superior. What could they know? What had they experienced? Blinking, tube-tanned office girls and young insurance drones wearing two-tone shirts. It was easy, consoling and delicious to justify my latest binge as a sign of frustration, an advanced intellect, overdeveloped sensitivities. As my head thumped, I planned the perfect future.

And so I would reach my destination proud of my condition. I took pride in my piss-hole eyes and badger's breath. They were signs of distinction. They were the products of my creative spirit, as valid as a poem or a song.

The act of drinking, even if solitary, gained me admission to a club with millions of members. I could recognise fellow spirits in novels, in plays, in the feature pages of newspapers. I belonged with them. I had a history: the drunken poet, the hell-raising actor, the tortured, self-destructive genius. Alcohol was theatre. I became a player by raising my glass.

But Bannock was not designed to encourage fantasy and delusion. The Bunters were woven from familiar, sensible cloth. My hostility was reflected back by those glassy pairs of eyes which had been pinned to the heads by brass skewers. Directed inwards.

Butcher, draper, fruit bannock baker. All jolly Bunters together. And me. Slouching along the wakening streets. Wanting to disappear.

'Good morning.'

'Morning.'

'Lovely morning.'

'Isn't that the new man at the bank?'

'The usual today, Mrs Pruddle?'

'Weems, I believe…'

'And how is little Struan today?'

'George Weems.'

'Sorry, 'The Borderer' hasn't come in yet.'

'Oh dear.'

'From the city, I believe.'

'Oh deary me.'

'Can I get you something else instead?'

'He looks a bit ill, does he not?'

'Oh deary me, no. Nothing else.'

'Very puffy around the eyes.'

'Hello, Mr Weems.'

'Married?

'Nothing else….'

'You'll never believe what Norman did with the car.'

'No sign of a wife.'

'That'll be one pound forty-four, please.'

'Did you hear what happened to the Minister's daughter?'

'With Agnes Tochle.'

'And thanking you.'

'A small, fruit bannock please.'

'He'll be late for his work, will he not?'

'Thank you, Willie.'

'Maybe he has the day off.'

'Hey, Mr Weems....'

'And four drop scones.'

'Did you catch that mouse yet?'

'Morning.'

'Morning.'

'Lovely morning.'

Winkie looked carefully at his watch as I struggled with the keys at the door of the bank:

'It's nice weather for a day off, Mr Weems.'

'Yes indeed, Derek. Don't let me stop you if you've any plans. You know, rowing the Atlantic, discovering Australia, anything like that.'

'You don't look too good today, Mr Weems.'

'Well, thanks for letting me know, Derek.'

'A bit under the weather?'

'That's right, Derek. A bit under the weather.'

'Late night last night, Mr Weems?'

'Derek, have you no work you could be going on with?'

Christ, had Winkie been there last night? Even if he hadn't, he would get to hear of it sooner or later. There were no secrets. And what about Kathy? She had hardly said a word this morning. She might refuse to work beside me. Her trade union would fight her case. It would be in the papers. And Macroom: 'We can't have you sullying the good name of the bank, George.' That stupid woman. She should be locked up. A public apology, that's what was required. I would have to talk to Stan at lunch time. He would have the answer.

Winkie opened the door to customers and a few straggled in. A wasp droned above my head. I shuffled the files on my desk, spread around a few papers. My pants and my vest felt wet with sweat. Figures and names blurred before my eyes. I was afflicted with a combination of boredom and unhealthy nervous excitement.

I slit open that morning's mail and piled the letters and documents in a wire tray, substituting order for effort. At the top was a standing order form from Welp, the man from the hardware store. The trap. The mouse.

I slowly pulled open the bottom drawer of my desk. There were fresh, black droppings inside. Open more. The tip of a long, ringed tail. Quickly. Snatch. Wide open. The trap had sprung. It had snapped shut, crushed. In its jaws was a large, pink mouse. It was around nine inches long. It had long protruding teeth. Around its neck was a collar and a black bow tie. It wore a white waistcoat on which was printed a star and the words: 'Marlon Mouse'.

I touched the furry, nylon body with my index finger. Marlon emitted a loud squeak. For a single second, Winkie turned from the counter where he had been dealing with a customer. He let out a strangled snort through his nose. As he returned to his work, I could see his shoulders shake silently as he flicked through a bundle of used notes.

Coming And Going

Once upon a time, a young man left home to go to live in the big city. He left, not because he was unhappy but because he wanted to study, to become smarter than he already was.

Stanislaw Kowalik went to university to study History. He liked reading about the past. He also liked hearing about it from his father, Janusz Kowalik, a Pole who had lived through some of the most important events in twentieth century Europe.

Stan lived in a very historical place: Bannock, the 'Borders Cockpit'. His mother's family had lived in the town for hundreds of years. To her and her family, Bannock's past was all fuzzy dates and places, Kings and Chiefs, fairytales and annual pageants. Stan wanted to cut his way through all of that. He wanted to investigate, to research, to truly understand the components that had combined to create himself, the Polish Bunter.

When he finished his studies, he would teach others. He would make the past come alive, as it had come alive for him in the Polish club listening to the memories of his father and of his father's friends. Alive, not like the annual waxworks in the town square, but in the sense of the past being truly part of the present, the earth from which today sprung.

Stan enjoyed university. He liked the academic work and also the wider social activity in the city. He got to know a lot of people, both male and female. Making friends had always come easily to him.

Janusz and his wife both missed their son. Over the years the boy had become more and more important to each of them. When Stan went away for the first time, the couple realised how little they had left to say to one another. They looked forward to the end of term when Stan would return and the house would fill with talk.

After his first year, Stan's uncle fixed him up with a summer job behind the bar in The Ploughman in Bannock. His mother did not like him working in a pub, but at least it meant he could spend more time at home. Janusz began to drop into the bar each evening his son was on duty, just to keep an eye on him. This was a pleasant arrangement because it gave Janusz an excuse to have a few beers and whiskies in a good cause.

Stan was breezing through his exams. At the end of his second year he was accepted into the honours History group. His tutor was most impressed with his work. Stan even had time to do a few extra courses in the Department of Slavonic Studies.

That summer, he planned to save up his cash from the job in the Ploughman and pay his first visit to Poland. It was an exciting prospect. His father began to hint that he might even shut up the shop and come with him. He probably still had cousins in Tuszyn, although they had lost contact. The hints changed to probabilities, then to certainties. Janusz had caught a fever from his son.

At night, after the pub shut, the travellers looked at maps of Central Europe and planned out a route by train. Visas and so on would have to be arranged immediately. Accomodation might have to be booked in advance. It seemed a long time to wait. Both of them felt like leaving that very minute. Meanwhile, there was the atlas. Once, Janusz traced the boundaries of Poland with his finger and shook his head as he read out the names of towns and cities on the Soviet side of the border. Tears stood in his eyes: 'My mother had relatives in Lwow, you know,' he told his son. 'I know, Dad, I know'. They began to count off the days on the calendar hanging in the kitchen.

No one knew what happened. No one had been given the slightest hint. One minute the trip was planned, the next minute it was off. One evening, Stan walked into The Ploughman and told the manager he would not be coming back to work. He had to leave, go back to the city. He couldn't explain.

Janusz closed for business and disappeared into the flat above the shop. The Kowaliks, father and son, were the sole topic of conversation in the Polish club, where a farewell party had been organised in honour of the trip. Contact with Janusz was broken. All kinds of rumours spread among the closed community. They knew Janusz had been displeased with his son's choice of career. Had this led to an argument and a split? Michnik claimed he had seen Stan board the bus to the city. He was sure the boy had a black eye and a badly cut lip. Kociolek swore the mother was behind it. Stan had wanted to attend mass with his father. She wouldn't have it and had given the boy the boot. It was only a matter of time before Janusz left too. That's what happened when you married outside your own.

Tired of speculation, despairing of the shop ever reopening, Tadeusz Szydlak and Joe Orszulik decided to call in at the flat to see what was wrong.

'   The door was opened by Mrs Kowalik. She sniffed when she saw who had rang the bell. Szydlak and Orszulik bowed their heads. Janusz's wife always filled them with apprehension. In her company, they always felt as if something nasty was going to happen. She made them feel they were about to be interned or deported as undesirables. In conversation with Janusz, her name was never mentioned.

Mrs Kowalik gestured over her shoulder towards a closed door. 'He's in there,' she told the pair. 'Hiding.' The woman left them standing on the landing and went back to the kitchen where a washing machine shook on the linoleum floor. 'When you're ready to go you can take him with you.'

70

Szydlak knocked on Janusz's door but there was no reply. Orszulik coughed and shuffled his large feet. They heard a noise. The door opened.

Janusz looked older. He was dressed in slippers and a dressing gown. He motioned them in to the darkened room.

More Travelling

The Bannock Explorers by Struan Winkie

The second in an occasional series of monographs published by the Bannock Historical Society.

Many men have set off from Bannock in search of_____

_____
_____drives them? _____
_____gone before, those who have_____light for the world _____
_____history _____
_____out of all proportion to its_____

What thoughts were_____
_____Major George Tait, late of the_____maps and charts deep into the night on board_____
Hobart,Tasmania?_____
journey frozen wastes_____
_____reach the South Pole by means of human muscle power___

_____
_____
_____selecting the fifty members of his expedition, he included six men

72

who had been reared within a ten mile radius of_____, a ship's carpenter; Dr David Dick, the expedition's medical _____

_____

____Rob, ex-K.O.S.B; and John 'Jock'

_____

_____

As we all now know,_____
_____failure and tragedy.____
____pack ice in the Ross Sea,_____

_____
_____scientific gear was lost
_____sit tight and wait,_____

_____

_____

_____, rescue _____

_____'that angel from a balmy heaven: Shackleton'. _____
_____almost exhausted____
_____found thirty-eight_____
____Rankie, who had fallen to his death while attempting to scale_____
_____Crum had lost both_____
_____ malaise
_____ entire limb _____
____who seemed to escape from the ordeal relatively unscathed, both physically and mentally, was George Tait himself. He had spent his time as constructively as he_____
_____standard maps_____
____Tuckeridge_____ice shelf.

_____never returned to the Antarctic, despite several attempts __

_____
_____Scott's expedition of 1910 but_____
___'petty jealousy' on the part__
_____Byrd's air expedition but _____

_____
_____in a letter as 'one of the fathers of modern_____
_____ at his Borders home in 1946, aged seventy-seven years. _____
outlived by the one-armed Sergeant Rob,_____
_____legacy from the major, erected a memorial at the gates of the estate in honour of what had become _____'Bannock Expedition'.
_____six foot high marble pillar rising from a granite plinth on which is carved the names of all those who ventured _____

_____
___Atop the pillar is a statue, not_____flightless bird._____
_____scientific memorial_____
extinct 'Tait's Penguin', whose purple crest and yellow breast was first seen on an ice-bound island in the Ross Sea by those men, now gone, who took part in_____

William Jeffrey's exploration of the dark heart of Africa

An Angry Man

My name is George Weems. I am thirty-eight years of age and I will be thirty-nine this coming August. Like most people, I worry about getting old. Time seems to pass so quickly, even when you're not enjoying yourself. And when I go, when I pop off, when I cross over the great divide, what then? Who will remember me? What will I leave behind, apart from a pile of rusting paper clips?

This is one of my major concerns. Not death itself, but the world after I am gone. Sometimes I lie awake at night worrying that no one will attend my funeral, that no one will even notice I have vanished. Then, worst of all, weeks later, sympathy will be expressed when my neighbours hear the news. Poor man, nobody came to see him off. Didn't he have any family? Terrible shame.

Feeling wonderfully superior, Mrs Bogie and Mrs Logie will settle back on their big, fat arses and pour themselves another cup of tea, happy that they have a moronic husband, a dribbling son or a gibbering sister to tuck them safely under the sod and give them a decent send off. Isn't that nice wallpaper? I will disappear for good, never to return.

Pathetic, isn't it? The preoccupations of a diseased mind. Why can't I turn round and say 'fuck it'? Or, better still, the full English breakfast: 'FUCK IIIIIITTTTTT!' Give us another: 'FUUUUUCCCCKKKKK IIIIIIIIIITTTTTTTTTT!!!!!' That's the ticket. Those winds need to whistle round my brain for an hour or two, to clear out all the unhealthy air.

Why do I concern myself with trivia? Why do I spend time thinking about the Bogies and the Logies while my life swirls down the waste pipe?

Once I had a dream which seemed to last for hours. I was on the beach with my mother and father. I was digging with a plastic spade, making a tunnel for my toy cars, when I discovered a silver sixpence in the sand. This excited me, so dug down more deeply, foot after foot after foot, searching for other coins. Occasionally, I was successful. Each time I found a sixpence I would clean it with saliva, then put it in my pocket.

When I had a pocketful, I ran up to show my parents. My mother and father were sitting in the sand dunes with a picnic spread on a rug before them. There were sausage rolls and cakes and glasses of lemonade. 'Look,' I said, and held out a handful of sandy sixpences towards them. They smiled and looked behind. The dunes changed from sand to piles of silver coins, not just sixpences but shillings, florins, and gigantic, shining half crowns. I dropped my tarnished discovery and ran off. My parents continued to smile. I don't think they were being cruel. It's just that they were better at seeing the joke than I was.

I was a pretty humourless little boy, even when I was fully conscious. What most interested me was collecting and saving stuff up. I also liked putting things in order and neatly arranging all sorts of junk – socks, toy soldiers, comics, model aircraft – on shelves and in drawers. Pity I couldn't have sorted out my brain cells while I was at it.

When I was round about nine or ten, I went through a hoarding phase. I would ask for a drink of lemonade and take it to my room. Behind the closed door, I would drink half of it and pour the rest into a bottle which I hid in my toy cupboard. There, behind the Lego and Scalextric were other bottles full of bubbleless cola and silted-up limeade, boxes and jars of mouldy biscuits, jelly babies and squares of fruit 'n' nut bar. I never ate any of it. I just wanted to save it up. What was I waiting for? A nuclear war?

I don't know if my parents discovered my secret supplies. If they did, it certainly wasn't mentioned. Maybe they thought squirrelling food was normal. Maybe they were hoarding too.

Certainly, my father liked saving money. It's not that he was mean: My mother and I were always well dressed; the larder was always full; each year, we went on a fortnight's holiday to the seaside. No, my father was just careful. If he had any spare cash, he didn't spend it on drink or fags or a new telly. He stashed it away in his little, blue Post Office savings book. He told my mother he wanted to make sure she was well provided for if, one day, he should 'pop off' unexpectedly.

If my father had a highly developed sense of his own

mortality, it probably stemmed from his wartime experiences. The tank crew he served with had been fried by a shell from a German 'Tiger' while he was in hospital suffering from amoebic dysentery. His brother, George, had disappeared while on A.R.P. duty, reduced to tiny, unrecognisable fragments, vapourised by an exploding land-mine. My father thought that he might disappear one day too. He was worried he would leave behind a destitute widow and a little, hollow-eyed Oliver Twist.

The death of his brother had a large impact on my father's life. Uncle George had run the family butcher shop after the death of my grandfather, and he would have continued to do so if it hadn't been for the intervention of the Luftwaffe. My father had also trained as a butcher in the shop but the business was not big enough to support them both, especially if each married and had a family. ('Had a family' – that would be me, Even then I was having an impact.)

So my father had the pilot and bomb aimer of a Junkers or a Heinkel to thank for his inheritance.

He later paid homage to his lost brother by naming his first born (and, it was to turn out, his last born) son 'George'. I often wonder if he imagined that I, in turn, would enter the family business. I don't know because he never told me. He died before we could discuss the matter. He died before we could discuss anything at all. We had a quiet, undramatic, on the whole friendly relationship, but I cannot remember anything I ever said to him, or anything he ever said to me. We must have talked about something. I was thirteen when he died. Thirteen years is a long time. I can remember him coming home from work; I can hear the slam of the door of the van. My mother would tell me to clear up my toys, put my paints away; get washed, ready for tea. He would smell of soap and his big, freshly-scrubbed hands would dangle from the sleeves of his jacket. I could hear the stubble on his neck rasp his collar as he kissed my mother. He would turn to me and smile.

I can see my father's mouth move, but in my dreams, nothing ever comes out. He was mute and I was deaf, and now it is too late for us to learn a new language.

Going And Coming

Once upon a time, a young Bannock Bunter called Stanislaw Kowalik fell out with his father. No one knew what the argument was about. The father, Janusz, refused to discuss the matter, either with his wife or with his friends in the Polish Club. The son, Stanislaw, was not available for comment. After the bust-up, he left Bannock to return to the city where he was studying History at the university.

It was a mystery. The two had been planning a trip to Poland at the end of the summer. The were both excited about the prospect and had spent their time together looking at maps and railway timetables. They had seemed more like close friends or brothers rather than father and son. Then, without warning, Stan was on a bus heading north and Janusz was locked in his room, refusing to come out.

Apart from Mrs Kowalik, the first to see Janusz after the argument were Tadeusz Szydlak and Joe Orszulik. The shop was closed, so they called in at the flat to see what was wrong. This was a brave thing for them to do because Mrs Kowalik didn't like Janusz's friends. She referred to them as 'that bunch of smelly old men'. Tadeusz and Joe were a bit frightened of this woman. She made them feel insecure, as if their papers were not in order.

A farewell party had been prepared for Stan and his father at the Polish club. Everyone wanted to feel they had a small part to play in the trip. Some planned to entrust Janusz with messages and gifts for the family back home. Others had asked him to visit cemeteries and villages which no longer existed, or to track down missing brothers and sisters. He told them he was going for weeks, not months, but the requests, the pleas, the demands piled up. Everyone in the Polish community had a stake in what came to be known as 'The Expedition'.

Then it was all over. Everyone was shocked; some were resentful. A lot of hope and emotion had been invested in the trip. The old Poles had become like little children looking forward to Christmas. All their thoughts had been concentrated on this one event, and they had been able to forget the daily disappointments and depressions which before would have fallen like bags of cement.

Someone had to be blamed. Janusz's wife seemed the likeliest candidate. The Poles were like toddlers whose ice cream had been snatched from their lips. A semi-hysterical atmosphere filled the club. Some action had to be taken to right this wrong. The boy had to be brought back. There had to be a reconciliation. Old men paced the linoleum floor in front of the bar, almost crying with frustration. They now truly felt like strangers in a foreign land.

The incident fuelled the paranoia which lay barely beneath the surface of most of the Poles. None of them had lost the sense of being aliens in a country which, at best, only tolerated them. The Poles' superficial success and integration masked a disdain for the host community, which in turn was born of fear. Even now, after twenty five years, they felt they could be turned out at any time. To go where? They no longer had anywhere to go. And who had this power to dispose? The fat shopkeepers and empty-headed housewives of Bannock, who thought Poland was the capital of Russia and that the Oder was a bad smell. The dunderheads who bought newspapers whose print rubbed off on their hands, who spent their time in bookmaker's shops losing their social security money.

However much the Poles despised Mrs Kowalik, and sneered at her ignorance and narrow-mindedness, she had one great advantage which they envied: she belonged. This, they felt, they could never experience again. The most they could hope for was to enjoy that reassuring warmth vicariously through Stan, who was their living link with a form of permanence. Now he was gone. Someone had to be blamed.

Despite spending an hour with Janusz in his darkened room, neither Tadeusz nor Joe could find out what had happened. The man just refused to talk of what they wanted to know, instead reminisced about Stan's rugby matches, and about the time Tadeusz baptised the boy in the sink behind the bar. He seemed distanced from reality. Joe said the man was 'carrying a great grief'.

When they reported this back to the club, the other Poles were of the opinion that Janusz was protecting the mother. Somehow she had driven the boy away, had caused the son to sin against his father. She was jealous of The Expedition. She knew that it was a sign of the boy's feelings towards his Polish heritage. By ruining the plans, the mother could punish both Janusz and his friends. But what could they do? They had never felt so powerless.

Eventually, Janusz re-emerged into the world. The first anyone knew of it was when the shutters on the shop were taken down and the sign in the door changed to 'open'. After the visit of Joe and Tadeusz, many of Janusz's friends were wary of approaching him and confined their contact to waves from the street outside. Kociolek reported that 'the patient' was looking much like his old self; Michnik claimed the man looked 'near death'. After this report, Janusz looked up from the counter one afternoon to see the faces of seven Poles peering at him through the window of the shop, examining him like a troupe of doctors with a wonderfully diseased patient.

Two weeks later, Janusz attended Mass for the first time since Stan's departure. Father Dwyer had heard of what had happened but had not attempted to interfere. He did not understand the Poles and sensed he was only tolerated in their company because of his position. Instead of going to the club as was usual, Joe and Tadeusz walked with Janusz from St Margaret's back to the house. They did not talk a great deal. Stan's name was not mentioned. As they left him, the two old Poles invited their friend to the club for a few drinks. Janusz said he would think about it.

In fact, he did not go back to the club for another month. Even then, his visit was short because he sensed some of the others felt awkward in his presence. In addition to this, Janusz felt guilty about letting everyone down over the trip. As he left that evening, he turned to the half dozen members at the bar and said to them: 'I'm sorry'. The old men nodded to him and felt his pain in their tears.

Cartoon Time

Kathy said she would take the mouse home for her youngest.

'I thought Derek would have outgrown this sort of thing by now,' she said loudly as I unpinned Marlon and handed him over. 'I thought you moved on to plasticine last week, did you not, Derek?' she asked the boy as he stood facing the empty customer floor, his shoulders still rocking.

I felt pathetically grateful to this woman I hardly knew. It seemed a long time since anyone had been kind to me, had protected me. I wanted her to hug me too. Maybe invite me home for a bowl of hot soup and a plate of buttered rolls. We could pass the time pulling Winkie's limbs from his torso before throwing the pieces on her log fire. God, had I failed to grow up? Did I still need a mother to save me from the rough boys?

Macroom was late. Was he consulting with our superiors as to my fate? What was to be done with the roaring assistant manager? The pervert, the drunk. It couldn't be tolerated. Not in Bannock. What about standards. He had been told about the importance of fitting in. Further promotion had been mentioned. He would have to go. Back to the city where perhaps such behaviour was considered normal. There was no room for it here, that much was certain. Perhaps his whole future with the bank should be questioned.

Macroom liked questions. These are some of the ones he had dealt me since my arrival:

1. Do you play golf yourself?
   No.

2. Are you a fisherman, George?
   No.

3. Any luck on the house front?
   No.

4. When do you expect your better half to join you?
   Never.

5. Made much headway with the Society publications?
   No.

6. Settling in now, George?
   No.

7. Getting to know the customers?
   No.

8. Is Mrs Tochle looking after you?
   No.

9. Finding your way around?
   No.

10. Any problems?
    Yes.

And now there was to be another:

11. Can you account for your behaviour last night?

I haven't always been so timid. At one time I was actually quite confident, within my own, rather limited horizons. Until I had the stuffing knocked out of me. Let that little, overused metaphor come to life. Imagine your favourite Teddy being systematically beaten with a bottle until the straw bursts from his mouth and his seams split apart.

Macroom appeared at half past ten. As usual, he had untidy folders of Historical Society crap under his arm. As usual he dropped one on the floor on the way to his office. Winkie scrambled to pick up the papers. Macroom smiled benevolently at his fellow Bunter grovelling at his feet and then turned to face me as I sat at my desk pretending to do difficult sums.

'Grand morning, George.' His round face beamed as if it had been burnished. He hadn't heard. I was so relieved I

82

almost stood to attention.

'Certainly is, Mr Macroom.'

Macroom gestured towards Winkie's greasy head: 'It's good to see the younger generation still has some manners.'

'Yes indeed, Mr Macroom.' I too directed a smile towards Winkie.

'Busy today, George?'

'Not overly so, Mr Macroom.'

'Well, keep up the good work.' Still grinning, happy with the world and his place in the grand, systematic order, he disappeared into his hole in the wall, watched admiringly by Winkie.

'Have you nothing to do, Derek? What about those new current accounts?'

'Yes, Oh Master.' The boy salaamed before me. 'Your wish is my command.' He grinned insolently, realising my powerlessness. Like most childishly cruel people, he had developed a great sensitivity in detecting weakness. His smile revealed long, pointed incisors. Something would have to be done about Winkie.

Something would have to be done. In the future. Safely tucked away behind today. I was paralysed. Every morning I woke up and said to myself: 'This can't go on.' But of course it did. I walked and I talked and I filled in forms; I smiled and scratched my backside and picked my nose; I cut up fried bread and dipped it in my egg; I drank tea and coffee and milk and water; beer and whisky too. I lived on, extended into another day, used up possibilities.

'What do you want on your sandwiches today, George?'

Was it that time already? Another morning over. Doesn't time fly?

Stan, of course, didn't turn up to see me at lunchtime as he had promised. I wasn't surprised. I was a quick learner.

Instead, his wife appeared in the bank that afternoon, shouting loudly that the automatic cash dispenser had swallowed her card. I looked at her over the top of a pile of files, hoping she wasn't going to cause a scene that I would have to become involved in. She was wearing the same waxed jacket but this time had her hair pinned up, revealing small, delicate ears. I could feel blood surging in my head. My hands shook as

I scribbled gibberish on my blotter. I imagined she would accuse me of another offence. The police would be called and I would be led along Bridge Street in handcuffs, then locked in the pokey until a lynch mob broke me out.

To me, the woman seemed demented, capable of anything. She was obviously so deranged she was incapable of feeling embarrassment, pity or any other emotion which might modify her behaviour. She could sweep me up like a wind taking control of a dry leaf, and deposit me under the wheels of a car or on top of the Bannock flagpole.

As Kathy reasoned with her and Winkie tried to extricate her card from the back of the machine, Stan's wife puffed on the end of an enormous cigarette and blew extravagant puffs of smoke into the air. She looked around and talked about a twopence halfpenny piggy bank in a Mickey Mouse town. She referred to Macroom as 'The Gnome of Bannock'. She called Winkie 'the village idiot'. I felt her eyes on me and cringed. At any moment she would turn on me: 'The Groper'; 'Johnny Fingers'.

I leaned my left elbow on the desk and supported my chin on my hand. Beyond a curtain of fingers I could see her looking at me through the armoured glass above the counter. Winkie held out her card and she snatched it from him.

'About bloody time too,' she said. 'Now can I have some money?' Kathy took her card and inserted it into the desktop terminal. 'Fifty. I thought these things were supposed to cut out hassle. God, Bannock. The land that time forgot. How does it feel to be living in a black hole?'

Kathy gave a tight smile and silently handed over a slim pile of notes. The woman went on, even as she walked towards the door: 'I don't know why I bother. There's nothing to spend it on here. Big woolly jumpers and stale buns. Give me strength.' She was gone.

'That woman.' This was Kathy.

'She ought to be locked up.' Winkie.

'No wonder her husband is never at home.'

'Did you hear what she called me?'

'Poor Stan.'

'Did you hear what she called Mr Macroom?'

'The nerve of her.'

84

'I ought to tell him.'
'Damn cheek.'
'He should bar her from the bank.'
'I ought to have said.'
'Take her cards away from her.'
'But then, there's no telling some people.'
'Close her account.'
'What did you think of that performance, George?'

Well I'll tell you: I'm happy to have escaped unnoticed, unscathed, unembarrassed. For that I am grateful. As for everything else, I couldn't give a monkey's nuts. Does that answer your question for you? Thank you very much indeed. And good night.

Sleep Tight

'Good night, sleep tight, hope the bugs won't bite.' When I was a child, those were the last words I heard most nights before going to sleep. They would be spoken by my mother or by one of her two sisters or by my grannie. They said those words to me each night up until I was almost twenty, until I had to plead with them to desist. They couldn't understand what the problem was.

'Listen, Grannie, do you think you could stop saying that.'

'Why, Georgie?'

'Well, I think I'm getting a bit old for that kind of thing.'

'I don't care how tall you grow, you'll always be my wee boy.'

'Grannie, it gets a bit embarrassing when you're nearly twenty.'

'Embarrassing? But there's no one here to get embarrassed about.'

See what I mean?

After my father died, my Auntie Isa came to live with us

in the flat above the butcher shop in Corsock Street. It was going to be a temporary move and was intended to help my mother over the worst of the shock of her bereavement. After a few weeks, my Auntie Betty seemed to move in too. I say 'seemed to' because it was difficult to establish exactly when extended visits became permanent residence.

I had seen a lot of my aunts even when my father had been alive. As neither of the elder Beaton sisters had married, they both still lived at home with my gran and grandad in Dalriada Street. This was just round the corner from where we stayed. That's how my father and mother had met. My mother used to buy sausages for her tea from my dad's shop.

After her marriage, my mum remained close to her two sisters. They shopped in town together every Saturday; on Wednesday evenings they went to the pictures; in between, they visited one another almost daily. Looking back, I can hardly remember a time when my aunts were not around me, either in our house or in Dalriada Street.

So, I grew up surrounded by women: my mum, my two aunts and my grannie. Dad was working at the shop. Grandad, a large, silent man who smoked a pipe, always seemed to be out, although no one ever mentioned where he went to. He would just disappear, dressed in a brown Crombie, pulling his Jack Russell, 'Barnie', behind him on a lead.

One day, six months after my father's death, Barnie came back alone from one of their outings, whining and trailing his leash. Before the smell of pipe smoke faded from the curtains, grannie had sent Barnie to the Cat and Dog Home and moved in with us. Our little household became complete.

As you can imagine, I received a lot of attention from these women. It was not unpleasant. I was the centre of a little, self-contained universe. I was the most important thing in the world to each of them. My name was top of the list at Christmas. No one forgot my birthday. After Saturday shopping trips into town, there were always packets of crisps and bags of sweets in the cabinet drawer.

It was difficult, but I tried not to take advantage of the situation. All I had to do was to mention some new, super-duper Airfix kit that had appeared in the shops and I could be sure that someone would buy it for me. If I talked of an impending issue of stamps, Grannie would slip me some cash and tell me not to tell my mum. I grew up surrounded by temptation.

I never asked my mother how long Grannie and my aunts were going to stay with us. It just seemed natural that we should all live together. One day I came back from school to find that a brass plate with the name 'Beaton' on it had joined ours above the letterbox on the front door. It seemed a sign of permanence. After a while I came to feel as if things had always been that way.

Grannie referred to me as 'the man of the house'. When we went to church on Sunday, all five of us linked arms as we walked along the road in our best clothes. I was always squeezed in the centre of the four women. It felt good to be surrounded by so much friendly flesh.

We had no money problems. My mother had dad's savings book and also the butcher business, although we took very little to do with this. The shop was looked after by Tommy Traynor, who had once been my father's apprentice. Our name was still above the door but in reality, Tommy worked for himself, paying my mother what amounted to rent each week. In addition to this, both my aunts had jobs: Betty, the oldest sister, worked behind the counter in the local sub-Post Office; Isa was manageress of a small ladies' outfitters. Life drifted on, the calm interrupted only by the gentle swell of birthday parties and trips to the seaside.

After the death of my father, my academic career took a turn for the worse. I had been a bright little chap in Primary and my parents had made the decision to send me to the City Grammar School. This meant they had to pay fees and buy a load of books and sports gear and stuff but they considered it worthwhile. After all, I was all they had.

I did well in my first year at the Grammar and even finished top of my class (although, to tell you the truth, I was only in 1B: 1A was where the real brainboxes were to be found). English was my best and my favourite subject: I won the Hewison Essay Prize for the first year with a composition entitled 'The City In The Year 2000'. Mr Pewitt, my teacher, wrote in his comments that it was 'a work showing great imagination and maturity'. My mother kept the essay and showed it to all the neighbours.

But the glory days didn't last. The beginning of my second year was disrupted by dad's death, and after that things began to go wrong. It started off with homework. There always seemed to be something better to do: building models of the Graf Spee and the Catalina flying boat; sorting out a three pound bag of used stamps; reading an Isaac Asimov omnibus; tidying my sock drawer. Every school morning I woke up in a panic because I knew I was in for a day of lies, confrontations and punishments. The day of rest was ruined because I could see the school week looming up after 'Sunday Night at the London Palladium'. Saturday became the day before Sunday, every tick-tick of the clock bringing closer that smell of floor polish and stewed tea which filled the corridors of my prison.

The solution, of course, was simple: sit down and do the fucking homework. But I couldn't. It wasn't because it was too difficult: I could cope with most of it while being rattled around on the top deck of the bus to school. No, it wasn't the difficulty, it was just a problem with my brain, like a stutter or a stammer. I would dump my briefcase on the floor and it would lie there, accusingly, until next morning. Every time I looked at it I would begin to feel anxious. Yet if I extended my hand towards a textbook a lump would come into my chest and it would grow until it threatened to fill my insides, closing out all life and all possibilities of pleasure.

And yet on the rare occasions I did complete the work at the correct time and in the proper place, I felt a tremendous sense of satisfaction and relief. So what was the problem? Experimental animals make similar connections every day: pigeons strut around the test area and peck at the correctly coloured disc; brown rats memorise their cardboard maze. In turn, they are rewarded with raindrops of corn and squares of mouldy cheese. But in my case, the correct reinforcement mechanism did not seem to be in place. I needed a few sessions with a sunken-cheeked Skinnerian to get my saliva glands back in working order.

Instead, I took the easy way out: I became 'delicate'; I became sickly; I became a 'not-well boy'. I caught every bug that was going and invented the rest. Nothing could have been simpler: I was surrounded by four women who thought the sun shone out of my arse. The sicker I got, the more sweets were bought, the higher the 'Airfix' kits piled up, the fatter became my stamp albums. We all became entangled in an unspoken conspiracy. Mum and Gran liked my company at home. Auntie Isa and Auntie Betty wanted excuses to buy me presents. I wanted to lie in my dressing gown, reading science fiction books and watching the 'Woodentops' on the telly. Presumably the school was happy too, since they received a substantial sum each term for providing me with a desk and chair which were rarely used. I was the perfect pupil.

To keep up appearances, my mother sent the school regular sick notes which chronicled the course of my bogus illnesses. She wrote them on paper my father had ordered from the local printer before he died. We had twenty-four boxes of this paper at home and more in the safe at the shop. At the top of each sheet was a drawing of a basket full of roasts, pies, and joined-up sausages. Underneath this image was a little motto in red ink. This is what it said: 'Weems – The Family Butcher – We Meat Your Needs'.

City Slicker

Once upon a time there was a Bannock Bunter who fell out with his father. The disagreement was so serious that the son ran away from home and did not return for over six years.

While he was away the young man, Stanislaw Kowalik, completed a first-class honours degree in History at the City University. Stan had planned to go from there to Logie College, where he could obtain the teaching diploma which would equip him for the profession he had always planned to enter. Stan had been a man with a vocation. Stan had been a man with a mission to explain. He had thought that a lot of empty heads needed filling.

Stan had wanted to show people that conscious time did

not drop from the sky; that we did not wake up one morning to find a world newly invented. Stan had believed that our lives could only be understood through a knowledge of the past. (One of his tutors at university had compared present reality with fungal sprouting on the surface of a midden. Stan thought this was a clever and an apt metaphor: he remembered how easily the toadstools in Irkdean woods were swept aside by his boot; how feeble were the etiolated growths from shaded stumps. History was compost – decayed weeds and vegetable matter; the grass clippings from the lawns around war memorials; a touch of blood and bone.)

Stan might have made a good teacher. He knew his subject and had an easy way with children. They liked him. He knew how to make them laugh. He knew exactly when they expected to see a sad or a happy face. Stan had learned to press all the right buttons.

But Stan never went to Logie College. He never got that certificate, never became a teacher. Sometimes things happen. Sometimes your life can change without you even noticing.

The Giant Arse

Some days, it just never stops. After toothless Charlie Trummle, Marlon the Mouse, Winkie, Macroom and Mrs Stan, came Roderick and Bruce, twin cheeks of the giant arsehole of Bannock.

One at a time.

After lunch, which for me consisted of two bites of a salad roll and a carton of Ribena, I settled down at my desk again, hoping for the chance of a snooze. I leaned my head on my left palm and in my right hand held a pen poised above an important looking file. Each time I dozed, my head would nod forward then violently whiplash back just before I crashed into the pages of mortgage applications. Neither of my fellow employees could avoid noticing my bobbing and snuffling.

Winkie, of course, saw it as an opportunity for a bit of sport at my expense. Vaguely, through my doze, I could hear him commenting in the background.

'What is it you call that disease? St Vitus's Dance, is it?' Then:

'One, two, three, DOWN we go. No, not quite. Back up. Try again.' Then:

'Snore…Snore…Snore.' Then:

'Wait for it, wait for it. Kerluuunk!' Then:

'Whew, that was close. Nearly wiped out another mortgage holder there.'

I heard Kathy telling him to shut up but Winkie couldn't stop. This was one of the funniest things that had ever happened to him. He also found excuses to come across to my desk to wake me up:

'You haven't seen my pencil sharpener have you, Mr Weems?' Or:

'How many zeds in snooze, Mr Weems? Or:

'Mr Weems, do you mind if I go home. I'm feeling a wee bit tired.' Hilarious, eh?

I was forced to wake up when Kathy reminded me she was to leave early to take her daughter to the dentist. I had to be ready to take over at the counter, smile at the customers, twinkle those eyes that looked like a spaniel's balls. I slipped another Polo Mint into my mouth to hide the smell of stale booze.

It was just my luck that Roderick, the left arse cheek, arrived as Kathy left. Five minutes earlier and I would have escaped. Winkie was counting out pennies from a woman's gigantic leather purse, moving his lips as he slid the coins over the formica towards his tummy. Roderick, whose name was unknown to me at the time, whose face I had never seen before, rapped his knuckles on the counter to attract my attention. I raised my head and loathed him on sight.

Roderick looked to be in his early thirties, overweight and jowly, with a dark shadow on his chin. A large, swollen lower lip shone pink against the stubble. His large nostrils gaped black. A frown wrinkled his brow. He had one of those faces on which, through the lines and sags of age, it is still possible to see the petulant features of a spoiled child.

He wore a tweed jacket, a checked shirt and a Bannock Rugby Club tie. On his head, crowning his five feet eight inches, was a deer-stalker hat. Who was he? The great detective? Big game hunter? Wrong. Gluteal alarm. Confirmed sighting. Left hemisphere. One of a pair.

'Is he in?' Roderick looked at me as I moved towards him then rolled his eyes in the direction of Macroom's bolthole. I felt like being awkward. I think it was the hat.

'Who are you referring to, sir?'

Roderick sighed. He looked towards Winkie who had broken off from his penny counting. Winkie sighed too. Then they both decided to ignore me for a little while:

'How are things with you, Derek?'

'Not too bad, Roddy. And you?'

'Oh well, you know what they say: 'Hark a spoon, cast a loon'.' 'Roddy' glanced briefly back at me. Winkie sniggered. I could only imagine that I was being discussed in Bunter-speak. 'You must tell your dad I was asking after him.'

'Will do. How's the rugby?'

'Oh, not too.....'

While all this was going on, I was standing, listening, waiting. Like an idiot. I had to act. My hangover was making me ratty. I imagined cracking Winkie's head with a roll of pound coins. Screaming 'Aaaaaaarrrrgggghhhh' in 'Roddy's face and punching his hat.

'You were asking for.....?' Roderick gave me his attention once more:

'The manager.'

'Have you an appointment?' This was power. I heard Winkie sniggering again. Where was that roll? Roderick bowed his head, took off his deer-stalker and wiped his brow with a handkerchief. He was balding and had arranged long locks of hair across his scalp. He swept them back into place then replaced his hat. He looked at me pityingly and spoke as if I had the intelligence of a small pimple:

'Mr Macroom will see me. Just tell him I am here, if you please.'

'I'm sorry, if you don't have an appointment.'

'Just tell him.'

'I'm afraid the bank cannot run for your convenience.'

'Just tell him.'

'Mr Macroom is a very busy man.'

'Just tell him his son is here to see him, will you.'

Bastard.

'Roderick Macroom.'

Bastard.

'I'm sure he will manage to fit me into his busy schedule.'

Bastard. 'Roddy' dismissed me by turning his back and walking from the counter, He stood, looking at the street outside through the clear glass of the 'B' in bank. He was confident I would follow his instructions. Confident I would not leap the armoured plate and garrotte him with the draw strings of a cash bag.

'Mr Macroom, your son is here to see you.'

'Roddy? Show him in, George, show him in.'

I was now a butler, a valet, a lackey. The Right Honourable Roderick Macroom, and Lady Lucinda Fart. Pardon my dick, m'lud, I'll cut it off. 'Roddy' would be spilling the beans about me inside: 'Terrible fellow. What's his name? George Weebs? My god, is that the fellow who raped the woman in The Old Mill? Call the police.'

Father and son emerged half an hour later, just as we were about to close. The two stood at the door to the street beyond. As Roderick left he turned. His eyes glazed when they met mine. I did not exist:

'Bye, Derek, see you soon.'

'Bye, Roddy. Give Inversnook 'Hell' on Saturday.'

'We will.' He patted his father on the back. 'Bye for now, Poppa.'

'Remember me to Pamela.'

'I will.' He left.

Macroom sighed and closed the door behind his son. 'Oh well,' he said. 'Back to work.' He glanced up at the clock above the counter. 'Oh my goodness, is that the time. I must rush.' His rate of shuffling increased. 'Lots to do, lots to do.' He went back into his room and came back out in a few seconds, dressed in his hat and coat, carrying the Historical Society files under his arm. 'Man the fort when I'm gone. I must run.' He did. Almost.

New names, new mosquito bites as time passed.

Roddy. Tochle. Fondle. Marlon. Macroom. Stan. Missus. Charlie. Winkie. Bannock. Bunter. Mouse. Trap. Divorce. Pin. Feckle. Loon. Spoon. Nook. Toast. Inver. List. Snook.

Although I had been in Bannock only a short time, I could already walk the streets on automatic pilot. My feet knew the route from the bank to Mrs Tochle's boarding house, knew when to take a detour to The Old Mill. Not tonight. Barred. Maybe my face on a mugshot above the bar.

I found myself 'home' before I fully realised I had left work. Had I locked up? Only an anxiety spasm. I remembered inserting the key and wondering what it felt like to be part of such a silky, well-oiled fit. Home. A smell of air-freshener. The aerosol stood on a half moon table behind the door. 'Rose Bouquet'.

Also behind the door stood a couple of suitcases. Tan, with black rubber corners. They looked familiar. They were mine.

'Misteghh Weems?' A thin man had emerged from the door of Mrs Tochle's 'Private Lounge'. He was about my own age, his face dominated by almost colourless eyes and topped with hair waved like a crinkle-cut crisp. He gurgled his Rs on his palate, closing the airflow above his tonsils with the back of his tongue. 'Misteghh Weems?'

'My name is Bghhuce Tochghhe.' Ls too. 'Mrs Tochghhe's son.'

'Pleased to meet you. Could you tell me what...' I looked towards my cases. 'You know, just what is going on.'

'That's what I wanted to speak to you about, Misteghh Weems.' We both pressed ourselves close to the wall to allow Wilton, the Jehovah's Witness, to squeeze past. He stepped over my cases and almost tripped on my golf umbrella which lay behind.

'Evening.'

'Evening.'

'Ghhoveghhy evening.'

'New arrivals?'

Tochle Junior gurgled towards Wilton's back. 'Grrarggggh.' Then we were alone again.

'Why have my bags been removed from my room?'

'That's just what I wanted to discuss. Would you ghhike to step into the pghhivate ghhounge?'

'Not really. I just want to know what the idea is.'

'You'ghh sughh you don't want to...?'

'Will you get on with it.' Bruce sighed then took a deep breath:

'To put it quite bghhuntghhy, Misteghh Weems, my motheghh would pghhefeghh if you made aghhteghhnative aghhangements for youghh accommodation.'

'What the hell do you mean?'

'My motheghh says theghh have been seveghhaghh in-cidents, Misteghh Weems. She mentioned some damage to the waghhpapeghh.'

'A pin. I put a bloody pin in ......'

'Not onghhy that but appaghhentghhy theghh was some sort of incident ghhast night.'

'What..'

'My motheghh wasn't theghh you undeghhstand, but she heaghhd of some unpghheasantness in a pubghhic house: The Oghhd Mighh, to be exact.'

'Oh..'

'And then with you not even coming back hegghe ghhast night.'

'I'm sorry, did I break curfew?'

'You must ghheaghhise, Misteghh Weems, my motheghh is not a young woman any moghh. She is not ghhunning a hosteghh foghh Heghh's Angeghhs and Punk Ghhockeghhs.'

'Jesus Fucking Christ..'

'Misteghh Weems, I must ask you to modeghhate youghh ghhanguage. This is a Chghhistian house.'

'A Christian house? What about me? Where am I sup-posed to go?'

'That is not my concegghhn, Misteghh Weems. My conceghhn is the weghhfaghhe of my motheghh.'

'Well, you can tell your mother where she can stick her wallpaper.'

'Ghheeghhy, Misteghh Weems. I do not think that is caghhed foghh.'

I picked up my cases and began to leave. My heart was beating strongly. For some reason I felt exhilarated. I wanted more: 'Fuck you, you Bannock twat.' The sweat dried on my back.

'I must pghhotest. I and my motheghh aghe both customeghhs of youghh bank.'

'Is that right? Fuck your current account too.'

'You can be sughhe none of the otheghh ghhandghhadies in Bannock will take you in eitheghh.'

'Screw them and all.'

'Misteghh Macghhoom wighh be heaghhing fghhom me.'

I suppose he would be. I now had to work out if I really cared.

Hobbies Page

By the time I was seventeen I had read hundreds if not thousands of science fiction books, watched billions of hours of television, constructed eighty-seven Airfix models, accumulated a stamp collection with a catalogue value of £2,752, and passed two 'O' Grades, one in English and the other in Geography.

My favourite science fiction books were the Robot series by Isaac Asimov, *Fahrenheit 451* by Ray Bradbury, and *The Day of the Triffids* by John Wyndham. My favourite television programmes were *Doctor Who*, *Top of the Pops*, and *Z-Cars*. My favourite models were the Sunderland, the Chance Vought Corsair, and the Heinkel HE 219. I specialised in the stamps of the United States of America but also had a little sideline in Malta and Cyprus.

I must have been mentally retarded.

If not mentally retarded, then emotionally so: drifting from minute to minute, year to year, as if drip fed on Librium. I smiled a lot, and people smiled at me. I was happy because I was not aware of any reason to be unhappy. Even traumas like the death of my father seemed to wash over me. I was a chucklehead.

I caught bugs and viruses every Sunday night as I sat in my dressing gown watching the telly. As The Tiller Girls grinned and kicked and contestants tried to Beat The Clock, I would cough and splutter over my mint humbugs. 'I don't like the sound of that boy's chest,' my grandmother would say. Another week off school. Oh, paradise on earth, to wake up 'sick' on Monday morning.

And so, a large part of my life was spent at home in the company of my mother, my grandmother, and my two aunts. They seemed to think I was normal. Just a bit sickly. Gran used to enjoy taking my temperature and feeding me cough mixtures. Playing nurses and patients. I suppose it kept her occupied.

I formally left school the year I passed my two 'O' Grades. I had scraped the English on native wit, passed the Geography, due to, I'm sure to this day, mistaken identity. With my passing into manhood, my mother decided it was time to convene a family conference to discuss my future. She took this seriously. One Saturday evening, all five of us sat round the big table in the livingroom, facing each other as if we were at Yalta or Potsdam. Mum had a pile of notepaper in front of her, each sheet having the Weems' basket of roasts, pies and joined-up sausages printed at the top. In her hand she held a pencil I had won at the carnival the previous Christmas. It was rainbow striped, and at the blunt end was glued a pink rubber in the shape of a monkey.

The butcher shop was out. That was established right at the start. It was not the kind of environment suited to a person whose health was not robust. I was relieved. I was friendly with Tommy Traynor, who had run the shop since my father's death, but he had always seemed to me like a being from another world. In a sense, this was correct: Tommy was an earthling, I was a Tube from the planet Tuba.

(Young Tommy had thick, hairy forearms below his blood spattered coat. His hands, pink through repeated washing, were constantly mobile: juggling chops and tying roasts; slicing steak and mincing mince. He was only six or seven years older than me but seemed decades further advanced. At the time of my careers conference he had a moustache, and was married with two kids. Once, when he had called in at the house to see my mother about something to do with the shop, he picked up the model of a 'Stuka' dive bomber I had been working on. His fingers, like a bunch of Weems' special pork links, closed over the fuselage as he admired my work. Then he tried to spin the propeller and the whole front assembly fell off. Tommy bowed his head before me. I could see he was deeply ashamed of what he saw as his clumsiness. He offered to buy me a new kit but I explained that a bit of glue would repair the damage. We seemed to get on well together after that.)

'It's too cold and damp in that shop,' Aunt Betty said. 'The boy would catch his death of cold.' Everyone, including me, nodded in agreement.

'Anyway,' said my mother. 'I wouldn't like Tommy to think that we were edging him out.' This time, everyone shook their heads. There was a pause while the adults considered the alternatives.

'What about a doctor?' asked my grannie. 'It would be nice to have a medical man in the family. 'Doctor Weems'.'

'I don't think Georgie's got the qualifications for that, Mum,' explained my mother.

'What? Are you saying my grandson's not clever enough?'

'No, not that, Mum. It's just that George missed a lot of school. He got behind in his work. He doesn't have the passes on paper.'

My grandmother still wasn't satisfied: 'He's a damn sight smarter than some of the doctors I've been to.'

'I'm afraid that isn't the point, Mum,' said Aunt Isa. 'Flora is right. George can't become a doctor with two 'O' Grades.' Gran thought for a few moments:

'I suppose a dentist is out too?'

'Och, Mum.'

'Don't worry, George.' Gran placed her hand on my arm. 'You don't want to spend your life rummaging around in people's mouths anyway, do you?'

I grinned and shook my head. I looked at my watch. *Doctor Who* began in half an hour.

That particular meeting ended without the question of

my future being resolved. Each of the adults said they would make enquiries as to what sort of careers were available for a boy of my abilities. I was urged to give the matter some thought. I couldn't spend my life sitting at home. This, I think, was the first hint of reality to enter my life.

A few weeks later, at our third conference, Aunt Betty came up with the solution. Maisie Troup, who worked beside her in the Post Office, had a brother who was married to a woman whose father was a bank manager. Now, Maisie knew for a fact that the bank was always looking for new recruits. If it was agreeable, she would speak to her brother, who would speak to his wife, who would speak to her father, to see about getting George an interview. It was quite straightforward. Mum and Gran and Aunt Isa were enthusiastic. It sounded quite good: 'My son works in the bank, you know.' 'George? Oh he's in banking now.' 'My grandson, the banker.' Already I was a Rockefeller.

What did the young man in question think?

I imagined working in a bank to be concerned mainly with counting out small hummocks of money. This appealed to me. I liked counting and sorting things into piles. I agreed to the process being set in motion. Everyone was delighted. My mother pressed the tip of her pencil to the sheet of notepaper before her. The final full stop. We sat back, triumphant.

I was successful. The aptitude test was simple. Well coached by my family and devoid of any normal inhibitions, I breezed through the interview. Eight weeks after our final conference, a new bank clerk was born.

Let There Be Light

The Inventors of Bannock by Roderick Macroom M.A.(Hons)

The tenth in an occasional series of monographs published by the Bannock Historical Society.

'In the engine rooms of our _____Seas; mapping new canals and railways in far away____; constructing bridges and roads through _____ _____find the men of Bannock.'[1]
_____hundred Bunters and I will build you a nation.'[2]
_____hint of the esteem in which the men of Bannock were held by at least two of the chroniclers of our now forgotten_____sphere of activity Bunters_____scientists, the technologists. From our farm-steads and firesides we_____: bringing food where there was_____; light where there was darkness.
But why_____ _____world prosperity?_____education system is monasteries of _____

1. 'The Borderer Abroad' by J.A.____and McHale, 1931); p17.
2. 'Out East: The Memoirs of General Sir Roger Wheale' (Dodder _____ p168.

100

_____envy of the_____
become known as the 'Bannock Geft',
that facility_____
____practical application _____
naturally to those born in 'God's
Welk'.[3]

_____
frontiers of human understanding.
ingenuity, have made_____
_____prosperous, or a happier
_____:the
inventors and the discoverers of
Bannock.
The Second World War_____
_____potential. In 1939 Dr
Wallace Pumphry, son of the Bannock
manse,_____
University._____volunteered
_____
____seconded_____
_____

_____
_____twelve he had supervised
the construction_____
_____
_____
Ferguson tractor _____
chicken droppings.
_____fifteen,
Pumphry_____
undergraduate. His precocious talents
amazed students and _____
_____abrasive personality.
Dr Robert Arthur called_____

3. For an explanation of this term, see_____
_____

101

_____ '4 _____'torque
in semi-rigid structures', work which
_____attract
national_____up the
chair in_____

_____
only thirty_____active service_____
___turned_____
_____research _____

_____Boffin Barracks', had been set
_____technology _____

_____
freedom he needed to_____
_____war against Hitler.'5 ___

_____
____The Pumphry Group'. _____
devices,____converted barn well away

_____

____'Pumphry Bridge', a compact,
easily portable_____
_____Allied advance through the

_____
_____'P-Strip' and the 'P-_____
_____immensely strong matting_____
_____temporary airstrips_____
Construction Battallions_____Pacific
Theatre during_____
_____'Mulberry' harbours
__D-Day_____'Pumphry was 'ere!').

_____
_____remembered _____

4. 'Camelot': _____
_____
5._____
_____.

the 'Pumphry Wheel'._____

_____the minefields of occupied Europe,_____inspiration to his_____

'The Rollin' O' The Ring,' he later recalled,_____sight of the smoking circle bowling down Mill Street towards the River Irk. Around the circumference_____flaming brands,_____spectacle_____
_____I sought.'

_____feet in diameter, _____at great speed, detonating_____

_____metal flails attached to_____

_____chemical rockets positioned along_____

_____same manner as the brands
_____
cheers from often hard pressed infantry.

_____
___threads of _____
_____Bechtel_____
_____greatest construction and _____, tunnels, dams and_____
_____globe.

_____New Mexico with his Canadian _____to revisit the place of his _____

_____
___The Rollin' O' The Ring which inspired him all those years ago.

The experiments of Arthur Crum, the Bannock-born inventor of television, rank with those of

103

Breeding

Once upon a time, there was a clever Bannock Bunter called Stanislaw Kowalik. At the age of eighteen, Stan went to the city to study, hoping to become even smarter than he already was. Sure enough, after attending university for four years, Stan graduated with an enviable degree. In his final term, he submitted an honours thesis which his tutor later described as being among the most original and the most intelligent he could remember. The title of this work was: *The Invention of Polish History*.

During this final year, Stan also found time to get married. The new Mrs Kowalik was a rather beautiful girl from the city called Briony Parr.

Briony was a student too. She studied Chemistry at the City University. She liked to find out exactly how little pieces of the world combined to form bigger pieces. In the laboratories, she listened to things bubble and fizz and pop; she watched the air cloud with smoke.

Stan and Briony had known one another vaguely for almost a year before they first got close at an end of term dance organised by the university's Historical Society. They got so close that, two months later, Briony confirmed to Stan over the telephone that she was pregnant.

Stan laughed when he heard the news. He laughed because he was happy. He had fallen in love with Briony and her condition gave them the ideal excuse to get married right away. He was also happy about the idea of becoming the father of a child. He felt he would make a good dad and couldn't wait to try it out.

When Stan laughed over the phone and talked about how excited he was, Briony cried. She cried because she was happy too. Briony was also in love. She wanted to marry this man and live with him for ever. As they laughed and cried together, Briony patted her flat tummy and thought of what lay inside.

They had a quiet wedding in the Registry Office. Stan's

104

side was represented by his mother and an aunt from Bannock. He explained that his father was ill and had to stay at home. When they heard the news, Stan's new in-laws said: 'Oh, dear. Isn't that a shame.' Briony's parents helped the couple to rent a small flat near the university and they moved in after a week's honeymoon in a caravan on the coast.

Stan graduated in the summer and his baby son, Daniel, was born three weeks later. The new father earned money labouring for a squad of bricklayers he had met during a holiday job on a building site. These men called Stan 'The Professor' and teased him about his name and his education, but Stan didn't mind. He liked them, and he knew they liked him. They drank together on Friday nights after they were paid, slapped one another on the back and told each other jokes and old stories.

Occasionally, Stan still thought of going on to Logie College, but his vocation had disappeared. He was offered the chance of post-graduate work at the university, but turned that down too. His thesis had burned him out. He wanted to leave History behind him. Anyway, with a wife and child to support, he needed instant cash. The future 'would look after itself'. Everything would 'sort itself out'.

When possible, Stan worked seven days a week: as many hours as he could find. During every one of those hours he thought of his new family and smiled or laughed. The world was a fine place.

Briony had successfully completed her second year while carrying Daniel. She completed her third year successfully too, helped by her mother who looked after the baby while his parents were working. That summer, she gave birth to another son, Adam. With the responsibilities of two young children, her studies in her final honours year suffered. Stan helped all he could but his time was limited. Briony's mother became an almost constant presence in the tiny flat. Sometimes, tempers would begin to overheat.

Briony was awarded a Lower Second degree instead of the First she was capable of. That same week she learned she was pregnant again. 'Haven't they ever heard of birth control?' asked her father when his wife told him. 'Where are they going to keep this one? In the coal bunker?'

In fact, the Kowaliks bought a larger flat. It was situated in a rather undesirable part of the city, but it had five bedrooms and it was cheap. They moved in just in time for the birth of their third son, Joseph. Mr Parr counted those rooms and looked at his daughter suspiciously. He was right. Fifteen months later, the fourth child, a daughter, was born.

When little Heather joined the crowd, Stan's father-in-law asked him if he now considered his family to be complete. 'It's a bit uneven as it stands,' Stan told him. 'Three boys and one girl. We'll have to try to balance it out a bit.'

'It's alright for him,' Mr Parr said to his wife later that night. 'He doesn't have to look after the little beggars.' This was true. Stan adopted a rather traditional view of the family unit. It was Briony's job to feed, clothe, clean and wash the growing number of small children. It was Stan's job, as he put it, 'to keep us out of the workhouse'.

After Heather came Ishbel; after Ishbel came John. 'It's her own fault,' said Mr Parr of his daughter. 'She's a grown woman, not a prize sow.' Each time Briony announced she was pregnant, her mother cried. In the beginning, these were tears of joy. After the third child, the nature of Mrs Parr's tears changed, as did her attitude towards Stan. 'Can't you do something, Charles?' she asked her husband. 'What do you want me to do?' replied her husband. 'Castrate him?'

In family discussions, the Parrs tried to explain this philoprogenitiveness in terms of Stan's background. 'He's Polish,' Mr Parr would say. 'All Polish peasants want dozens of children to look after them in their old age.' 'He's a Catholic,' Mrs Parr would say. 'They can't use contraception. They want to flood the world.' To people of such modest habits (Briony was one of only two children), reproduction on such a grand scale was rather obscene; slightly animal in nature. Mrs Parr in particular found it embarrassing when her friends enquired after Briony's health. 'How many has she now?' they would say. Or, 'What's the news from Maternity Ward 10?' Or perhaps, 'Soon have a little football team, won't they.'

But what of the parents of all these babies? How did they feel about things? Stan always laughed when his in-laws raised the subject. He told them they should be happy with all their

106

grandchildren. 'Think of all the birthdays you can celebrate throughout the year.'

And Briony? She told her mother she loved Stan and she loved her children. What could be simpler? 'But how long can it go on for?' asked her mother. 'Ten? Fifteen? Twenty?' In the end, mother and daughter avoided the subject by mutual agreement. Discussion always degenerated into argument.

The Parrs could only hope their daughter and their son-in-law would burn themselves out. After the birth of little John, which gave her daughter six children under the age of eight, Mrs Parr began to undergo treatment for anxiety symptoms. She had a horrible sense of things spinning out of control. Worst of all was a recurring dream in which Briony gave birth to a litter of puppies.

'It's all right,' the worried grandmother would explain to the gawping neighbours who had somehow found their way into the delivery room. 'They're all going to good homes.'

What About Me?

I had nowhere to go. I was on the streets of Bannock with my two suitcases and soft rain was beginning to fall. My feet took me in the direction of The Old Mill, my liquid womb, but I knew that was lost. There was no welcome there any more. I walked towards the river.

Market Square was empty. Shops and offices and schools were closed and most people were back home watching the telly, or doing their homework, or listening to mince and potatoes cook on the gas.

Pigeons rested on the statue of William Jeffrey and on the green wooden benches beside the bus stop. They called to me as I passed by: 'Grp, grp, grp'. Several fluttered towards me looking for crumbs or an empty crisp packet. They pecked at grit on the paving stones and chuckled as they bobbed from my path.

The buildings on the square and in the streets leading off were faced with blonde sandstone or red whinstone. The tallest were three storeys in height, and all were topped by steeply pitched roofs of blue-black slate. A few of the shops had striped awnings shading their windows, and a candy pole revolved outside the gent's barber. Beside the grilled door of 'Border Antiques' a pair of small, brightly painted cartwheels was bolted to the wall.

Many of the windows above the shops advertised offices and businesses behind. 'Dod, Jack & Tait – Solicitors and Notaries Public'; 'J.J. Murgle – Dentist'; 'Calder & Son – Auctioneers and Valuers'. On the edge of the square, growing in its own traffic island, was the town's war memorial. A bowed, helmeted soldier stood on a white marble plinth which bore the names of Bannock's dead. Abernethy and Arthur; Bannerman and Bun. Pumphry and Paton; Tulp and Tod.

Radiating at right angles from the sides of the square were four streets: Lower Main Street led in from the south and exited towards the north as Upper Main Street. To the east, back towards Mrs Bogle's boarding house was Banner Street. To the west, leading down the hill towards Temple's Bridge over the River Irk, was Mill Street.

At each corner of the square was a statue of a famous Bunter: clockwise, from William Jeffrey in the southeast, were Arthur Crum, Robert Winkie, and Thomas Bogle. Jeffrey, the explorer, held a bible in his hand and wore a sola topi on his head. Arthur Crum, the inventor, from whose lap Stan Kowalik had pissed on my umbrella, studied a valve through a magnifying glass. Robert Winkie held aloft the ring which condemned John Heddington. Thomas Bogle, the first Master of the Guild, waved a bronze flag on which could be seen the coat of arms of Bannock.

At the corner of Market Square and Lower Main Street was the bank where I worked. I half considered going inside for shelter but I saw shadow movement through the window and heard the noise of Mrs Weir's vacuum cleaner drift through the door. Pubs beckoned too: 'The Ringman'; 'The Square Bar'; 'The Ploughman'; 'The Turk's Head'. I knew, however, that all heads would turn as I entered, and a silence would fall for several seconds while I mumbled my order and fumbled for change. I didn't want company or questions from strangers. I wanted to press a button and wake up far away. Home. Wherever that was.

As I walked down Mill Street I heard more clearly the sound of the Irk. When I crossed over Fogorig Row and entered the park which ran along the banks of the river, I could see the water, swollen by the recent rain, rush under the arches of the bridge. Branches of trees and pieces of timber were being swept along in the muddy flow which lapped at the lowest points of the grassy banks.

With my handkerchief, I cleared rainwater from a bench and sat down with my feet resting on a suitcase. I raised my umbrella and sank down into my damp coat, rolling my shoulders to relieve the cramp caused by my forced march in the damp air.

My mind was strangely empty. I felt as if I had cast myself adrift. I could suspend my will and float with the current. Decisions pained me. I would give them up. Give up worrying too: it didn't make things any better. Just let things happen. Relax; go limp as a leaf in the river. Be swept out to a sea of tranquillity.

I could smell a Sunday dinner being cooked in my mother's kitchen; I could hear the laughter round the table as I carved the salmon cut for the first time. A hand was in my hair as I bowed my head in embarrassment.

I lay on the carpet before the gas fire. Rain ran on the windows. I could smell model paint and feel dried adhesive on my fingers. The taste on my tongue was the gum from stamp hinges.

My wife and I sat together in the living room of our house. We were both silent. She began to weep but when I moved to comfort her she let out a cry and ran from me.

In room number seven on the second floor I wrote down jumbled thoughts and drank whisky mixed with tepid water from the tap. Below, on the street, was the sound of a couple going home, her feet racing to keep up with his stride through the drizzle. They laughed together. They did not know I breathed above them.

I would take up fishing; buy a small dinghy; perhaps learn to sail. Come the summer, I could travel to places I had never been. There would be a woman waiting for me at the end of my train journey, at the end of my flight. We would talk and I would make her laugh. We could hold hands and climb to the top of the Eiffel Tower; we could look from the Golden Gate Bridge, down, into San Francisco Bay; we could lie in a gondola and kiss as water sounds filled our ears.

I could breath a new me on this bench, in the rain.

'I thought I recognised that umbrella.'

I had not heard the car drawing up behind me. I looked over my shoulder and through the park railings saw Stan leaning out of the window of a large, expensive-looking saloon. He waved to me:

'How are you doing?' I couldn't speak. 'I'm sorry I couldn't make our appointment at lunch time. I've just been looking for you.'

'Oh, have you?'

'Yea. Peter at The Old Mill said you hadn't been in today. He wondered what had happened to you.'

'He wondered what had happened?' I repeated. What was going on here?

'Yes. He's got used to seeing you at this time.'

'Oh.' Was he trying to take the piss?

'Then I went to Mrs Tochle's. She said you'd left. She says she still owes you for the rest of the week. Found somewhere better to get the old head down?'

'Well, in fact,' I looked around the park, 'I was thinking of kipping here for the night. It seems to be the only place that's open to me these days. Thanks to you and that wife of yours.'

'Yes, I must apologise for that.' Stan opened the door and stepped out of the car. He leaned against the railings and looked at me through the bars.

'Apologise?' I stood and faced him. 'Do you know I've been thrown out of my digs over what happened last night.'

'Oh, so that's it?' Stan laughed. 'You should be thanking me. I've heard Mrs Tochle's breakfasts are rather hard on the digestion.'

'Oh, I should be thanking you? Do you know I've been banned from every other boarding house in Bannock too?'

'What? Who told you that?'

'Mrs Tochle's son.'

'Oh, Bruce?' Stan laughed again and rubbed his big, broken nose. 'You shouldn't pay that much attention to Burny Bap.' Stan's levity was beginning to annoy me. What was this Burny Bap stuff? Why had everyone to speak in a foreign language? Perhaps Stan began to sense my irritation. He became serious. 'Listen, don't get too worried about last night.'

'Don't get too worried? I was accused of indecent assault in front of dozens of people. Where does that leave me?'

'Perhaps I should explain.' Rain was still falling. Stan looked up at the sky and pulled up the collar of his jacket. 'Listen, there's no point standing here getting soaked. Come on up to The Old Mill and I'll buy you a pint.'

'You must be joking. I'm never going back in there again, that's for certain.'

'Well what about The Square Bar?' I shook my head. 'Or The Ringman?'

'No.'

'Jesus, you must be worried.' He thought for a moment and looked up at the sky once more. 'Look, this rain's going right through to my skin.'

'I'm not exactly the driest man in the world either.'

'Come on home with me and we can have a drink and a chat and maybe sort something out.' He saw me about to speak. 'Don't worry. Briony is up in the City, visiting her parents.' So that was her name. It seemed to fit. 'She's taken the kids too.' I hadn't thought of them having children. What were they like? Half a dozen broken nosed little boys and girls. A broken nosed baby. 'What do you think?' I thought. 'Don't make me feel even more guilty than I do now.'

The rain began to fall more heavily on my umbrella. It was now dark. Float like a leaf. Out to the Sea of Tranquillity. I shrugged my shoulders:

'I could certainly do with a few whiskies.'

Stan grinned and walked to join me at the park gate. 'That's the man.'

Cured

At the age of sixteen years and ten months, I went to work in the Lowland Road branch of the Royal Northern Bank. Two months before my seventeenth birthday, still only an occasional shaver, I embarked upon, as Mr Prewm the manager insisted all we new recruits put it, my 'banking career'.

It was great. I enjoyed it. All my illnesses cleared up at once. After two months in the job, my mother swept all my medications out of the cupboard in the bathroom, put them in a large plastic bag, and dumped them in the bin behind the house. I became a new boy. Maybe even, hesitantly, a new man.

My grannie was the only one who seemed a bit miffed about all this. Her favourite patient had been discharged: I no longer wanted to lie around in bed all day being dosed with cough syrup and smeared with chest rub. She, of course, still insisted that I 'looked a bit peaky' and that I could 'do with a wee day in bed', but I was having none of it. I had become a superman: I was impervious to cold germs, flu bugs, dysentery, sleeping sickness and bubonic plague. I felt as strong as Young Tommy. I wanted to flex those muscles that had lain unused for so long. I had woken up.

But Gran needn't have worried. Her time was yet to come. She didn't have to put her nursing skills into permanent cold storage. I had one last viral strain incubating inside of me.

What were the things I liked about my new existence? Tell you what. I'll set this out in an orderly fashion, as befits an analysis of this period in my life when I entered my orderly career, when I became an orderly person. The period in my life when I put aside childish things and escaped from emotional anarchy. Temporarily. Yes. Set things down neatly. Put those thoughts in order. Show you're organised. That there's more in the noddle than just a jumble of nerve endings and synapse farts. What'll I do? Make a list.

A LIST OF THE THINGS I LIKED ABOUT GOING OUT TO WORK FOR THE FIRST TIME.

1. I had a new, concrete identity. I was George Weems who worked in the bank. For the first time I felt as if I had a purpose. For the first time I felt as if I could participate in life instead of trying to avoid as much of it as possible.

2. I bought and wore a suit (later, suits) and an assortment of shirts and ties. Previously, my wardrobe had consisted of items of school uniform, assorted 'leisure clothes', i.e. baggy twills and nylon casuals, and mounds of well-worn pyjamas.

3. When I travelled to work on the bus, I began to sit upstairs. This gave me a whole new outlook on life.

4. I bought a newspaper each morning and the man in the newsagent got to know me by my first name. He would have my paper ready for me as I entered his shop at eight o' clock on the dot.

5. I received wages each fortnight. Some of this I gave to my mother to pay for my lodgings. Some I put into a savings account all new recruits had opened in the bank. The rest I could spend as I wished.

6. I bought a long leather wallet and carried this in the inside pocket of my jacket. In the wallet I kept, for that time and my circumstances, quite a substantial amount of money: one ten pound note, one five pound note, five single pound notes and, until they were scrapped, four ten shilling notes. Whenever I spent any money, I would replenish the wad, either from wages or savings. I had always dreamed of having a store of crinklies in a large leather wallet since reading of sixth formers in Billy Bunter books peeling off cash to pay for super feeds in the cake shop. Yaroo. Billy Bunter. Was that an omen? Cripes.

7. I got on well with my fellow trainees. They called me Weemsy and listened to what I had to say, valuing my opinion. They laughed at my jokes. This was rather startling as even I did not find these jokes and cracks in any way funny, and only told them because I thought that was what people did in the outside world. This atmosphere of bonhomie made me feel

relaxed. I did not feel threatened. Everyone was as dim as me.

8. My immediate superiors were dim too. They recognised my dimness and felt relieved. They welcomed me into their world and told me I was a boy with a future. This increased my confidence in handling the world that I had avoided for so long. All day long, everyone smiled at one another, sank deeper into the comfortable decrepitude of the bank.

9.   found I had an aptitude for the work. I liked it best when a shopkeeper came in with a huge bag of mixed change, and I had to sort it into the different coins and count it and total it. My totals were always right. I was given all the big counting jobs to do. My talents were recognised and valued.

10. For the first time in my life, I came into contact with women other than my immediate family. Most of these women were customers, a few were other members of staff. I liked them. I think they liked me. I had no inhibitions. I did not want anything from them except a smile and a few friendly words. I knew that other levels of contact existed but somehow I did not believe such activity related to the real world outside of the telly and salacious literature.

11. When I began to be a working man, my mother and my aunts solicited my views on all sorts of things. 'Do you think we should redecorate the living room?'; 'Should the Americans pull out of Vietnam?'; 'Will we have a goose for Christmas dinner?'; 'Who should I vote for in the election?'; 'Should we buy a new vacuum cleaner?'; 'Ought I to complain about Mrs Lump's Alsatian?' 'What about the bomb, Georgie? Should we do without the bomb?'. My family thought my brainpower and wisdom had increased overnight. I was a Solomon, an Einstein. Maybe I should have been a doctor after all.

'Not Waving, But Drowning'

The Flags of Bannock by G. Gordon Tummle.

The seventh in an occasional series of monographs published by the Bannock Historical Society.

_____known in every country in _____finest flags and bunting, and the products _____glorious, the most turbulent, the most _____ _____world's history.
The bunters and broontailers of Bannock have _____
____led its inhabitants,_____
____adopt the generic_____
soubriquet _____
___contribution to the affairs of men.

1. BANNOCK GOES TO WAR
_____not a warlike people, yet, ironically, a_____
_____some of the most devastating conflicts that have_____
_____our products to proclaim their__
_____proud and_____
___drooped above broken_____
____powder and gore;_____by the desert wind and sprayed with _____ conquering

115

armies, but have also wrapped _____burial.

A comprehensive _____ _____to give a hint_____ selectively on the order book of J.G. Thwaw and Sons of Fogorig Row, an archive which dates _____ _____ destroyed in the devastating _____ _____ merchant area on Easter Sunday 1761._____ _____back into the past and catch a hint_____

10th March 1809 – _____Quarter-master-_____, London:_____ _____complete sets of sema-phore equipment; two hundred each, standard national flags, Spain and Portugal.

5th August 1861 – From: Mr Courcy DeWitt, Charleston,_____ _____ flags of the Confederated States of America, as per _____. Sizes: various, as_____

_____Russian Imperial War_____of naval signalling flags (waterproofed; salt resistant).

23rd June 1903 – From: Japanese _____signalling flags (waterproofed;_____

1st February 1908 – From: Russian
_____, St Petersburg
(repeat____): Four hundred complete
____signalling flags_____;
salt resistant).

_____Serbian
_____Regimental flags,
ceremonial_____and designs
enclosed); five thousand (two thousand each sizes D and _____ size
A;____H). _____miles of assorted
medal_____

23rd September 1916_____, St
Petersburg: Full sets of_____
_____previously agreed designs
already in the possession _____
_____the follow-
ing:_____

_____of Supply, London:
five miles assorted bunting, type 1(d);
_____double weave, type
12(b) (amended); leather end-pieces,
type_____

_____conjure up the
past: the smoke and the smell
_____ horror. _____not
Bannock's only customers.

2. ROYAL BANNOCK

Last year's coronation of King An
Wan Lee of Malabbar was only the
most recent of

117

Floating

Stan took the suitcases from my hands and carried them to his car. 'I used to be a taxi driver, you know,' he told me. 'Amongst other things.' He laughed to himself as he stooped to throw the bags in the back seat.

It was a big car. The type that smells expensive. When he began to drive, I could barely hear the engine. I looked around the leather seats, the cockpit dash. 'You seem to be doing all right for yourself.' I knew exactly how well. I had rummaged through Stan's current account statements.

'What?' He caught my drift. 'Oh, not so bad.' He laughed again. What was so funny all the time? 'I earn it, Briony spends it.'

'About your wife...'

'Listen, as a favour to me, forget about all that, will you. I'm afraid Briony's not been herself recently. She would apologise herself if she was here.'

'But everyone...'

'Don't worry about that. Everyone knows what Briony's capable of. She's one of the main topics of conversation around here. You're seen as the injured party. Everyone feels sorry for you.'

'Sorry for me?'

'And a bit embarrassed. You know what I mean: new man in town not being treated with due respect. Peter at The Old Mill has got a big line of free drinks for you behind the bar.'

'But Tochle...'

'I told you, you're best to ignore Bruce. Close your eyes and hope he'll disappear. Believe me. I know.'

'And Derek Winkie...'

'Ditto. Anyone with the remotest connection with the Historical Society doesn't count. I can see I need to set you straight about Bannock.'

This was too much for me to take in. Apparently I was not the villain but the victim. Free drinks at the bar. I was almost a hero.

The road outside was black, lit only by the headlamps of the car. A tractor appeared round a corner causing us to slow. Light filled the windscreen and Stan turned to look at me:

'Are you all right? You don't look too well.'

'Just a bit hungover.'

'Well, we all know the best cure for that.' We slowed again and the car took a sharp turn right. I heard the wheels crunch on gravel. 'Here we are.' The headlights illuminated a double fronted stone villa covered with ivy. All the windows were dark. Somewhere close, dogs barked. 'That's Joe and Julie,' Stan explained. 'They look after the house when there's no one at home. Stay in the car until I sort them out.'

When Stan unlocked the front door of the house, two large shapes came bounding out past him, did a quick about turn, then wagged their way back to their master. One of the dogs came sniffing over to the car and peed against the wheel below my window. Stan waved, a silhouette against the light of the entrance hall. 'They're okay now.' Both dogs watched and followed me in. 'They won't touch you now they know everything is all right.' One of the huge Alsatians stood on its hind legs and placed its front paws on my chest. Stan rapped it on the nose. 'Down, Julie. Sleep.' Joe and Julie padded over the black and white tiles and disappeared through a door which Stan closed behind them. 'Never been burgled yet.'

There were real leather chairs in the room and the walls were lined with books. It was the kind of room I had always wanted for myself, a room where I could think really deep thoughts and write majestically, where I could accumulate a casual jumble of manuscripts and important papers whose correct order and significance would be known only to myself and my loyal, loving, personal and extremely private secretary. There were decanters on a silver tray, full of stuff I felt like drinking, and a bronze statue of a woman on a table pressed to the wall. French windows led from the room to the blackened garden, but these were closed now and obscured by heavy curtains. A simple gas fire burned in the hearth, its rays providing extra illumination in the comfortable gloom which shadowed the delicacies of the moulding on the high ceiling.

'Cheers,' I said, not for the first time. My face burned with the heat from the fire and from the alcohol which had

119

raced, then strolled round my system. Stan had ignored the contents of the decanters and instead had pulled a bottle of whisky from a cabinet which was, I was delighted to see, healthily stocked with a broad range of liquid comestibles.

'Cheers,' Stan said in return. He seemed to be drinking with what I can only describe as violence, as if there was someone at the bottom of his gullet he was determined to drown. His glass was completely encased in his fingers and he stared at it from time to time as if he was contemplating its destruction. He gave us both a refill with what was left of the bottle. 'Let's see,' he said, looking through the glass and the liquid illuminated by the flames. 'What can we make a toast to?'

'The Bannock Bunters?' I suggested. 'Macroom? The Winkies? The Tochles?' I was in fine form. My needle on my fuel gauge was pointing towards 'full'. I was everyone's friend. The world was a wonderful place.

'What do you think would make the best toast?' Stan asked his glass. He looked at me. 'What do you think is the best time of your life? The future, the present, or the past.'

'Some of the past. It's all right if you can pick and choose. Select your moments.'

'What about the future?'

'That is okay. But it depends on your mood at the time when it's being considered.'

'And the present?'

'Well, it's not too bad now.'

'Let's make it the present then. The others are too problematical. The present. Here's to us, and this glass of whisky, and the heat from the fire.'

'Here's to them. Here's to us.'

'Cheers.'

'Cheers.'

Stan opened another bottle. Everything was just as I had imagined. I could have cried with happiness. I thought I had found a friend.

Other Friends

At the beginning of the second year of my new career in the Royal Northern Bank, my life began to change in a significant way. On one day in each week, the bank's City branches sent all of its trainees to the Abernethy Technical College to study for the Grade I and Grade II Certificates in Banking Knowledge and Practices. I attended college with two other trainees from Lowland Road: Billy Coakley and Jim Peeps. Altogether around fifty young men and women from banks all over town sat in those lime green classrooms listening to lectures on exchange rates, balance sheets and ledger work. Among these one-day-a-week school chums was the woman who was later to become my wife.

We were all pals together. We didn't have a single worry between us. We were all happy and we laughed and kidded around in the refectory during breaks. To my amazement, everyone seemed to like me. I still couldn't understand this: my only experience of affection up until joining the bank had been from my immediate family. I thrived on this uncritical acceptance. I felt like a prince. I felt my heart swelling. Excitedly, I began to catch hints of a whole new world of possibilities. I had power to change my life, to give it real direction towards an adult existence: something I had always considered to be beyond me, stuck as I was in the soft toffee swamp of permanent childhood. I felt in control, no longer swept along by mother, teacher, T.V. schedule, aunt. I could be George Weems, King of the Dopes.

I listened to the others talk of parties and dances, heard them drop the names of people they had met at weekends. I nodded and shook my head and laughed at what I hoped were appropriate moments but said nothing, hoping the others believed that I also took part in such things. Billy or Jim might ask, 'What are you getting up to at the weekend, George?' and I would shrug my shoulders and say, 'I'll just wait to see what turns up.' Of course, I knew exactly what would turn up: I

121

would watch the telly from my favourite spot on the settee and crunch salt 'n' vinegar crisps and suck mint humbugs, and listen to my gran tell me I would ruin my teeth if I kept eating all that rubbish.

I knew what I wanted. I could see it, almost feel it without actually experiencing it. I had seen the outline, smelled the scent of what it was like to fit in. Now I needed more. I felt I had to catch and hold on to this shadow, and then all the other gifts would be available to me: happiness; fulfillment; acceptance; normality. I wanted to possess what I thought other people had, what I thought made them so enviably different to me. I wanted to be an unnoticed part of the whole, not the boy who didn't go to school, not the boy who stayed in bed, not the boy who was alone.

Then, someone suggested going into a pub after college was over for the day. I went along and tasted alcohol for the first time. Jim Peeps gave me a cigarette and I filled my cheeks with smoke. I peeled notes from my Billy Bunter wallet and grandly handed them over the bar. A girl's elbow rubbed against my side and I smelled the smooth scent of her hair. I smiled and she smiled at me as she had done before in the rooms of the college. Billy Coakley stuck his elbow in my other side. 'Get in there, George,' he whispered in my ear. I looked at the girl again and my throat dried. I sensed this was different from laughing and joking in the canteen. I took a slug from my glass of beer and puffed in smoke which caught in my throat. As I doubled up, two hands pounded air into my lungs. The smaller of the two, belonging to the girl at my side, remained after I straightened.

'Are you all right, George?'

'Yes, thanks, Joyce.' Billy Coakley elbowed me again and ostentatiously turned away to give us some privacy. Joyce smiled again and patted the small of my back just above the waistband of my trousers.

The following weekend, against the advice of my grandmother, I sold my stamp collection to a dealer in town and bought myself a new suede jacket.

A Country Estate

Once upon a time there was a Bunter who went home to Bannock. His name was Stan Kowalik. He had been away for six years. Six years without a single visit. Then he went back. Why? Who knows for sure. We only have his wife's opinion on record, and how can we depend on that? Anyway, this is not the time or the place to discuss that particular issue.

He did not go back alone. He brought with him the above wife, Briony, who was a big city girl. Also four children. The boys: Daniel, Adam and Joseph. And baby Heather. Still to come, still to be born in Bannock, were Ishbel and John. Stan had become a real family man.

When he graduated from the City University, he did not use his degree to find a job in teaching, or research, or in business, or in the Civil Service. Instead he worked on a building site: carrying bricks in a hod; stacking concrete blocks; mixing mortar and carrying it on his back up a three storey ladder. He enjoyed hard physical work: it made his body and his brain feel good. It also brought in a lot of cash, cash that was needed for his growing family.

In the little spare time he had left, Stan did a little buying and selling of second-hand goods. He found he had an aptitude for trading. Maybe he inherited this from his father, Janusz, who owned a second-hand shop in the town of Bannock. On second thoughts, maybe not: Janusz was not a success. Stan was.

Stan was often asked questions relating to his peculiar hobby. 'What do you do in your spare time?' some one might say by way of conversation at a party. 'What is in those boxes in the bathroom?' his mother-in-law might ask when she arrived to baby-sit. 'What are you punting today, Stan?' an aquaintance might ask in the pub. Stan's answer was always identical: 'A little bit of this and a little bit of that.' He even had a stock music-hall gesture to accompany this reply: he would hunch his right shoulder and extend his forearm, then move

123

his hand, palm down, as if he was stroking the upper half of a football or the swell of a woman's breast. Sometimes he would say these words in a Cockney accent and try to look like a wartime spiv. It was all great fun. Stan thought play acting was hilarious and much more enjoyable than real life.

The trading remained a hobby until Stan had a bit of luck. He ran into what his fellow entrepreneurs might have called 'a seam'. It was a seam of gold and it made Stan a whole lot of money. So much money he was able to give up his job with the bricklayers. So much money that the growing family could move to a bigger house. Out of the city to where the sun shines bright for little boys and girls. And where better to bring up such a family than in the countryside, where the air is clean and perverts are few. And where better to bring up such a family than in 'God's Welk'. In the crooked arm of the Irk, shadowed by the Shieldon Hills. 'The Maister's Ain Gairden'. Home of the Bunters. Dear old friendly, welcoming, home-smelling Bannock.

'Hail, laddie, an' feckle in the nook'.

(I know you want to know how Stan made his money. Why is that? Do you feel jealous? Or perhaps you want to find out so that you can make a wad too? Stan didn't want people to find out the secret of this seam. Not because he was ashamed of what he did. No, he did not want to advertise because what he did was very easy. If the information was generally available, everyone would want to join in, and then, where would that leave him? Wheeling a wheelbarrow? Teaching the History of the World to people who couldn't remember what they had for breakfast? He told me the 'secret', but then he knew I was not the type of person who was cut out for a business career.)

What about Briony? How did she feel about this major move? After all, she wasn't a Bunter. She had never even visited Bannock. Was she a willing partner or a dutiful wife? She was leaving behind the city she had been born in; her friends, her mother, her father: everything she knew. They were moving to a bigger house, more room for the growing family. But Bannock was not the only place where big, old houses could be found. Stan was returning home. She knew that. Was prepared to accept it. But there was something more.

Stan wouldn't tell her what. Maybe he didn't know himself.

Stan's mother helped them move in. She had a pot of tea waiting for them as they arrived at the house with the removal van. She stayed to help them unpack and tended to the children as their parents got things organised. Stan's father did not appear. Not that Briony expected him to. He was a non-person. Neither Stan nor his mother ever mentioned him so he had ceased to exist. Briony knew of the argument between father and son but had learned not to talk of it. It seemed nonsensical to her but she knew how deeply Stan felt. In the beginning she had tried to promote a reconciliation: 'It's so trivial,' she would say. 'Can you not forget about it?' 'It's all water under the bridge,' she would say. 'Can you not patch things up?' 'Whatever happened,' she would say, 'is just history now. Can you not forgive and forget?' But how could Stan forget the past?

However Briony felt about things, she kept quiet. She had decided this was the best thing to do since discussions always ended in victory for Stan's point of view or in interminable, high-decibel argument. Instead, she concentrated on what she could influence: the children. She immersed her life in theirs to the extent that she almost vanished as a discrete entity. Every day revolved round the routine of bathing, clothing, feeding, teaching, scolding, changing, powdering, burping, consoling, entertaining the growing swarm. Briony was a mother. Every other human function and potential was secondary to this large, dominating, biological fact.

After Stan moved to Bannock with his family, he began to make more and more money from his secret enterprise. Stan didn't consider salting this money away to provide for the future. He believed in conspicuous consumption. He wanted to show his fellow Bunters that 'the Pole' had become a success.

Following the birth of John, the Kowalik's fourth son and sixth child, Stan bought a large house in Eckford, six miles out into the valley of the River Eck. The house had been built in 1849 and was the family home of Major George Tait, the famous explorer. The Major had died in 1946, leaving no direct heirs, and since then, Eckford House had been left unoccupied.

Stan bought the house and five acres of walled, wooded grounds for a bargain price. Renovations and landscaping took four months to complete. When the Kowaliks moved in, Eckford House looked as splendid as it had done in the nineteenth century.

Outside of the walls, beside the gate lodge, stood an eight foot high memorial to those men who had travelled with Tait to the Antarctic. It was overgrown and covered in pigeon shit. Stan cleaned it up and restored the bronze statue which sat on top. It was a statue of a bird, the now extinct Tait's Penguin which had been discovered by the Bannock Expedition of 1906. Stan's kids called the bird Polly the Penguin. This label was innaccurate since, judging by the crest on its head, the bird was certainly male. This can be confirmed by reference to photographs of the last known examples of the species: a non-breeding pair which died in 1916 in the city's Zoological Gardens.

The Kowaliks were very happy with their new home. The children loved playing in the woods. They climbed the squat, knotted beech trees, and swung from their low branches. They hid in the trunk of the hollow oak. They explored, and in overgrown corners hunted imaginary big game with cane bows and arrows. Briony developed an interest in gardening. She grew sweet peas and experimented with cross-pollination. The colours of her creations exploded in the summer light; their scent perfumed the still air within the old stone walls.

Stan's mother was a regular visitor to Eckford, as were Briony's parents. In addition, special times of the year were set aside for family get-togethers. There was Christmas, of course, when Stan would order a fifteen foot spruce tree and erect it on the lawn outside the house. There was New Year, when even the youngest would stay up until midnight. There was Easter, when the children would roll hard-boiled eggs down the short hill which stretched to the road. And, most spectacularly, there was Guy Fawkes Night, the fifth of November, when the Kowalik kids built the biggest bonfire they could and gathered round it after tea time to watch the fireworks display prepared for them by their mother. This was not the fart and splutter of shop-bought sparklers, but a pyrotechnic display of imagination and genius prepared over the preceding three weeks.

Briony had been making her own fireworks since, as a child, she had been given her first Junior Scientist Set. At university, using all the facilities of her Chemistry Department, she had learned how to make fat, heavy volcanoes; howitzer star shells; rockets which burst and reburst in overlapping colours; Roman candles that could turn night into day; and Catherine wheels the size of dinner plates which flared and spun with enough power to shake the trees.

At other times, on warm summer evenings, grandparents and parents would sit on chairs on the raised terrace behind the house and watch and listen as their babies played on the lawns and in the trees. The family's pet dogs took part in the games. Jill, the labrador, would run and jump and roll; the spaniel, Jack, added his bark to the shouts and squeals of the children. Sometimes, during those long, calm, windless days, it was easy to believe that the world did not exist outside of the walls of the gardens; that all contentment, all joy was contained within their field of vision. On one occasion, as they sat in the fading sun listening to bees buzz in the soft, end-day air, Briony gripped her mother's hand and said: 'Mum, I don't believe I could be any happier than right now.' Mrs Parr had smiled and her eyes had filled with tears for her daughter.

Twelve months later, one year after what she thought was the happiest day in her life, Briony's first born son, Daniel Charles Kowalik, was dead, and things had changed forever.

Daniel, the child that had grown from their first, powerful love, was ten years old when he died. It happened in a private room off medical ward 14 in the Royal Children's Hospital. The young, pale boy was unconscious; he felt no pain. With him were his father and mother. Each parent held one of their son's hands. Each parent felt their son's life leave the body. Each parent looked at their son's face, hoping that what they knew was the truth was somehow a lie.

Daniel died of leukemia, as children sometimes do. He was diagnosed as having the disease in October of one year and died in August of the next. Their family doctor and the staff at the hospital said it was very unfortunate: some young children lived for years after the discovery of the cancer and would perhaps go through a whole series of remissions of their symptoms. Others, like Daniel, succumbed very early in the

127

course of their illness. It was just one of those things.

The boy was buried in a medium-sized coffin as befitted his size. The funeral was, as you might have expected, traumatic. The sense of loss and anguish was so powerful it seized people by the throat and prevented them from speaking.

A huge crowd attended the bleak ceremony. Half the town seemed to be there. Stan's mum and Mr and Mrs Parr stood by the graveside in a state of numbed shock. Only one person seemed to be missing from the crowd of mourners: Janusz Kowalik, the grandfather of the dead child. Somehow, it had been made clear he would not be welcome, even at the service held to commemorate the life of the grandchild he had never seen. The estrangement was to continue, even in the face of tragedy.

Briony's grief drove an irrational anger. She wanted to blame someone or something for what had happened to her child. Each night in the house they had built together, her pain would erupt in the face of her husband as she sought to establish guilt where there was none. Was this the inheritance he had given his children? A coded message which had lead to the death of a son and caused agony for the others. Who would be next to suffer from those warped genes? In Briony's mad eyes, Stan had become the devourer of his own flesh and blood.

Junk

Stan and I had talked a lot by the time we finished the second bottle. We had a lot in common. I had known that this would be the case, as I had already run through those conversations up here, in my head, in advance of actual events. Now, sober and more rational, I am unable to tell you exactly what our common ground was. Maybe I sensed that, despite our different circumstances, Stan was just as much a stranger as I was.

Talk seemed important as we sat in the darkness of the

conservatory, looking through the glass at the clearing sky. The importance for me lay, not in the words themselves, but in the contact forged by their utterance. We conducted a dual monologue and I felt close without really understanding. Do my memories have any real basis in fact? Perhaps I just wanted to experience that sensation and so willed it into existence.

There certainly was no element of comprehension. I never understood Stan, even when I left Bannock and, from a distance, saw his weakness amongst his strength. But for that matter, I can't say that I understand myself either. Insight has never been my strongpoint. It seems that all I can hope for is to feel a little happier, a little less uneasy, while locked up inside this head.

Stan had apologised half a dozen times for Briony's behaviour towards me in the pub. He felt bad about anything that slipped beyond his control: wife; dead child; most things that had ever happened. He wanted to make everything better for everyone, whether they wanted it or not. He had the correct prescription made out for the whole population of the world and they were going to swallow their medicine, come what may. Just give him enough time and he would sort everything out. Unfortunately, this involved everyone becoming like him. That was his major problem: lack of imagination. He got worried when people were unhappy but could only envisage one solution: the creation of millions of little Stans and Stanettes. He couldn't understand why some people might not like that, couldn't understand that some people might be happier with their own, personal, unhappy lives. He couldn't recognise that he was a prisoner as much as anyone else. He had the delusion that he acted rather than accepted, that he had broken the constraints of his past and was now the author of his future.

Leaning back, he looked up through a weaving grape vine and pointed towards the sky. 'Do you see that bright star? There. Down there. Yes.' He estimated, wrongly, that I had focused correctly. 'There could be some of me inside that light.' He spoke in a meaningful sort of a way. He wanted to tell me something. Maybe he wanted to show me how significant a person he was. I think he had to prove himself to everyone. 'Come on,' he said and walked me towards the doors which led out on to the lawn. Before we went outside we both topped up from the third bottle. 'Cheers,' he said.

'Cheers.' I slurred this word. I was very drunk. The arse of my trousers was damp and green-stained with moss which grew on the stone seat from which we had been spouting. I didn't care. My heart burned with the alcohol flame of friendship.

'Do you know what that is?' Stan indicated the same area of the night sky. A sharp point stood out.

'Alpha Centauri?' I was no Galileo. The grass was wet and slippery and I almost fell.

'Mir.'

Only blankness from me. I sipped my drink and weaved. The sky and the stars were making me feel dizzy. I lost Mir then found it again at the end of Stan's arm, through a silver swirl. 'Star, is it?'

'Soviet space station. It's burning up now. It'll soon be gone. Just gas and space dust.'

'Anyone in it?' I was now in a disaster movie.

'Not for years. Everyone's gone home.' We walked along a crazy paving path which led to what looked like a stable block. Floodlights illuminated the front. The stone had been cleaned and repointed. The moon shone on the black, square slates on the roof. Stan unlocked double wooden doors and drew them outwards on silent hinges. 'Come on. Have a look inside. It's my little savings bank.'

I stood on the threshold and looked in but I could see only shadows. Stan's hand bent round the corner and flicked a light switch. Four strips above my head sizzled and stuttered then beamed a flat whiteness. The barn was full apart from a square space before me. The walls were concealed by piles of boxes and jumbles of equipment, some looking new, some obviously old and battered with wires and insulation spilling out like fish guts. I looked round and saw cash registers, typewriters, fax machines, photocopiers, juke boxes, calculators, word processors, video games, slot bandits, cash dispensers, remote control units, toy robots, digital watches, alarm radios, central heating timers, portable telephones, microphones, microwaves, disco laser light shows, synthesisers, electronic keyboards, radio controlled toy cars, electric guitars, computer games, joysticks, printers, monitors, bits of washing machines and televisions, hot drinks dispensers and hi-fi equipment. I was in the ultimate, electronic junk shop.

'What do you think?' he asked me. I couldn't think of anything to say. 'It might not look much but you should ask my bank manager.' Stan looked at me for a moment then laughed. 'But then, you would know, wouldn't you, George.' I did. I did.

'What is it all for?' The sight of this junk cave had sobered me up.

'Recycling, George. Recycling. We all bear a responsibility for the environment.'

'But what do you do with it? Where does it all go?'

'Poland. Land of my ancestors. Home of the Kowaliks. Starved of foreign currency and the humblest chip. By the container load. This lot makes the trip tomorrow.'

'Do you mean they pay for junk like this?'

'Pay for it? Well, not exactly.'

'What do you mean, 'not exactly'?'

'Well, they pay for it, but not in cash. The day of the fully convertible zloty has not yet arrived.'

'What then?'

'Coal.'

'Coal?'

'Coal. Thousands of tons of the stuff over the years. Enough to keep the Kowalik home fires burning for the next ten squillion years.'

'But what do you do with it? All that coal.'

'Sell it, of course. Without even seeing it. It's all done on paper. Warsaw, Rotterdam, Bannock: the energy triangle. Dollars. The universal currency. Or from time to time I might trade a few loads. I enjoy that. You can barter everything for anything in this world you know.'

'What sort of stuff?'

'Oh, a little bit of this. A little bit of that.'

I looked again at the piles of junked electronics. 'They really want all this?'

'Every last chip. That's what they're interested in. Even the most basic. There's always a need, if they're cheap enough. And who else wants the electronic guts of a scrapped washing machine? Then, of course, there's the more sophisticated stuff. Arcade video games, for example. They can't get enough of them. They'll even buy them new, if it can be arranged. There's a lot you can do with the chips from video games.' Stan turned his back on all the junk and looked out again at the starry sky, now clouding with the threat of rain. He flicked the light switch off and the dark blue curtain was illuminated as if with a back light. 'Lots and lots you can do with those little buggers.'

He didn't seem to want to talk any more. We were both silent as we walked back to the house. He gave me a large refill and showed me to a bedroom where I flopped out, not even bothering to take off my clothes. Before he closed the door he wished me good night, whispering the words as you would to a sleepy child. He turned off the light and with its click I left his world.

Zlotys

Once upon a time there was a man called Stanislaw Kowalik who occupied himself by doing 'a little bit of this and a little bit of that'. Stan was loath to elaborate on this rather vague description of his profession, not because he was ashamed of what he did, but because what he did was so simple and so lucrative he feared that if the secret got out the market would be flooded with rival entrepreneurs.

When Stan lived in the city he worked as a bricklayer's labourer. This was an unusual choice of job, as Stan had a first class honours degree in History. But Stan was not frightened of being unusual. That was one of Stan's strengths in the early days. He wasn't frightened of very much at all. But I suppose we all have a weak spot, however much we try to hide it, whether it's fear of spiders, fear of the dark, fear of a wife, fear of heights, fear of not being loved. There's usually something there somewhere, if you pick under the skin with a sharp little scalpel.

In his spare time, Stan did a little buying and selling. He enjoyed the adrenalin rush of the transaction. It didn't matter how small that transaction might be. It could be selling a watch in a pub; it could be buying six boxes of Christmas teddy-bears; it could be trading a television for two hundred jars of mint humbugs. The interaction, the uncertainty, the manipulation was the thing. The money did not matter. It was a by-product. Welcome but not crucial to enjoyment. If anything, Stan used it as an indicator of success. But it might just as well have been gold stars in a primary school exercise book or a piece of paper which stated academic achievement. All of these provided transient pleasure but they were intrinsically useless. What then was useful? Love? The love of a father, of a wife, of the world? Perhaps.

Briony, Stan's wife, secretly thought this barrow-boy activity demeaning. (Labouring on a building site could, as long as it didn't last too long, be seen as romantic, adventurous: the horny-handed academic; the poet with mud on his boots. Many men who later became famous and successful had worked at jobs like that early on in their lives: they stated as much on the dust jackets of their books. Briony could tell herself and her parents and others that this was merely a learning experience, a preparatory stage, before Stan settled down and decided which of the many career options before him he would choose.) In indulging in the buying and selling which fascinated him, Stan associated with men whose sideburns were long and sharp, whose hair was over-oiled, whose faces, thin and dark, were worn with lines denoting cunning and moral bankruptcy. (One pair, two brothers, smiled lecherously at Briony with large white teeth, smiles which made Briony uneasy, suspicious that they had seen her naked in the bath, that they had intimate knowledge of her which they might use to their sexual advantage when they considered the moment to be correct. These brothers were impervious to her disdain, in fact they seemed rather to like being treated badly. Such abuse would make their eventual triumph all the more enjoyable.)

Briony did not like to listen to the bad language which these men used without thinking. She did not like to look at the piles of goods in which they dealt: radios in bashed cardboard boxes; canteens of flashy cutlery; synthetic shirts with sleeves too narrow to fit. She did not like to touch the bundles of money which travelled from their pockets into those of Stan.

Briony banned Stan's fellow traders from the house, in the same way that the first Mrs Kowalik banned Janusz's Poles. Neither women had a feel for the romance of foreign languages.

One evening, Stan and Briony attended a little party in the Department of Slavonic Studies at the City University. The party was in honour of a visiting trade delegation from Poland. Stan was invited because he did some translation work for the department when they had a rush job. He was a man of many talents. No wonder the others in the bricklaying squad called him 'The Professor'.

At the party, Stan got talking to a man called Tadeusz Kurowski. Kurowski was a short, fat man with a thick moustache. He came from Poznan but lived and worked in Warsaw where he was employed by the Trade Ministry. Tadeusz liked drinking: while in Stan's company he consumed nine glasses of beer. Before he drank each one he shook his head and whispered in ragged English: 'Piss in one end, piss out the other'.

Tadeusz complimented Stan on his command of Polish, especially his use of demotic language. Stan explained he came from a long line of foul-mouthed bastards. Tadeusz laughed and slapped Stan on the back and grabbed two more beers from the free bar. 'Piss in one end, piss out the other.'

Back in Poznan, Kurowski claimed, his grandmother had a cat which could piss better piss than the piss he was drinking now. Stan offered to buy this Kurowski cat. He said it would be a huge success if installed in any of the university bars. He said its product could be described as Premium Polish Lager. You knew you were drinking when you had a few back home, Kurowski said. You could feel it right down to the bottom of your boots. But, Kurowski had to admit, even the beer back home wasn't as good as Czech beer. Now those skinny Czech bastards really knew how to brew a barrel. What was the situation like in Prague, Stan asked. Could Kurowski get hold of any Czech moggies? Tadeusz laughed again and told Stan that he reminded him of his brother. Now there was a man who knew about drinking. Stan could visit them both in

134

Warsaw if he ever managed to pay a visit back home. Then all three of them could go out to some real bars and drink all the cats dry. Stan grabbed two more beers. 'Piss in one end, piss out the other.'

They talked some more. Stan mentioned he was involved in business in a small way. He did not specify exactly how small 'small' was, but instead gave the vague impression that he dealt in imports and exports. Tadeusz showed some interest. He asked Stan what kind of commodities he traded in. Stan replied. 'A little bit of this and a little bit of that.' Tadeusz looked interested. He took a long drink of beer and looked at Stan curiously over the rim of his glass.

One week later, Stan received a phone call from his new Polish friend. The phone call contained an invitation. An invitation to a pub where they might have a meal and discuss some slight business. Stan accepted. He was excited. He sensed that something was about to happen.

In the time since the reception at the City University, Korowski had checked out Stan's credentials and had discovered the meagre truth about his business activity. He had also ascertained from the Professor of Slavonic Studies that Stan possessed a brain which he had not yet put to use. It all sounded very promising.

When Stan learned what Kurowski wanted and what he was offering in return, he could not quite believe what he was hearing.

'Things like that, you mean?' he asked, pointing to the electronic till behind the bar.

'Exactly,' said Korowski. 'We do not care about condition. The little brains inside are the important factor for us. We have a great shortage of these little geniuses. The Americans do not like us any more. They tell us we are not moving in the correct direction, or at the correct speed. They imagine they are teaching us to dance the cha-cha.'

'How many do you need?'

'We need as many as you can give us, as long as the price arrangement is to our mutual advantage.'

'But no cash.'

'Unless you request us to deposit zlotys in a bank of your choice in Warsaw.'

'Zlotys.'
'Zlotys.'
'In Warsaw.'
'In Warsaw.'
'But I live one thousand miles away.'
'Yes, you live one thousand miles away. But little pieces of paper money are not the only things of value in this world.'
'Could you expand upon that.'
'What about cement. We make an excellent product. It could be made available to you to trade on the open market.'
'What do I want with cement?'
'What does anyone want with cement? The world is built with cement. You should know that.'
'How do I sell a load of cement?'
'You are a clever man. You use your wits. You can sell cement. You can sell coal.'
'Coal?'
'Top quality. You burn it in your power stations. The lightbulb above our heads is probably lit by the power generated from a little piece of your father's homeland. Coal is as valuable as those paper notes you carry around in your pocket. What if your National Union of Mineworkers should call another strike?'
'Would you not support them?'
'Trade is trade. The world must go on. You are a businessman. You know how things are. Did your father not teach you?' Kurowski took a drink from his glass and looked at Stan over the rim as he had done a week before at the reception. He finished what was left and spoke in English: 'Piss in one end. Piss out the other.' He looked in his wallet for money and ordered from a waitress. 'We could maybe even arrange for you to take delivery of some decent beer. Now you would have no difficulty in disposing of that.'
'Polish beer?'
'Polish beer. But not just for anything.' Korowski nodded towards a video game which bleeped and whirred in a corner. 'We require machines like that. We might consider beer for a consignment which suited our specifications.'
'Are you short of fun in Poznan?'
'That's right. We need something to occupy ourselves

136

during the long winter nights. We are particularly keen on certain of the larger machines. The ones that are to be found in the amusement arcades. Not the whole machine. Just certain parts. For certain special toys we might find you a load of Czech beer.'

'Do they like playing too?'

'Very much so.'

This is too much for me to take in.'

'I will give you a list of what we require.'

'I'll have to think about it.'

'You would like Czech beer, Stan, I know you would.'

'How would I find all the stuff?'

'Perhaps your father would help.'

'No. I don't know.'

The waitress came with two more glasses. Korowski smiled at her then at Stan, then raised his glass: 'Piss in one end, piss out the other.'

Married Life

Joyce and I were engaged for eight years before we were married. We went out together for two years before we became engaged. We didn't want to rush into things. It's not that we were unsure about our commitment to each other. We were as sure as any two people can be.

We wanted to save for a nice house with nice furniture. Not some crummy flat with only orange boxes to sit on, but a proper home with a proper garden, like Joyce's mum's. Joyce's mum told us she had seen many a marriage come to grief because the couple were ill-prepared or because financial problems caused stresses and strains which sent the poor unfortunates reeling to the divorce courts. We agreed. We said that we didn't want to end up like that. 'Do you want another Garibaldi, George?' Better to wait. Get things started on a good foundation. 'Maybe just a little drop more tea, Mrs

Hewison.' Anyway, we had our whole lives in front of us. Joyce's dad was thirty-eight before he got married. It didn't do him any harm, did it? 'Pass the milk, dear, would you?'

When the day did arrive, we had a big church wedding and a reception in the Twin Firs Hotel. My mother was there to support me, of course, as were my aunts and my gran and some other, more obscure relatives. Jim Peeps was my best man. Billy Coakley was there too: after all, we joked, he was the man who had elbowed us together. We spent our honeymoon in the Clifford Hotel in St Ives in Cornwall. It rained almost all of the time we were there. The barman in the residents' lounge annoyed me by continually saying, 'The weather won't be bothering you now, Mr Weems, will it?' He would then wink and suggestively polish a sherry glass with a towel wrapped forefinger: 'Married bliss,' he would sigh. 'Married bliss.'

Due to our years of prudence, Joyce and I returned from our honeymoon to take up residence in a new, detached three bedroomed villa, paid for with a substantial deposit and a subsidised mortgage from the bank. We had bought the house fifteen months before the wedding but had not yet spent a whole night there on our own. On our visits we had occupied our time putting up curtain rails and measuring the floor for kitchen equipment. Sometimes we would sit on the staircase and fantasise about our life to come. We were both very happy living in the future.

And so, when we arrived as a married couple, the house was fully carpeted and furnished down to ashtrays and automatic corkscrews, woolly toilet covers and spare bin liners. All the decorative work had been done, and prints and family photographs hung on the walls. Our few personal possessions sat on shelves or were packed in drawers. My model aircraft were in cardboard boxes in the roofspace.

Joyce's dad had sorted out the garden for us. He had dug it over with a rotovator and removed all the rubble hidden under the topsoil. He had laid lawns and planted out flowerbeds. He had constructed a rockery round the back which could be seen through the patio doors. From a fountain at the top, a little stream trickled over boulders into a shallow, kidney-shaped pond where goldfish swam. Joyce's dad was a handy man. He couldn't do enough for his daughter and his new son-in-law. He was a saint.

Looking back now, I'm not sure what kind of a marriage Joyce and I had. I suppose it was normal. We were not unhappy. We did all the things people in our position usually do: we ate together, slept together, made love together, watched telly together, played badminton together, went to the pub together, took our holidays together, planned for the future together, looked at wallpaper books together, walked our dog Skipper together, talked about work together, visited our parents together.

I don't think I loved Joyce. But then, maybe that's normal too. I don't think I even really knew her. Sometimes, perhaps sitting at the breakfast table eating cornflakes, I would look at her over a newspaper or through my fingers and I would wonder who this woman was and what she was doing here. At other times, I would suddenly become aware of myself: dressed for work; fresh egg stain on my tie; in mid-sentence. And think: how did it all happen? All those years had passed and now I had arrived at that precise, conscious moment in time. It was on one such occasion that I experienced my first attack of anxiety, the first of those deluging sweats which later almost drowned me. My lifeboat was the album of photographs my gran had given to me the day I left the house in Corsock Street to be married. This album contained photographs which showed me as I once was: blank, uniformed; in pyjamas, opening Christmas presents; nervous, first day at the bank; acrobatic in a nappy. Photographs of my parents: a wedding; a bicycle trip; a holiday beach. The Tartan Terrors. Those photographs convinced me I was more than a dislocated point; they showed me I extended backwards, told me I could reach forward into the future.

But for most of the time, I was content. I had merged in with the background. I was indistinguishable from any other happily married man. At various times I had not believed this was possible. As a child, lying in bed pretending to be ill, I had considered that a normal life was not for me. It was reserved for the people I watched on television, for the people I saw in the street from my window. They could cope with life's dangers. I was destined to construct an existence from stamp

139

hinges and Airfix glue. Don't misunderstand me: I was not altogether distressed with this prospect. In some respects I accepted it with more than just resignation: I was instinctively a believer in a stress free life. (Also, I had seen at first hand that worry and guilt, however misplaced, could be fatal.)

So I was prepared to accept what I was given. I was prepared to be grateful for crumbs. Because I had once thought that I could not expect to receive anything at all outside my self-imposed universe of vapour rubs and nasal decongestants.

I wanted us to have children: three would be a nice number, I thought. Certainly not just one: I argued it would be unhealthy for a single child to be the focus of so much attention from parents, grandparents and aunts. But Joyce insisted we should wait before 'starting a family'. (That phrase: as if we were considering setting up a rabbit ranch.) We should wait until we had paid off the car; until we had taken that holiday in Austria; until we had built our garage; until we had installed a toilet in the broom cupboard under the stairs. I acquiesced in this: I did not want to 'rock the boat', 'upset the applecart'.

I was still a keen reader and had the vague idea of embarking upon something creative in the literary field. (Perhaps this urge to produce occurred in the absence of opportunities to breed.) One Saturday, I bought a box of science fiction books at a Red Cross jumble sale. Among *Best S.F. Six* and *Worlds Apart* was *A Moveable Feast*, a book by Ernest Hemingway about his life in Paris in the 1920s. I read it and, inspired, made a little study for myself in one of the spare bedrooms: desk and chair; bookcase; adjustable lamp; wire baskets; portable typewriter; jug full of sharp pencils. Sometimes I would go up there and pretend to be a writer. My productivity was very low. I did not have anything to write about and spent most of my time day-dreaming, but it gave me something mysterious to hint about at work. Then Joyce began to complain that she was being left alone for long hours while I 'scribbled' and 'tapped'. So I stopped. Just like that. Without a murmur.

At times of stress, I would remember winter nights glueing and painting on the paper-covered table in the living room at Corsock Street. One rainy Sunday I climbed up the ladders to the roof space and blew dust from the boxes which contained my old models. I took a few of them out, just for old time's sake but there was neither the light nor the space to appreciate them fully. I backed down on to the landing holding a load in my hands but was only half way there when I became aware of Joyce observing me. She did not say anything, just stood with her arms folded, looking at me with her head tilting towards one shoulder. I took one more step towards the floor. Joyce compressed her lips so that little lines stretched in the skin, and blew air through her nose. She began to tap one foot on the carpet. I took the models back up to the attic and closed the lid of each box.

What did Joyce want from me? In the early years, I don't think she gave the question much thought. Marriage was something everyone did. Since she was someone, she got married. Maybe if Jim Peeps had been available she would have married him. Maybe if my friend Billy had caught smoke in his throat that day in the pub, Joyce would now be Mrs Coakley. My presence, unremarkable though it was, lent her a certain status which she considered to be superior to 'unattached'. A glove puppet would have served just as well as long as it could perform husband-like roles in public: Sooty mowing the lawn; Sweep washing the car. What was going through her mind all of those years? Was she, like me, not really aware she was functioning for most of the time? Were we both sleepwalkers, waking only in moments of panic?

If Joyce was one of life's somnambulists, then one day she awoke from her dreams and decided she had had enough.

141

A New Career

The morning after my introduction to Stan's cavern full of junk, I woke up in a crumpled suit, cramped in a strange bed. My chin was damp with spittle and my eyes were glued. As I slowly opened one lid, feeling the lashes ungum, a pair of eyes met mine.

'Mummy!'

I jumped up and my head hit off the underside of the bunk above me. A little girl was exiting from the room.

'Mummy! There's a strange man in my bed.'

I then heard a woman's voice, a voice I recognised, coming from a distance. 'I know that, darling. Just find your socks and come down to the kitchen.'

The girl reappeared in the doorway and entered shyly. She was about nine or ten years of age, slight and pretty with short, dark hair framing an oval face. As she pulled open drawers I pretended to be asleep, curled, corralled like a baby in that impossibly small space. The sound of giggling from close by made me open an eye once more. Two other heads had appeared round the door. These spectators, one younger male, one older female, closely resembled the drawer rattler and I took them all to be Stan's children. As the giggling continued, the smaller of the girls turned towards the noise and threw a jumble of clothes towards her brother and sister:

'It's not funny!' she shouted, stamping a bare foot. 'How would you like it if some smelly old man was sleeping in your bed?'

'Mum!' shouted the older girl. 'Ishbel's throwing her clothes all over the room.' The boy laughed then was hit in the face by a flying sweater. 'Mum! She just hit Johnny on the head!' The older sister looked at Ishbel then held her nose between her thumb and forefinger while pointing at me in the bed. 'Phewweee.' Johnny laughed again.

'Mum!' shouted Ishbel. 'Heather's making fun of me.'

'Ishbel, will you come down with those socks!' shouted

142

the mother. Now Johnny grabbed hold of his nose:
'Phewweee.'
'Mum! Tell them to stop making a fool of me.'
'Right! All three of you down, socks or no socks.'
Heather stretched her mouth with her thumbs and pulled down her eyes with her fingers. Johnny followed her example. Both of them danced a jig in front of Ishbel.
'Mum!'
'Right this minute!'
I checked my watch. It was twenty past ten. I was an hour and a half late for work, trapped in a strange house, surrounded by jeering children and a woman who was capable of any personal outrage. I drew the covers over my chest and awaited an opportunity to escape unnoticed

Muffled sounds and squeeks and yells continued downstairs for some time. I heard heavier footsteps ascending and the sound of young male voices from the room next to the one I found myself in. Then they too went away and there was the sound of a door closing and a diesel engine turning over. There was one last shout from that voice I recognised: 'Heather!' Then doors closed once more and the tyres of a car sounded on the gravel driveway.

I leapt out of bed and drew the curtains from the window. Through the trees I could see a large estate car drawing out of the gate, turning left towards the town. I ran to the bedroom door and listened. Silence. On the landing I found a bathroom where I washed my face in cold water and tried to avoid looking at my puffed, blotched image in the shaving glass on a shelf above the basin. As I turned to leave, I was caught in the reflection of a full length mirror which was attached to the bathroom door. There I was: Tommy the Tramp, rising from a refreshing night's kip under a hedge in the park. All I needed was a few leaves in my hair and a piece of string round my waist.

I was halfway down the stairs which led to the front door when I heard a car arrive outside. This was a petrol engine. I heard voices. Men. Then a key in the door. I backed up the stairs.
'Briony!' There was, of course, no reply. 'Briony, are you there?' I crouched down and saw the top of a head. The grey-black hair was thick and stood up straight. I recognised a

broken nose.

'Stan?'

'Jesus, George, you gave me a scare. Did you sleep well? I'm afraid I couldn't be bothered looking out spare sheets for you last night. You haven't seen Briony or the kids, have you?'

'I think your wife left about ten minutes ago.' Stan picked up mail from a table in the hall and disappeared from my sight:

'I don't know what excuse she's going to give to their teachers this time. She was supposed to be back from her mother's in time for school.' He reappeared, looked at me through the bars of the banister. 'Are you going to stay up there all day, or what?'

'I was wondering if you could give me a lift into town.'

'What for?'

'Work.'

'No work for you today, boy. At least not in a bank.'

'What do you mean?'

'I phoned Macroom this morning. It's all arranged. I told him you wouldn't be in today.'

'What?'

'In fact, I told him you wouldn't be in for the rest of the week.'

'What do you mean?'

'You looked as if you could do with a break.'

'But what did you say?'

'I told him we'd had a slight accident in the car last night. Nothing too serious. Just whiplash injuries. I told him you'd been advised to spend the rest of the week in bed.'

'By whom?'

'Your doctor.'

'But I haven't got a doctor down here.'

'Well you have now: Doctor Murgle. Don't worry: he's an old school pal of mine. He'll fix you up with a medical certificate. Maybe even a surgical collar, to add that little touch of authenticity. He could probably arrange for you to have a month off if you like. What about recuperation somewhere in the sun? How does that sound?'

'What did Macroom say?'

'He told me to extend to you his best wishes for a speedy recovery.'

144

You mean he believed you?'

'Why not? Not everyone is as mistrustful as you, George.'

'Did he not ask why you were phoning, or where I was staying?'

'Mr Macroom's much too discreet. He doesn't want to offend one of his best customers.'

What could I say? The prospect of having a week off appealed to me. As did the idea of handing control of my life over to someone else. Stan and I were the ideal match. He was the stream; I was a little boat made out of folded newspaper. But what about...?

'But what about...?'

'Don't worry about where to stay for the time being. We've got plenty of room here.'

'But what about...?'

'We'll fix you up with your own room this time. We can't have Ishbel thinking that the man at the bank is called 'Mr Goldilocks'.'

'But what about...?'

'And I've told you: don't concern yourself about Briony. If anyone should be worried, it should be me.'

'But...' What was the point. He could read my thoughts. He had all the answers. I decided to float with the current.

After coffee and a shower and a change of clothing I met up with Stan outside the old stables. 'This is the plan,' he told me. 'The container arrives at two o'clock. While we wait, we box up some of the loose gear. We should finish loading at around six. Then, your work is over for the week.'

'Do you mean the two of us are going to shift all the stuff in those stables?'

'Malcolm Jeffrey will lend a hand. He's driving the truck. And my two oldest boys will help when they get back from school. But we're not short-handed just now, you know.' Stan leaned in through the stable door. 'Hello in there!' There was the sound of cardboard being shoved across a floor, then a smiling face appeared in the sunlight:

'You called, master?' Charlie Trummle seemed to have more teeth in his head than had been the case the last time I had seen him. He spotted me and the grin widened on his lined face. 'Hello again, George. Moved house again? Have you no home of your own to go to?'

'Hello, Charlie. And how are you?' I was smiling too. I was happy. I felt like I was one of the gang. Like it had been back in Abernethy Technical College. All those years ago. I almost did a little dance on the grass. If I had been wearing a hat I would have tossed it in the air. I felt like I could....Wait a minute.

What was happening? In the space of a few days I seemed to have dropped off the edge of the known world. People I barely knew conversed with me intimately; my life was being arranged by a man who had once pissed on my head; I had been thrown out of a boarding house for sticking pins in the wallpaper; I had abandoned my career; I had been publicly accused of indecent assault; I had spent the night sleeping in a child's bunk; I was engaged in activity which, for all I knew at that time, might well have been criminal.

And what was my reaction to all of this? How did I feel about being in free fall without a parachute? Buoyed by the euphoria of buddydom and the remnants of the previous night's piss-up; my pores unbunged, clear of sweat; anxiety inducing clouds: Macrooms, Brionys and wives, gone, drifted beyond the horizon; I was just the man for anything anyone could suggest.

'Let's make a start.' I was now a man of action. My energy was unlimited. Stan and Charlie looked at me then at each other.

'Let's go.'

'Show me those empty boxes.'

'Let's get this show on the road!'

We waded in. What a team.

146

Meanwhile

What was everyone else up to while I was loading a container full of junk? It is important not to lose contact with the rest of the world while concentrating on my own little history.

I will slice across the town with a sharp knife: take a cross section. It is four o' clock in the afternoon. I am having a little rest, recovering from my exertions. The smell of something cooking is coming from the kitchen. I am strangely restful. Meanwhile.

Mr Macroom is in his office at the back of the Royal Northern Bank. The door is closed. One bar of the electric fire is on and it warms his legs as he sits behind his desk. He is humming a little tune, a traditional air which is sung by the folk of the town on the occasion of The Rollin' O' The Ring. The song is called, 'Once There Was A Fair Maid'. It refers to the Fair Maid Of the Loch, whose life was saved through the intervention of two Bannock Bunters, namely Mary Dunlin and Robert Winkie. While Macroom hums, he consults texts which lie open before him, and makes notes in a pad which sits on his lap. He finds pleasure in his task. He is composing a new monograph for the Bannock Historical Society. Its working title is: *A Far Flung Bannock: The Bunters Of America*.

Mrs Tochle is in her kitchen. She is baking 'ring baps'. These are doughnut-shaped currant buns which, traditionally, are eaten for breakfast by the people of Bannock on the day of the ring ceremony. They can be taken toasted or just as they are; they can be eaten dry or spread with butter or with jam, or even with both together. Mrs Tochle is preparing a large batch. When they are ready she will put them in the freezer until the big day. She always plans well in advance, ever since the year her buns incinerated in an untried oven and, to her great shame, the family had to go without. Somehow, the story of her disaster leaked out, and that day her son, Bruce, returned from the festivities in tears, complaining that the other boys were laughing at him and calling him 'Burny Bap'.

147

Leaning over the counter in the Royal Northern Bank is Derek Winkie. He is in conversation with his cousin, Cowan Winkie, who, at the Ring Supper three months earlier, was elected to be this year's Ring Bearer. At the ceremony to come, it will be Cowan's task to accept the ring from The Fechtin' Lassie, then set fire to the brands which are attached to its edge. When they are alight and smoking, he will roll the ring to four Winkie Boys who, with the aid of long poles, will control it on its course down Mill Street towards the River Irk. All of the polemen will themselves be former Ring Bearers. One of them will be Derek, who was elected to the position two years previously. In the empty bank, Derek and Cowan are discussing plans for the evening. In the week leading up to the ceremony, the main participants sport about town in their costumes and, as a matter of custom, can demand solid or liquid sustenance from any man they meet within the area of God's Welk.

Bruce Tochle is balancing on a ladder twenty feet above the level of the streets. He is looping the cord of a banner round a steel peg inserted for that very purpose in the wall of his mother's boarding house. One end tied, he descends, moves the ladder along the pavement, and climbs again to secure the second cord to a second peg. The banner now stretches high above the front door of the house. It was made thirty-two years ago in the craft room of J.G. Thwaw and Sons, Fogorig Row, Bannock. It was woven in two colours from fine, silk-like thread, and finished to a standard difficult to find in these modern times. Green lettering shows boldly on a pale pink background. The banner spells out this imprecation: 'Oot John Heddington! Oot Surly Andy!' John Heddington was the traitor who, over seven hundred and fifty years ago, betrayed the Fair Maid of the Loch. 'Surly Andy' refers to Andrew Rankine, the Maid's half-brother, who sought her destruction. Now, seven hundred and fifty years after the deaths of these men, Mrs Agnes Tochle and her son, Bruce, are once more telling them to bugger off out of Bannock and leave decent people to get on with their lives in peace.

Roderick Macroom, M.A. (Hons), son of Mr and the head of the History Department at Bannock High, is in the school gymnasium, sweating. Roderick is pumping iron, lifting weights, getting strong. Roderick has been working out for almost a year, since the time he heard he could well be in line to take on the role of The Sinning Wretch in The Rollin' O' The Ring. Nine months after this first hint was dropped, Roderick's election was confirmed at the Ring Supper, and his training increased in intensity. The Sinning Wretch, clothed in black, symbolises the twin threat of Heddington and Rankine, the evil which is exorcised at the ring ceremony. The man elected Wretch needs strength because he stands braced inside the ring as it rolls down Mill Street amid the smoke from the brands which burn around its rim. Since his election, Roderick has been heaving heavier and heavier weights, absorbing advice from previous Wretches, becoming prepared physically and psychologically for the greatest honour a Bunter can receive. Now it is almost time. He is almost at his peak. It has been hard work over long, painful hours. Whenever his enthusiasm has flagged, whenever the weight on the bar has seemed just too much to bear, Roderick has muttered to himself 'Assistant Head Teacher, Assistant Head Teacher' and found miraculous new reserves of strength. It is not unknown for Wretches to find themselves with greatly improved career prospects after that three minute spin down towards the River Irk.

You might ask how I know all of this. You might ask how, while snoozing on a bed in Stan Kowalik's house, I managed to be in four other places at the same time. You might ask how I gained knowledge of the secret thoughts of others, or of actions which took place before I arrived in the town of Bannock. The answer to these questions is simple. I made it all up. It is pure invention. But that is not to say that it is any less true than what has gone before or what is still to come, or, for that matter, the stories that you yourselves invent day after fictional day.

Lying in Bed, Worrying

For a few moments, awakening from a deep sleep, the world can seem changed.

You experience a dislocation. Perhaps the furniture has been moved in the night. Perhaps you have been carried to a strange room in a strange house.

The transmigration of souls. The woman at your side no longer breathes. You have opened the eyes of another body.

The room is grey, colourless. If you could only find my way back to the warmth and the light.

But as your brain clears, as your eyes open fully and focus on a curl of hair or a crease in my pillow, you know that this is the real world, the one in which all of us have to live out our lives.

Perhaps Joyce, my wife, felt the same sense of unreality when she awoke from her dream. Perhaps, in the beginning, she also wished to return to that calm equilibrium which lies somewhere between life and death.

If she did experience this desire, she resisted it. Brave woman. She willed her senses to sharpen and breathed in cold, refreshing air which blew dust from clogged synapses, uncovered dendron clusters from drift-layers of choking, silky loess.

Charlie Trummle's Big Chance

A container is just a metal box. But an extremely big metal box. A metal box which takes an awful lot of filling. Especially if you are filling it with a whole variety of objects, some of which, individually, are the size of a small fingernail. Luckily, there were bigger objects too. Unluckily, some of these were very heavy. Then there were the boxes. Lots and lots of cardboard boxes. What was in them? Ancient bronzes? Jade carvings? Rare books? No. Junk. Just junk. Lots and lots of it: heavy, light, loose, wrapped, sharp, shiny, rattling, crackling junk.

We were still loading when Briony returned with the children. We heard the sound of the car, then doors opening and closing; feet, young laughter and shouts, then that familiar voice.

'Stan!'

'Yes!'

'Oh, so you're here.'

'What is it? We're busy.'

'Oh, you're busy are you. Well you can just unbusy yourself and look after the children. I've things to do.'

'Hold on.' Stan put down the box he was carrying and ran towards the voice. 'Hold on.' There was the sound of a car door once more, then an engine, then tyres on gravel. Stan came back. 'Carry on yourselves for a while lads, will you. I've got to fix the kids' tea.' I received a huge, wrinkled wink across a box. 'No comments, please, Charlie. I've had enough today.'

'I didn't say a thing.'

'You don't have to say anything, Charlie.'

Charlie laughed, but there was no humour in his expression. We were all getting tired. We were all hungry. Not much seemed funny any more. 'What about Adam and Joseph?'

'Not here. Rugby practice.'

'But...'

'Not a word, Charlie. There's no need. I'm thinking it already.'

Stan left. Charlie threw the box he was carrying to the floor and sat down on top of a visual display unit. 'That's it.'

'You might break that,' said Malcolm, the lorry driver, as he passed with a load.

'Bugger off.' Charlie lit a cigarette.

A hoop rolled into the barn, wobbled, hit a pile of keyboards, jumped, then fell to the ground at Charlie's feet. Running behind it came John, Stan's youngest child, a solid little boy dressed in school uniform, about eight years of age. Charlie picked up the hoop:

'Is this yours?' The boy came to a halt, hesitated, then

nodded. He put both hands behind his back and silently looked from Charlie, to me, to Malcolm, then back to the hoop. Charlie bent the hoop and examined it closely before flipping it back to the boy. 'Your father ought to know better.'

'Are you rolling your ring?' asked Malcolm as the small boy turned to go. John nodded, his back towards us. He spoke a little above a whisper:

'We made them in school.'

'And who are you?' asked Malcolm. 'Are you The Wretch?'

'No,' said John. He swung his arm once, then twice, then flicked and spun the hoop. It rolled along the concrete slabs which led to the side of the house and John raced in pursuit, his legs kicking high in the air. He shouted, loud; released. 'I'm a Winkie Boy!'

'His father ought to know better,' said Charlie once more.

'Oh, shut up, you greeting faced old bastard.'

'Who are you talking to?'

'I'm talking to you. Come on, up off your arse and do some work.'

'Bugger off.'

Malcolm turned to me and gestured with his head towards Charlie. 'Some man we've got here. He'll work when the boss is around, then he skives off when nobody's looking.'

'No man's my boss.'

'No? Who are you, then? Small businessman of the year?'

'Bugger off. Away and play with the wee boy's ring.'

'Touchy, eh? We all know what's bothering you, Charlie, don't we.' Malcolm turned to me again and made the same movement with his head. 'Did you hear about old Charlie boy, now did you?' Charlie stood up. Malcolm placed a hand on his shoulder and pressed him back to his makeshift seat. 'Did you?'

'I think we ought to leave this and get back to work.' I was now a diplomat. My efforts were not appreciated.

'Why don't you bugger off too. Bugger off back to the city where you belong. What are you doing here, anyway?'

'Friendly, isn't he?' Malcolm still rested his large hand on Charlie's shoulder. The old man tried to brush it off but his

152

strength had gone.

'Why don't we just leave it?' I was a large, fluffy, untaloned bird, flapping ineffectually over the hyena's kill.

'Did you not tell Mr Weems here about The Rollin O' The Ring?' Charlie could only wait. Malcolm turned to me. 'Do you know, George, we've a famous Bunter here.' He squeezed the old man's shoulder. 'Charlie was once the Sinning Wretch. You know what that is, don't you, George? The man in the ring.' I nodded. 'Well, the year Charlie was honoured has gone down in history. Do you know for why? Do you have any idea? You've surely heard what happened?' I didn't want the answer to any of these questions. But Malcolm Jeffrey did not care.

'Old Charlie here got drunk, didn't he. He said later he was nervous. Nervous, would you believe it? A grown man. Anyway, here's old Charlie drunk, so drunk he can hardly walk. And what does he do? Does he say he can't do the job? Does he hand things over to someone else? Does he buggery. Charlie Trummle always thought he was the best man for anything that was going. Didn't you, Charlie? Anyway, that's what he used to tell everyone all of the time. So, anyway, Charlie goes ahead. He convinces everyone he's fine. He stands in the ring that's been made specially for him. They roll him down Mill Street. Everyone's there: every Bunter that ever was. Cheering and roaring and shouting, throwing their bonnets in the air, running after him towards the Irk. And what happens? You know, don't you?' I did, without remembering how. 'Old Charlie, drunk as a duck, falls out of his ring and rolls around on the street, and everyone, the whole town, gathers round him and watches him throwing up his stomach on to the stones. That's why Charlie's famous in this town. That's why Charlie doesn't like wee boys playing with hoops. Isn't that right, Charlie?'

The old man finally shook off the hand which had restrained him and walked from the barn. As he left, he brushed past Stan who was coming in with a tray of tea and biscuits.

'What's the matter with him?'

'It's that time of year.' said Malcolm.

'What?'

153

'No tea for me.'

'Or me.' Suddenly, I wanted to be back in the bank. 'Let's get this finished, for god's sake.'

And we did finish. Without the help of Stan's two sons but with Charlie, who returned to us after a fifteen minute absence.

We completed the loading in virtual silence. Stan attempted several conversations but soon accepted the mood of the company. My brain now clear of alcohol, the fireworks doused with damp sand, I was beginning to think ahead to the rest of the week amongst strangers like this. I wondered if Macroom would believe I had experienced a miracle cure.

The packing over, the container secure, Malcolm climbed into the cab. Stan spoke to him through the window then turned to me:

'George, help me direct the lorry on to the road, will you? Charlie, away in and help yourself to a drink.'

As the load disappeared in engine noise and blue exhaust smoke, Stan took a handkerchief from his pocket and wiped his neck and face:

'Another day, another zloty.' We walked back towards the gate. Stan stopped and wiped his face again. 'What happened back there?'

'Something about Charlie and the ring.'

'Jesus. Malcolm can be a cruel bastard sometimes. The town's never forgiven Charlie for that. Down here, we take our history very seriously.' He looked at the sky, the ground, then the walls which surrounded his garden. 'Even this place is historical, you know.'

'Oh?'

'Eckford House, home of the Taits.'

'And of George Tait?'

You've heard of him? You learn fast.'

'Remember, I work for Macroom.'

'Given you the benefit of his knowledge, has he?' We both smiled. 'Have a look at this.' He led me to one side of the gate. A statue stood there, eight feet high. On the granite plinth was carved a list of names. On top of a marble pillar sat a bird, a crested penguin, cast in bronze. 'The memorial to the 'Bannock Expedition'.'

154

'Really.' I moved closer to read the list of those who had died.

'It was built after the Major's death by Willie Rob, who used to live in the lodge house. The bird is 'Tait's Penguin'. The discovery of those birds was the sole scientific achievement of the expedition.' We both stood back to look at the polished image. 'I used to speak with old Willie when I was a boy, when I came out here looking for chestnuts or hunting for rabbits. He was on the trip with Tait, you know. Old Willie was quite a man. Ex-sergeant. Real dry sense of humour. He used to talk about Tait and the penguins all the time. He told me once why the birds were now extinct. I didn't know whether to believe him or not at the time. But now I do.'

'What did he say?'

'What did he say?' Stan shaded his eyes from the sinking sun. 'He told me that Tait's Penguin is now extinct because he and Major Tait and the other members of the Bannock Expedition ate them all when they were stranded on the ice at the South Pole. Oily flesh, he told me. Tasted like a week old herring.

'That's why Willie put the bird on the statue. He didn't give a shit about the expedition or the scientific achievement. He wanted to give thanks to his little black and white friends. Those penguins saved his life.'

155

In the Land of Opportunity

A Far Flung Bannock: The Bunters of
America by T.J. Macroom

The sixteenth in an occasional series of
monographs published by the
Bannock Historical Society.

The United States of America is, of
course,_____
_____
___creed and tongue known to man.
_____story to tell but surely no
story is more_____
_____Bannock_____
expansion_____mighty
country thousands _____
_____Atlantic waves.
_____Bannock-
American_____, Andrew
Tochle, the man who_____
_____industrial titans. Born
a Bunter in the year 1831, _____
_____immigrant
ship_____parents and
_____Pittsburgh
_____position
in the Pennsylvania and Erie Bank by
the founder of that establishment, T.J.
Dalrymple, a cousin to_____
_____some of the financial
flair which was later _____

In 1853, using funds from the bank,
Tochle bought out the ailing Scranton
Iron_____
business round, expanded, diversified
into_____
___Civil War_____
_____concerns in the country.
_____misery and loss of
_____stimulus to heartland
of_____American industry.
At the end of the conflict, the turnover
_____national
product of Belgium._____
railroads._____into
its own_____cont-
ributory factors to the Union
_____, James Fisk and Jay
Gould, Tochle brought the benefits of
modern_____mammoth
subsidiary, the Great Lakes, Southern
and Pacific Railroad_____
_____consolidation for the
Tochle empire. Tens of millions of tons
of coal were mined; thousands
of_____; countless _____
_____insatiable appetite_____

_____
_____

_____
_____innate shrewdness _____
sold out _____1893,
_____financial panic
money thus raised_____: oil.
_____John D. Rockefeller and
together_____
Standard trust_____four fifths
of_____

157

_____

_____

_____shortlived_____

_____1900, the dawning of a new

_____sold_____

Standard   Oil._____to   U.S.

Steel:_____end.

_____millions_____less

fortunate_____not   for-

gotten. The Tochle Memorial Hall,

famous as the site of the experiments

of   television   pioneer   Arthur

_____

_____

statue_____

_____public subscription:_____

_____

exploits changed the world.

It is a little known fact that Grover
Cleveland, the twenty second Pres

Natural History

Charlie didn't stay long after the loading was complete. Stan drove him back to town and left me to look after the three smallest children. In fact, Heather, Ishbel and John looked after themselves. As I sat drinking whisky in the room with the leather chairs, I heard them playing outside in the garden, singing Bannock songs and rolling their hoops.

When Stan returned, he told me Charlie was in quite a state. Apparently he always slipped into a depression at this time of year, as every conversation, every excited child, every banner, every display window reminded him of his disgrace thirty years before.

Stan had bought him a couple of bottles and a paper sack full of fish and chips. That, said Stan, would keep him off the streets for one night. There, whether from taunting children or disapproving adults or drunken Winkie Boys, only trouble awaited him in the week leading up to The Rollin' O' The Ring.

I suppose only someone born in Bannock could fully understand the mix of emotions on Stan's face when I asked him the obvious question: why Charlie Trummle remained in a town which brought him only pain, in a town where his shame was reflected in every pair of eyes; in the stone and glass and wood of the buildings themselves.

'It's his home,' Stan told me. 'It's where he was born and brought up. He knows no other place and has no great desire to find out. Maybe he doesn't like any of his fellow Bunter's, but then he doesn't particularly like anyone else either. It's the same for everyone: we're all drawn back to Bannock. All of us. There's no escape, even if we live five thousand miles away on the other side of the world.'

At that instant I thought of a scene from a natural history programme I had once seen on television. Soil was compacted between sheets of glass and in that clearly defined world a colony of ants constructed their tunnels and chambers, oblivious to the cameras and the technicians and the entymologists, even the other ant universes which existed somewhere beyond the millimetre-thick skin which contained their intense activity.

They reproduced and died; they cleared new spaces for eggs and drove through ventilation chimneys; they rolled aggregates of sand and soil before them, and groups combined to lift boulders four times their combined weight.

And then I saw my dream of the ant world as the observers left the lab, as the studio lights were packed up for the next assignment. The door would close with a final click, leaving silence among the test tubes and Bunsen burners. The only movement would be on the bench under the moonlight where the props had been left. There, noiselessly, the ants would turn on each other, the need for pretence gone. Driven mad by their confinement they would tear at one another with pincers and claws, and the chambers would fill with the smell of formic acid. Their eyes would not see through the glass: they would be directed inwards towards the rubble and ant-gore in the collapsing tunnels.

Other People's Thoughts

Once upon a time, a young boy died. He was ten years old and his name was Daniel Kowalik. He was a son, a brother, a friend, a grandson.

Daniel died because a cancer attacked his white blood cells. This leukemia killed him before the doctors who dealt with his case had time to do much about it.

Everyone at the hospital was surprised at the speed of the boy's decline. Most patients lived longer after diagnosis. The boy's parents received the sympathy of all concerned.

The doctors were philosophic about the loss of their patient. They had to adopt such an attitude, otherwise they could not function. They said: 'It's just one of those things'.

But why Daniel? The parents asked themselves this question night after screaming night. They tore themselves

160

apart looking for the solution to this problem but they could not find any answer.

In fact, the cause lay deep within their son. The answer lay inside Daniel's cells. Contained in each one, a hidden bonus from either mother or father, was an extra chromosome. Not whole, but broken: a fragment. But enough to pass on a poisonous message. From the moment he had been born, from the moment he had been conceived, Daniel's future had been laid down in a pattern no one could change. That had been his inheritance.

A form of madness took hold of the mother when her son died, but it burned itself out and a colder, more frightening anger took over. This anger could have been directed towards many people. Towards her parents, who offered sympathy but not understanding. Towards her remaining children, who now seemed to hold out the potential to inflict further pain. Towards those doctors, who could not prevent the inevitable. Instead, Briony focused upon her husband: the organiser, the provider, the comforter; the protector, who had stood powerless, silent, as he watched his son slip away from the world.

The mother wanted to hurt this man who had told her he could accomplish anything, conquer anyone in her name. The one who had shrunk in his clothes in the hospital-white room and cried like a child as he had watched his power evaporate. She wanted to damage him as she had been damaged. It might take time but it would be done.

While she waited, Briony retreated into herself and spent most of her time behind the walls of Eckford House. She cooked for the children, looked at photographs and went for solitary walks in the garden. Her only view of the outside world was through those wrought iron gates which guarded the driveway from the main road. On the other side of the bars she could see cars pass and she imagined the thoughts of their occupants. They would be engrossed in their own problems, oblivious to the pain which existed yards from their elbows. How else could it be?

On one of her walks Briony saw an old man looking at her from beside the statue at the gatehouse. She stared back at him, expecting him to move on, but he stood his ground. She walked towards him, thinking he would turn away, but he

advanced several paces. 'Briony.' She stopped. 'Briony.' He
was short and broad, his grey hair standing straight up from
his forehead. As he came closer, she could see his eyes: pale
blue; washed out with grief.

'Janusz?' It was the first time she had spoken his name.
Her hands shook as she drew the bolt from the gate.

Dissolving

When my wife awoke from her dream-life, when Joyce opened
her eyes at last and discovered a new world, there seemed to be
no place in it for me. I was still asleep. I recognised this: I was
not so unaware as to confuse conciousness with unconciousness;
but I had no desire to change. I knew of these other possibilities
but I was content as I was. I was worried that confrontation
with too much reality could be damaging. I suppose that,
somewhere in there, I was thinking about my father. He had
lived briefly in a world of heightened senses: where he could
smell blood and death on his tunic; where comradeship merged
with love; where a day was as short or as long as a lifetime.
Later, even thinking about such vivid experiences had been
hard work, had been so emotionally draining that there was
nothing left for anything or anyone else. It was then that he had
decided it was easier just to pop off, to bale out, to call it a day.
Bye-bye, everyone.

'George.' Joyce spoke my name one Sunday. She said it in
such a way as to imply there was something on her mind, that
something was going to come out: 'Geeoorgge.' She was
ironing handkerchiefs. I was watching a repeat of *Lost In
Space* on the telly. 'George.' (I was on that cardboard planet
with the Robinsons. I had a walk-on part in the episode where
the intergalactic trader....) 'George.' There was a puff and a
hiss from the steam-iron.

'What?' (... and Doctor Smith had just discovered he had
sold himself into slavery...)

'George, could you listen to me for one moment.'

'What? Go on. I'm listening.' (....ith could save himself if he could arrange the sale and delivery of young Will Robinson to the.....)

'No you're not. You're watching that rubbish on the television.'

'No I'm not.' (... but then the robot ...) 'I'm listening to you.'

'No you're not. I'm not going to compete with that drivel.'

So I never found out what happened at the end of that episode. So we had our discussion. So it all started. From such small beginnings.

'George.' She concentrated on the work before her. The wrinkles disappeared from my shirts. 'George, are you happy with things as they are?' She did not look at me. Arms were folded over on to chest. A neat square was formed. A pyjama top joined the pile. 'Do you never think maybe we're in a rut? Maybe we should think about....I don't know. It's just that sometimes I think I'm missing out on life. That the world is just passing me by. I'm sure there must be more to it than this.' The iron hissed again.

What was I supposed to say? A whole pile of words flew around in my head but none of them came out. They just bounced off one another and numbed the inside of my skull. I didn't want to deal with things like that. What was happening on the box? I felt dizzy.

'What do you think, George?'

I thought. The shirt was wet against my back.

'George?'

I thought some more. I became aware of sweat trickling down my face. A smell burst in my nose: Vick Vapour Rub and Nasal Decongestant.

'George.'

I was afloat on an ocean.

'George, are you all right?'

'I don't feel too well.'

'Maybe you'd better go and lie down.'

'Maybe I'd better.'

'Go upstairs to bed and I'll bring you up a hot drink and an aspirin.'

'O.K., Gran.'

'Gran?'

'Sorry.'

'You are sick.'

So it proved. My temperature was up. The doctor was called in and diagnosed a bad case of influenza. He told me to drink plenty of liquids to replace the fluid lost through my sweating. On his advice, I took a week off work. My first absence in fifteen years.

In the years that followed, I was sick a lot. Drained of energy, I would lie in bed for days on end, dissolving like an ice cream in the sun. The health I had discovered when I joined the bank had gone. I underwent all kinds of tests but none of the doctors or laboratory technicians could find anything wrong with me. Allergies, viral infections, tropical diseases were all ruled out. A research student attempted to write a paper on my case. He interviewed me, took samples of various body fluids, analysed my home and working environment, examined my medical and personal history. He abandoned the project before the work was complete. It was leading nowhere. It was all a waste of time. I was a mystery which was not worth investigating.

As I declined, Joyce gained in strength. She began to attend night school at Abernethy Technical College, sitting in the rooms in which we had met all those years before. In her first year she enrolled in a course on 'Assertiveness Training'. She came back from the first class full of energy and enthusiasm. She came back from the second saying she had discovered that new perspective she had been seeking. She came back from the third proclaiming that our lives up until that point had been a colossal waste of time.

Joyce told me this in our bedroom. I lay on our king-size divan, sweating into the sheets, a melting ice pack pressed to my forehead. As my insides came out through my pores, I watched my wife pace the floor. Through bead-prismed eyes I saw her stop and turn to face me:

'George, you've got to listen.' I nodded, but my heart wasn't in it. 'Things have got to change.'

'Yes, dear.'

Next, Joyce opted for *Introduction To The Social Sciences*.

Her tutor, an Irishman from London called Cathal McSwine, told her she had great potential and should consider applying for admission to a degree course at the City University, where he was a research student. The idea appealed to Joyce but she had reservations about giving up her job at the bank. The pain caused by this dilemma was dumped off on me. It was at this stage that Joyce fully formulated the idea that:

'You're holding me back. Every time I want to step forward, I feel you clinging to my ankles with your clammy little hands. God, I've got to break free.'

She shouted these words at me. She had started to shout a lot. I think that, somewhere along the line, she had picked up the impression that this was what talented, intelligent, creative, newly liberated people do when faced by inhibited, inhibiting saps like me. When she wasn't shouting, she was silent, apart from the occasional sigh or snort or sniff over the top of a book.

For her third course in a consciousness-expanding eighteen months, Joyce chose: *Feminist Perspectives: A Multi-Disciplinary Approach*. During this period, people I had never met before began to appear in the house: large women draped in ethnic fabrics; men with unusual accents who talked very quickly; nutty professor types in half-mast trousers; menopausal tomboys wearing dangling earrings. Sometimes, I found swarms of small children, presumably the offspring of the adult guests, bumping down the stairs, crawling over the kitchen floor. Exuding confidence and health, hair like upturned, silky soup bowls, they would be dressed in denim overalls and odd socks, little checked shawls with tassels round the edges, patched drawers, and the shapeless woollens favoured by coca addicts on the streets of Bogota. (These children would ignore me completely, unless I presented some obstacle to their enjoyment. Then they would yell for their mothers, and Joyce would appear, and look. And I would release a Stuka or a Hurricane, return it to those little hands which had prised open the cockpit and twisted the propeller from the fuselage. I would lift a pair of five year olds back on to a chair and smile weakly as their small fists hammered on the keys of my portable typewriter.)

Joyce had joined a variety of groups and organisations

and become a valued worker on their behalf. The members of these groups were the people who cluttered up my living room, took showers in my bathroom, used my newspaper to make hats for their children. They would chat over cups of my coffee then settle down to their meetings behind closed doors. From my exile in the kitchen or upstairs in the bedroom, I would hear muffled voices, the occasional shout; short silences then bursts of laughter; then doors opening and closing, and the shuffling of feet as the business of the day came to an end.

Joyce became membership secretary of one group, treasurer of another. Both organisations had very long names which were usually reduced to acronyms. A steel cabinet was purchased and installed in the room where I had once attempted to become Ernest Hemingway. It filled with important papers which then overflowed into a series of box files on the floor. Correspondence was typed on my typewriter. Figures were added up at my desk. Joyce bought a little square plate and stuck it on to the outside of the door of this room she had taken from me. On the plate was engraved a little pencil and a little pen and the word OFFICE.

Posters began to decorate this room. They were printed in bold colours and exclaimed messages in a variety of languages. Highly stylised figures strode forward towards the wallpaper, waved flags or fists, showed their teeth in smiles or shouts. I could not understand all of the words, but some of the messages appeared to be urgent: we were being urged to do something or support something else right now: there was no time to lose! Other posters seemed to be more celebratory: they hailed the anniversaries of heroic people or of significant events. They were designed to ensure that we did not forget the important dates in history.

Joyce took to saying things like: 'Where does all the time go?' and 'There just aren't enough hours in the day.' She pursued very long conversations on the telephone, in the course of which she would mention a whole series of people and places and events I had never heard of. She received two registered parcels in the space of one month. On these and on her letters from abroad were stamps I secretly coveted.

Everywhere Joyce went, she carried cardboard folders full of papers and leaflets. One day she came home with a leather briefcase and, on the kitchen table, solemnly packed it with her diary, notebooks, address book, calculator, textbooks, ring binders and file pads before exiting to her latest night class at Abernethy: *Sociological Images of Deviancy.*

'How is the sick man tonight,' she asked before she left.

'Not too bad.' I had been off work for a few days. The usual problem. Sitting in my dressing-gown, I was eating a bowl of tinned tomato soup. A drop dripped from my spoon to my already orange chin. I wiped it with my sleeve. Joyce looked to the ceiling, shook her head and sighed. I stopped in mid-slurp. She studied my far from debonair appearance:

'What in the world do you look like?'

'You tell me.'

'I don't have a large enough vocabulary.' She finished her packing. 'What in the world did we ever have in common?'

'We used to be able to talk.'

'Is that what you call it? You could have fooled me. At least now I know what real conversation is about.'

'Oh, what's that then?' I sneered.

'You probably wouldn't understand. I don't suppose you've ever had an idea in your life, have you?' I began to eat again:

'That's right.' Slurp. 'Not one.'

'You're impossible. Why don't you just go back to bed. I'll bring up your model aeroplanes and you can pretend you're a fighter-pilot.'

'At least I can recognise unreality when I see it.'

'What do you mean?'

'Nothing.' I felt tired.

'You wouldn't recognise reality if it bit you on the backside.' She looked at her watch. 'Nearly time for *Star Trek*. Will I put the television on for you?'

'You're very kind.'

'Enjoy you're rest while you can. Remember, it's only four months until I begin university. What'll you do then if you get the sack for malingering?'

'You know I'm sick.'

'Sick in the head, more like.'

Shortly after this 'conversation', Joyce moved into the spare bedroom. My sweats became worse and I began to sleep on a rubber incontinence sheet. I was off work and drinking a lot to no effect: the alcohol burst from my skin almost before it had cleared my gullet.

My mother came over to see why I hadn't been in contact. Letting herself in with a spare key she found me in bed, surrounded by week-old newspapers, sticky glasses and fly-blown plates, whisky bottles, empty bean tins. I was unshaven, unwashed; my fingernails were black, my eyes yellow; the flesh had dropped from my cheeks. She looked out some fresh clothes, cleaned me up and called a taxi to take me home.

'Home'. There I was again. Back in Corsock Street. The same furniture, the same curtains, the same carpets, the same smells. In the flat high above the butcher shop where my father had worked, where Tommy Traynor still minced mince and chopped chops. 'Young Tommy' came up to see me as I recuperated in the bed where I had once sheltered from school. He had put on a lot of weight and there were grey hairs in his moustache. We talked for a short while, then he wished me all the best and clapped his solid hand on my shoulder. I felt about eight years old.

My mother and my two aunts made a great fuss. They made pots of broth and fed it to me from a bowl which resembled a teapot. They pressed cold cloths to my forehead and bought a small electric fan which whirred day and night on a locker at my side. They brought me a selection of newspapers in the morning, collected books from the library, and hired a twelve-inch, remote-controlled, colour television for the foot of my bed.

Only one thing was missing: Grannie. Increasingly confused, cantankerous and befuddled, this still active octogenarian had developed into a problem too great for her three ageing daughters to cope with. With great heartache, and after long discussions with the minister, the family doctor, and various social workers, it had been decided that the best solution was to put Grannie into care, and so, two days before my arrival, she had been admitted to the John Knox Memorial Eventide Home For The Chronically Bewildered, situated on the western fringe of the city.

But how could long distance, failing sight, bunions and arthritic hips keep a woman from her only grandchild? On the

168

Sunday of the weekend after my removal to Corsock Street, my Aunt Isa put her head round the door of my room:

'George. Are you awake?'

'Uh?' I was not. I was conserving my strength for a return to work on Monday morning.

'George.' She whispered, insistently.

'What is it?' I sat up, rubbed my eyes, felt my lips with my tongue.

'There's a visitor here for you.' I immediately thought of Joyce. I felt damp. Aunt Isa disappeared and I heard muttering and scuffling from behind the door. Both my aunts came in and stood smiling by the side of my bed. I heard my mother's voice:

'That's it. Nearly there.' There was a bump and a scrape and heavy breathing, then that familiar head, the white hair thinning. Then a metal frame with a huge, black handbag swinging from a crossbar, and an arm supported by my mother. 'That's you. Through you go.' Grannie looked up from her efforts and saw my face above the blankets:

'Georgie,' she wheezed. Her Zimmer seemed to skim over the carpet and she was by my side. She studied me. 'You're looking awful peekie, son. No school for you tomorrow.'

Helped by my mother, Grannie sat in a chair by my side and slowly regained her breath. When she had composed herself, she bent down and produced a small jar fom her handbag:

'This is what you need, Georgie.'

I knew what it was before the lid was opened. The memory of the smell filled my nose, caught in my lungs. And as those old fingers rubbed Vick's Vapour Rub into my chest, I began to seep liquid again. But on this occasion, for the first time in a long while, it was my eyes, not my pores, that had sprung a leak.

An Evening In

'Daddy.' Ishbel's head appeared round the door. Stan broke off in the middle of his story and looked towards his daughter:
'Yes, dear?'
'Daddy.'
'What is it, Ishbel?'
'Daddy, can I talk to you?' Stan winked at me and stood up:
'Pour us another couple, George, will you.' He went to the door, bent down, and put an arm round his daughter. 'What is it, sweetheart?' Ishbel whispered in his ear but I could hear her words:
'Daddy, is that man going to sleep in my bed again tonight?' Stan straightened, put his head back, and laughed loudly:
'Don't you worry, sweetheart. Mr Weems'll be sleeping somewhere else tonight.'
'In Heather's bed?'
'No, not there either, pet. Away you go upstairs now. It's past your bedtime. I'll be up to see you in a minute.' Stan kissed his daughter then twisted her nose between his fingers.
'Daddy!'
'That's what you get for staying up late.'
The headlights of a car lit up the window.
'Is that Mummy?'
'Away you go up. You'll know soon enough.' As the girl disappeared, Stan turned to me. 'Give me that drink, George.' He drank a large whisky in one gulp. 'I might need this.'
'Maybe it would be best if you gave me a lift into town. I could stay at the hotel until I fixed something up.'
'Don't worry, George. You can't make things any worse.'
How could I be more at ease? There were the sounds of people getting out of a car, then the opening of the front door.
'What happened to you?' I heard Stan speak.
'Rugby practice. We told you.' The voice of a boy.
'But you were supposed to give me a hand.'

170

'You don't want us to be dropped, do you?' Another voice, similar to the first.

'Where did you get your tea?'

'Struan Tummle's. Mum knew we were going there.'

'She didn't tell me.'

'Well you can ask her now.'

There was a silence which expressed half a dozen emotions at once. I could almost see Stan clench his fist. I began to sweat for the first time that day. A drop dripped from my nose and fell on to the hand which held my glass.

Two boys came into the room and looked at me without much curiosity. Both appeared to be around fifteen or sixteen years of age, with Stan's broad frame and that thick hair standing up from the forehead. One of them, the older of the two, even had a broken nose, the bridge twisted to the left like that of his father. He lifted a chess board which lay prepared for play on a table in front of the french windows, and tipped the men into their box.

'You're not using this by any chance, are you?' he asked me. I shook my head and a bead fell on my chin.

'Tough luck if he was,' said the younger boy in a whisper designed for me to hear. And again as he left the room: 'Salvation Army time again.'

From somewhere came the sound of an argument. Stan's voice. Then the other voice. The voice I recognised. I could not hear the words, only the anger. Stan came back into the room dressed in a jacket.

'I have to go out for a while, George.' My face must have shown a look of concern. 'Don't worry, I won't be long. I just forgot something for Briony. Help yourself while I'm away.' I wanted to ask if I could come too. I was frightened of what might happen in Stan's absence. I started to speak, but Stan was gone. He waved: 'Ten minutes.'

Only one thing for it. I poured myself another. As I did so, I heard a noise from behind my shoulder. Then that voice. My shirt was sticking to my back:

'I'd like one too please, if you don't mind.' I heard her sit down on one of the leather armchairs. I half turned my head to pretend I was looking at her:

'What would you like?'

171

'Gin. Just straight with ice. My husband forgot to buy tonic for me this morning. Such a thoughtful man.' No tonic. One step from mass-murder. I brought the drink to her, avoiding her gaze. Her light brown hair was loose, freed from plaits and ponytail. 'Thank you. My goodness. You're sweating. Is it too warm for you in here?'

'No, no, it's fine. I think I've caught a bug or something.'

'My god, what sort of bug would make you sweat like that.' By now, a Niagara was pouring down my face.

'I've had something like it before.'

'Shouldn't you see a doctor?'

'It's not that serious.'

'I hope it's not contagious.'

'No, it's not.' She eyed my glass:

'And should you be drinking?'

'The doctor didn't mention anything about alcohol.'

'No? Who is your doctor?' Think, think, think:

'Doctor Murgle.'

'God. Murgle.' She shook her head but did not explain her obvious disapproval. Half of her drink disappeared in the kind of violent gulp I had seen Stan use to deal with alcohol. 'Well, are you not going to sit down? I don't want you to collapse in a heap.' I followed instructions. She was silent, looking at my fragmented image through the crystal glass she held before her eyes. 'You really ought to see about that, you know. You must be losing pints of fluid. Is that why you drink so much?' I looked down at my empty glass and smiled weakly:

'I think I'll survive.'

'Survival. Is that all there is to it? What about...' She thought for a moment. 'Oh, god. What's the point?' Her glass was now empty, like mine. 'We may as well have another, I suppose.' As I buttled, I heard her settle deeper into her chair. 'My husband informs me you will be staying as our guest for the next few days.'

'I hope it's not inconvenient.'

Inconvenient? Oh Lord, no.' She said this in a tone which suggested that it was, in fact, incredibly inconvenient, and that if she had her way I would be locked up for vagrancy.

'Very nice of you.'

172

'Don't mention it. Thank you.' She rested her refilled glass on the arm of the chair and made no move to drink from it. 'And how are you finding life in dear, old, lovable Bannock?'

'It's a beautiful place.'

'That's not what I asked.'

'Well, I suppose it takes time to settle into a new environment.'

'Oh yes. A long time. You haven't adjusted fully until you're settling into the soil at the bottom of a deep hole.'

'I get the impression that you're not fully converted to the pleasures of country life.'

'How could I say that? How could I be dissatisfied here? After all, you know how the Bunters refer to this happy wonderland of theirs: 'The Maister's Ain Gairden'.'

'I've heard it.'

'Yet another chosen people living in God's own country.'

'I suppose it has its attractions.' Briony looked up towards the ceiling in despair. What had I said?

'Why is it that everyone, no matter where they live, thinks that their particular little rabbit warren is the best collection of burrows in the world? It could be a village of cardboard boxes, or a collection of mud huts. It doesn't matter: there's no view like the one from their window; there's no air that smells so pure as the air that's in their nostrils. And as for the people, well, there's nothing like your 'ain folk', is there? They're the friendliest, or they're the canniest, or they're the hardest working, or they're the most honest. It doesn't matter that, in reality they all hate each other and derive their greatest pleasure from bankruptcies, and divorces, and house fires.'

'I wouldn't say that every...

'And as for Bannock: the good old Bunters spend their days biting little pieces of flesh from one another's bodies, then they puff up with self-righteousness when they watch the telly and see the floods and earthquakes that afflict those who don't look after their affairs correctly or fail to pay their bills on time.'

'I don't suppose that ...'

'Look at Charlie Trummle: hardly anyone will even pass the time of day with him because of something he did thirty

173

years ago. But he would never dream of moving to the next town. He would rather stay with the torment he knows and spend his evenings getting drunk and planning his revenge.'

She stopped. I had to make an effort: be sociable. Show an interest:

'Maybe...'

'Maybe what? Maybe Charlie would die in a city where no-one knows anyone else.' She was trying to read my thoughts. Had she learned this from her husband. This could become annoying.

'No, maybe...'

'Maybe what?' I took a long, hard pull on my drink and decided it would be advisable to be the perfect guest. I adopted a listening mode:

'Well, you tell me.'

'It's you who's interrupting.'

'Sorry.'

'And you're sweating again.'

'Must be the whisky.'

'Are you really sure you should be drinking?'

'Dr Murgle...'

'I know.' She nodded as if thoughts of Doctor Murgle, or perhaps my presence, or the utterance of my astoundingly boring thoughts were inducing a headache. She leaned her head on the back of the chair and closed her eyes, her hand still gripping the untouched drink. Flawless skin stretched over her face and neck and her hair flopped back to reveal small, delicate ears. I realised that Briony Kowalik was beautiful, and for one frightening instant, I felt drawn towards her pain.

She remained like that for several minutes until I thought she was asleep. I remained still in case I disturbed her until a cramp forced me to uncross my legs. Briony opened her eyes and spoke:

'Where are you going?' I jumped, as if I had been caught lifting her skirt:

'Nowhere.'

'Nowhere.' She repeated. She seemed to relish a hidden significance in my words. I resented the implication that they meant more to her than they did to me.

'Stan's late.' I looked at my watch.

174

'Stan's often late.' Briony liked mystery and ambiguity. It indicated she was one of the leading members of a club which I would never be able to join.

'Maybe he bumped into someone.'

'Oh yes. My husband knows lots of people. He even knows you, and you've only been in Bannock for five minutes. Stan needs to know everyone and he needs everyone to know him. That's why he left the city and came back here. He couldn't bear the idea of walking the streets, passing by all those thousands of people who didn't recognise him and know how clever and successful he was. He thought he had to return to be appreciated.'

And so it went on. And on. She had worked out her views on just about everything. I tried to care, but it was difficult. There was just too much. I became overloaded. It was as if she had never spoken before, as if a whole lake of words had been dammed up then released. Why was she telling me? But then I knew. She was not communicating, only picking at the scab which had formed over a wound.

The room was warm. I was full of whisky. I had had a disturbed night's sleep.

I could not help myself. My eyes closed and my head began to nod. As I dozed, I dreamed. Each time my head swooped down to my chest I awoke and Briony's drone mingled with the other world.

I was back at school.

'... ask him a favour. He loves doing little services for people in the community. It makes him feel ...'

I was happy.

'... giving birth to one of my sons, my husband was helping my neighbour to move her...'

I had finished top of the class.

'... never really going to be one of them...'

I was on a stage.

'... just laugh at him...'

I reached out a hand for my prize.

'... should be loved by everyone...'

I felt all their eyes upon me.

'... they can't resist...'

I was a liar and a cheat. The prize was not mine. I was not

the pupil they had called for.

'... truth, and his wole world comes tumbling down.'

Briony stopped talking and the silence in the room forced my eyes open. She was sitting perfectly still, holding her glass to her forehead, as if to cool a fever. Had she asked me a question? No. In her eyes I did not count any more than a sofa or a wall lamp. She did not expect any response.

Anyway, what was I to say? I could not pass comment on any of our lives. I could only report events as I had seen them. I could only give evidence, as if I had been called as a witness to a road traffic accident.

Grandad

Once upon a time, there was an old Pole who discovered a new world. When Janusz Kowalik spoke the name of his daughter-in-law and walked through the gates of Eckford House, he felt as if he had been readmitted to the human race.

After this first contact, the old man called about once a month, always when his son was away on business. Stan was not to know about the visits; neither was Stan's mother. It would be between Briony and Janusz and the five children who were sworn, uncomprehendingly, to secrecy.

Perhaps Stan knew of Janusz's trips into the countryside. It would be difficult to imagine he did not uncover any clues over a five year period. But if he did, he remained silent and, as before, never raised the subject of his father or even mentioned his name.

In a faint echo of Stan's beanos in the Bannock Polish Club, the five Kowalik children began to enjoy double birthdays. Some days or weeks after the normal, family party, a second, more subdued celebration would take place. Their long lost grandfather would call round and, after tea, would hand over a gift to the lucky boy or girl and solemnly shake a small hand. 'Thank you, Grandpa,' each child would say, looking shyly at this old man who combined the foreign with the familiar.

Five years. Around sixty visits. It could not be said that Janusz greatly touched the lives of his grandchildren, but they got used to seeing him pop up from time to time. They did not greatly look forward to his appearances, but they didn't resent his presence. That was enough for Janusz. A starving man will accept any food he is offered.

Briony felt sorry for the old man, and made him feel welcome in her house. Eventually, she grew to like him, and looked forward to him calling. Maybe they had a lot in common.

Janusz was a little uneasy in his daughter-in-law's presence, and this would make him rather stiff and uncommunicative during the initial part of the visit. After a while, Briony found that a couple of drinks helped to promote conversation.

They talked of the children, of events in the town, of the weather and the garden, of the health of the pet dogs. They might discuss television programmes or the news of the day, or plans for redecoration or a new car. But never the past. And never Stan. Neither knew how to begin, neither could utter those first words; so these subjects were buried. After each visit, Briony told herself she would have the courage next time, but of course, she never did, and the tension increased, like the stretched skin on a swelling boil.

Then, one day, Janusz failed to appear at the house as arranged. It had never happened before. Immediately, Briony knew what had happened. The old man had been unwell for some time, although he had never complained. When she contacted the flat above the shop, the telephone was answered by one of Stan's aunts. Briony replaced the receiver in its cradle without speaking.

Like the old soldier he was, Janusz Kowalik had faded away. But he had not disappeared completely without trace. Under a bright sky, in the small Catholic cemetery in Bannock, he was buried by his wife, a few acquaintances, and the ageing remnants of the Polish community. And by his new family. The old man would have been pleased to have seen Briony support the arm of his wife. He would have been proud to have known that his two oldest grandsons, Adam and Joseph

177

Kowalik, would be there to help lower him into his grave.

But look: another funeral, another missing mourner. No son. No Stan. A long memory. And for what?

For This

Once upon a time there was a Pole called Janusz Kowalik. In 1939, he served as a soldier on the eastern frontier of his country. There, in the September of that year, he carried out what he saw as his patriotic and religious duty by resisting invading Soviet forces. Later, Janusz joined the underground Armia Krajowa, or 'Home Army', and helped to fight the Germans until victory was achieved. In late 1945, when most of Europe was at peace, Janusz's war continued against the People's Army, the armed wing of the Polish Workers' Party. Six years without a rest. Six years without a home. Some people thought he was a hero.

In 1946 he left Poland, sick of war, tired of fighting, searching for peace and a new life. At that time, whole chunks of Europe were moving or being moved. Boundaries changed, countries disappeared, whole populations woke up to discover that their nationality had changed overnight. The roads were packed with people who carried their whole lives on their backs. Janusz Kowalik was one of them.

After a long, difficult journey, he reached the British Zone of occupied Germany. There, in a camp for displaced persons, he found work as an interpreter. He was well suited to this job for, although not well educated, he had an aptitude for languages. In addition to Polish, he had a good working knowledge of German, Czech and Slovak. Soon, he could speak English too.

Later, as a reward for his services, the authorities allowed Janusz Kowalik entry into Britain. This was not a purely altruistic decision. At the time, there was a shortage of labour in certain key industries. The Pole could help out.

Janusz had been a miner before serving as a soldier. When he arrived in his new country, he became a miner again, but not for long. He found he could not stand the darkness any more. He did not want to spend his new life burrowing through geological history. Instead, he felt a great desire to live in the countryside, where the air was pure, where he could see the upper world in the sunshine and in the rain.

He moved to Bannock.

There, Janusz Kowalik, the Polish refugee, worked, made friends, married, had a son.

There, the son, Stanislaw, the Bannock Bunter, grew, learned, won prizes, tried to fit in.

There, Stan, the historian, fell out with Janusz, the man who had lived through so much of the past.

There, a son decided that his father was not worthy of him any more.

There, a son decided to reinvent his father's history.

Why? Because a civil servant in Warsaw refused to grant a visa for Janusz Kowalik, a Pole, to visit his own country. Why? Because Janusz was not a desirable person. Why? Because Janusz had fought against people he could not understand.

This was not good enough for Stanislaw, the son. It did not satisfy him. There had to be more.

Some Poles had dressed in another uniform and killed their own people. Some Poles had helped to build walls across city streets. Some Poles had rounded up their neighbours and prodded them on to trains. Some Poles had pulled babies from their mothers' arms. Some Poles had collected hair for mattresses, gold teeth for ingots.

Some Poles. Some Poles. But not Janusz Kowalik.

But that did not matter. Since when has the truth counted in any analysis of the past?

The ability to improvise is what counts. A skill in tailoring the facts: little tuck here; a raised hem there; snip: an arm has vanished.

That, and the hidden anger fuelled by petty slights. And the frustration felt when your future does not unfold as you would wish. And the refusal to accept even the slightest disappointment. And the resentment felt at not belonging. And the desire to blame someone for your unhappiness. And the presence of an uncomplaining victim, one you know will cry rather than fight any more.

179

Sleep Tight

Stan did not return to the house until after midnight. By that time I was in bed, hiding from further conversation with Briony.

We had sat up until after eleven. She talked to the furniture, holding that glass tightly in her hand until I thought it must break. I tried to get drunk on whisky then brandy. But it was no use. As usual, the liquid exuded from my pores and did not pass through any other organs. I sank deeper into my chair hoping I could disappear between the cushions and come out somewhere in a different universe.

At no time during her extended monologue did she mention our 'meeting' in The Old Mill. She wasn't embarrassed about what had happened. It had merely slipped her mind. It had just been one minor skirmish in her undeclared war against her husband, a conflict in which she would resort to any weapon, regardless of civilian casualties.

In the middle of one long sentence, unpunctuated by pauses for breath, I slunk from my seat and muttered apologies, mumbled words like 'getting late' and 'brush' and 'teeth'. I needn't have bothered. She wasn't listening to anyone but herself. I took a quarter-full bottle with me, holding it close to my trouser leg in case it attracted her attention. Sleep seemed far away; I had forgotten what it meant to rest and wake refreshed.

Upstairs, where I had slept the previous night, the doors to all of the rooms were closed. A thin strip of light showed on the carpet and diffused softly into the darkness. As I shuffled towards it I could hear voices:

'For God's sake, move.'

'Hold on.'

'Move or I'll claim the game.'

'Hold on.'

'Move.'

'There: satisfied?'

180

'Checkmate.'

'You wee bastard.'

There was a sliding noise, then the sound of grunting and a loud thump as if something very heavy had fallen on the floor.

'Get off!'

A narrower staircase led upwards from where I stood. A full moon silvered the clouds and through a skylight illuminated half a dozen steps, then a small, square landing and a curtained window. From there, more steps turned back upon themselves and led to a narrow corridor and varnished doors. The floor was uncarpeted and a board squeaked under my foot. There was a circular light switch on the wall which felt smooth and cold to my touch. Flicked, it lit a bare bulb and peeling paint and cobwebs blowing in a draught from the attic above.

In one of the rooms I found a bed, in another, a pile of grey blankets and a rug which smelled of dog. Sweat had cooled on my body and I shivered as I burrowed into the musty mattress. Shoes wrapped in my jacket served as a pillow.

This was freedom. This was what it meant to be alive.

Bedtime Reading

The Songs and Verses Of Bannock by Frazer Ruill and Roderick Macroom M.A.(Hons).

The fourteenth in an occasional series of monographs published by the Bannock Historical Society.

1. A TRADITION IS BORN.
In the words of the Bannock farmer and poet, Wallace Wil: 'Whaur the Guid Lord

Nature

Stan said he'd been worried about me. 'I looked for you all over the house,' he told me the next morning. 'Everywhere. I even looked in everyone's bed to make sure you weren't Goldilocksing again.' This was a joke. I was too tired to laugh. 'Then I thought about upstairs. That's where the servants stayed in the old days, you know.' So what's changed? 'And there you were. Sleeping like a baby. Hugging an empty bottle of brandy.'

He was partly correct: the bottle had been empty. But I hadn't been sleeping. I had seen a light go on and heard footsteps and had closed my eyes. Not because I was frightened of ghosts but because I was frightened of human beings. I had seen Stan's shadow at the door, its shape blurred through my lashes. I had prayed, to no one in particular. Don't speak. I couldn't take any more words. I was full up. There was no more space left in between my ears. My prayers worked. The shadow had retreated. The door had closed, a light switch had clicked.

'You could probably do with a shower. That's Jack's blanket you were sleeping on. He was a spaniel. He's dead now.'

'Something catching?'

'No.' He remembered. 'It was Briony. She wanted rid of the dogs. You know. After Daniel, it was as if she couldn't bear them any more.'

I stopped eating my cornflakes. Suddenly, I wanted a drink.

'Listen, maybe I'd better go into town to look for some digs. I can't hang around here indefinitely.'

'What's your hurry. We've plenty of room. I'll fix up a proper bed for you tonight.'

'I feel I'm intruding.'

'Don't be silly. Stay.' This was not a command: more a plea. 'Anyway, you're supposed to be injured, remember? Where's your surgical collar?'

How had I got into this? Some simple answers: drink; despair; passivity; boredom; sloth; fecklessness; idiocy; an excess of morbidity. Who or what could I blame? My mother; my father; my aunts; my grannie; my wife; my employers; my fellow citizens; the government; a representative sample of world leaders; a selection of deities; the effects of background radiation emanating from the origins of matter; accidental knowledge of a constantly expanding universe; a gnat's fart in the darkness under my bed.

'Maybe Doctor Murgle could fix me up with one.'

'No surgery today. He's probably off fishing.'

Our roles had reversed and I didn't like the feeling. I wasn't ready for responsibility. I couldn't yet cope with people expecting things of me. My skin was wet and my clothes itched. I was trapped in a world I didn't want to understand. I wanted to yell like in the comics:

AAAAAAAAAAAAAAAAAAARRRRRRRRRRRRRRRRRRRGG GGGGGGGGGGGGGGGHHHHHHHHHHHHHHH!!!!!!!!!!!!!!

Instead, I took the Alsatians for a walk. Joe and Julie seemed to know where they were going so I followed them along a well-worn path through a thicket of decaying ash trees at the back of the house. The dogs led me to a locked iron gate through which I could see a lane overgrown and choked with whins, rushes and barbed brambles. Joe and Julie squeezed through a scraped hollow between the rusting bars and the ground, and disappeared in snuffling, wagging ecstasy into the undergrowth.

The bushes shook as the unseen dogs brushed against them. There was a growl, a sharp bark, then a tweet and a flurry of wings as a blackbird burst through the cover. The whins swayed again, further along the lane and I heard splashing then silence. I called the dogs names and whistled but they did not return. I called again and heard a bark from what seemed a long way off, then nothing. Stan had given me a lead for each dog. 'Headstrong,' he had said. 'Take a bit of handling.' I fingered the chains and the leather straps in my pocket and began to sweat, thinking of those large, sharp teeth sinking into woolly flesh; those hard bodies tipping a soft, round ball from a pram; pinning a pensioner: breathing dog-air into a crinkled face.

184

I felt and heard a trouser leg rip as I jumped from the top of the gate. The ground was soft underfoot and at intervals brown, stagnant water rose and bubbled around my boots. Wild raspberry canes scratched my hands and whipped viciously at my face; brambles wrapped themselves round my ankles and became entwined in my clothes. Overhead, the sky was blue and clear apart from a few white clouds. I could feel the heat of the sun on my shoulders and back, and on the top of my head where the hair was thinnest.

As I followed the old cart track the ground rose before me in a slight incline. About one hundred yards from the gate, a barbed wire fence blocked my way. Beyond this, a small stream crossed the path, and further on, a tall stand of willows obscured the view. I whistled and called again, and listened, but there was only the sound of high larks and the drone of a wasp.

Higher still, above the jungle, from the top of a dry stone dyke, I could see below the empty road, the high walls, and the house and stables. A car was leaving the grounds, turning left towards Bannock. It moved noiselessly, whatever breeze there was drifting the engine sounds away, over the gentle mounds and hollows which swelled softly down to the reeds on the indeterminate edges of the River Eck. Trout weaved in the Eck's waters, and salmon swam upstream to spawn. On both banks were the red and white and blue bursts of parked cars, and microscopic anglers twitching invisible rods. I breathed in deeply and felt the sun dry my shirt.

The wall led in a straight line almost to the top of the hill where it joined another, lower dyke which circled the crest like a jagged, irregular crown. Inside this ring grew rowan and birch and ash trees, scattered sparsely among the broad, iron hard stumps of long dead oak. As I stepped over the stones there was a cry above my head and I sensed the air move. I crouched defensively and, protecting my eyes with visored hands, looked up to the black and white swoop and soar of angry lapwings. The birds, two pairs, pursued me until they considered my soft shape no longer presented a threat, then they swept away on their broad wings and disappeared from view.

From the other side of the trees I could see the river

narrow and thread along its valley until it became lost in a series of identical, bare, sheep-spotted hills which stretched towards nowhere I wanted to be. Behind me, Stan's house could no longer be seen. Beyond, further obscured, Bannock waited for life to begin in a hollow of the Shieldons where the Eck joined forces with the Irk and swept to the sea. I had become invisible. I began to forget my own name. Here, unseen, I could re-invent myself and begin again. I didn't need the others. I could do this on my own.

The climb in the heat had made me tired. There was still no sign of the dogs and I did not feel like continuing the search. I whistled one last time and called their names then stretched out on the ground in the shelter of the crown where the sun had warmed the grass.

I had not slept well for some time. Almost as soon as I lay down I was dreaming: the bright, striking dreams I had experienced since childhood which at times seemed to be compensation for the poverty of my other life. I smiled and laughed without waking, and the world transformed itself into a joyous place. Then I felt fear and excitement, or love and fulfillment: all the emotions except the numbness and panic which dominated the other world.

From the hill I was in a bus with a pretty girl and as I made a joke she pinched my arm. The bus took me to a football field where I raced and jumped and fell in the soft mud. Cleaned and dried, a pavement walk turned into a fall through lung-bursting blackness. I ran through a park, past the duck pond where a thousand colours floated, breathing easily, feeling my legs strong. From the edge of a cliff I leapt into the air and my gently flapping arms took me higher and higher until I woke.

The silence had gone. Crows circled and called in the air above. Footsteps came nearer. I could smell her and hear the sound of her plaited hair on the waxed surface of her coat. She shadowed my face, then the sun hit my eyes again as she kneeled down behind my head. I had to speak but a finger pressed against my lips, feeling the dry contours. As she bent towards me, her hair, loosened, shaded and cooled my cheeks; circled, brushed my bared chest, feathered the skin. She pressed closer. Her lips kissed mine and she touched me gently with her fingertips, stretching and pulling until I had no choice but to accede to her request.

As I came in my pants, the crows descended and I could see their beaks and their bright, empty eyes. There was my dead father and at his side, my mother, holding his talons in her own. Behind them, flapping to slow their descent, my aunts and grandmother. Then a moulting greyback: Macroom, cawing and croaking. And in the middle of a flock of Bannock jackdaws, a wedge-tailed, crooked-billed raven called Stan.

I sat up and flapped my arms to ward them off, blinked in terror, almost feeling those sharp beaks tear my skin. I blinked again and stared wide, looking for the eyes, the feathers, those sharp claws, but they were gone and only white clouds moved in the sky.

On the grass beside me, one on either flank, Joe and Julie lay stretched, their heads resting on their front paws. Moving only their eyes, they looked towards me, the disturber of their dog-dreams, yawned, then returned to sleep.

That Feeling, When Things Begin to Drift Away

The Masters of the Guild by Dr J. B. Wham

The twenty sec

A Not-Well Boy

Luckily, no one was around the house by the time the dogs led me back from the hill. I changed trousers and scrubbed out my dream in a sink in the upstairs bathroom.

Stan had left a note for me on the kitchen table. It lay beside a plate of sandwiches and a glass of milk. It said that he would be back some time in the afternoon and that I was to make myself at home. My new bedroom was to be on the ground floor. I would be more comfortable there. He had left the door open so I would know which room it was. He would see me later. Bye.

High windows looked out on to the garden at the back of the house. A couple of towels lay on the freshly-sheeted double bed. On one wall, above a campaign chest, was a series of prints of battle scenes from the Napoleonic Wars: Wagram and Ulm; Jena and Dresden; Borodino and Austerlitz. On shelves was a collection of military artefacts: campaign medals; a blunt, two-edged bayonet; assorted steel helmets; several pairs of field glasses; a gas mask. But most striking of all in this mini-museum was the flag. Blue and white, it covered most of the wall opposite the window. In its centre was a golden, imperial eagle, and below this figure was silvered, Cyrillic lettering and the Roman numeral IV. The fabric was beautifully light and smooth; the needlework perfect. I picked up a corner and rubbed it between my fingers. And there, in tiny letters, was another name, an alien address: J.G. Thwaw and Sons, Fogorig Row, Bannock. I remembered where I lived.

That evening, I ate with Stan and his family. The table in the kitchen was opened out and we all crowded round bowls of spaghetti and sauce and salad and bread. We drank wine, even the children, who mixed it with water.

Heather and Ishbel and John made lots of noise and masked the silences of their dining companions. Adam and Joseph, the two oldest boys, ate quickly, excused themselves, and left before the rest of us were barely halfway through our beyond, where rogue strands wormed their way as far as the elbows which rested on the checked waxcloth. Stan disposed of his huge pile of food steadily and efficiently, concentrating on the job in hand, pausing only to select a piece of bread, load on some more salad, or fill up with wine. I sat with my arms pressed close by my sides, worrying if I had gravy on my chin, wondering if I could repair the tear in my trousers and if the stain in the crotch had rinsed out.

I offered to wash the dishes but Stan shook his head and gestured for me to go outside. Still cleaning his teeth with his tongue, he held me tightly by the elbow and muttered: 'Just leave Briony to it: she's not feeling too well today. I don't think she would appreciate the gesture.' There was the sound of a smashing plate. 'See what I mean? That could've been your head.' He did not laugh. 'Do you fancy a refreshment?'

'Why not.' I said this casually but I needed one. Right away.

'I'll see you in the car in five minutes.'

'Are we going out?'

'Sure. We can't miss out on the Ring Week celebrations.' I must have looked doubtful. 'Or maybe you want to stay here in 'Happy Valley'?'

'If you remember, I'm supposed to be laid up with whiplash injuries. With my luck, I'll bump into Macroom.'

'Don't worry. I've got just the answer. See you outside.'

I dozed off waiting for Stan in the car. As anyone except me could have predicted, he had taken half an hour rather than the five minutes he had promised. I was cold and stiff when I was wakened by the sound of him opening the driver's door. He slid in and dumped a brown paper parcel on my lap.

'What's this?'

'Open it and see.' We moved off, down the driveway, into the main road, past the penguin, towards Bannock as the lights in farmhouse windows began to shine in the gloom. I tore off the paper and found a cardboard box: 'Excelsior Medical Supplies: Semi-Flexible Surgical Collar'.

'Where the hell did you get this?'

'Murgle. I told you: he's a pal of mine. We're both in the rugby club. Go on: try it on for size.'

We stopped at a roadside pub to to test out my new

disguise. I sat at a table well away from the bar but I felt all eyes turn, ready to denounce me as a malingerer. As I waited for my drink I heard the barman ask:

'What happened to your friend, Stan?'

'Bit of a smash in the car. Whiplash.'

'Tsk, tsk, tsk. That must be the new man in the bank then. I heard you and he had been involved in a bit of a pile-up. All right yourself?'

'Fine. Just a bit shaken up.'

'And the car?'

'You wouldn't believe it: not a mark on her.'

'Well, would you credit it?' Quite frankly, no.

After a few drinks, the collar began to feel quite comfortable. I developed the technique of tilting my whole body back when gulping beer. I felt as if I was doing myself a bit of good: toning up the muscles. My round.

'I hear you've been in a bit of an accident.' There were sighs and nods of sympathy all round. A couple of women ignored their partners and looked at me in a motherly sort of a way.

'Nothing too serious. Dr Murgle says I've to take it easy for a few weeks.'

'You can't rush these things.'

'No indeed.' I was beginning to enjoy myself. It was just like old times. I grimaced with imagined pain as I lifted two pint glasses from the counter. The barman raced to attend to me.

'Here now, just you leave them. I'll bring them over.'

'Thanks very much. I just felt a slight twinge for a moment.' More shakes of more heads. Tut, tut, tut:

'Poor man.' I slipped very easily into a 'stoic-in-the-face-of-suffering' expression. I had plenty of experience in that line of work.

Stan and I laughed a lot on the short journey to the Irkdale Arms on the outskirts of the town. I was enjoying myself for the first time in ages. This was the Stan I had imagined when we had first met. This was the friend I had been seeking. We pulled into a car park decorated with large, balsa wood rings festooned with bunting.

'Wait here.' Stan ordered. He jumped out of the driver's

seat and I heard him open the boot. He reappeared and helped me out of the car. 'Use this.' We both sniggered. The walking stick certainly added to the effect. I let out a huge sigh, as if of fatigue and suffering, when I sat down at a table near the barely flickering fire. I heard Stan expounding up at the bar:

'Yes, Doctor Murgle recommended a wee dram before bedtime. It helps to deaden the pain, you know. Helps the patient get some sleep.'

'... poor man ...'

'... see the pain in his face ...'

'... tut, tut, tut ...'

'... dangerous injury ...'

'... got to watch out ...'

'...lucky it wasn't worse ...'

Stan placed a large whisky on the table in front of me. 'That one's on the house. With Jack's compliments.'

I looked up and there was Jack behind the bar, a large, fresh-faced man drinking from a mug. He smiled and several customers on stools raised their glasses.

'Cheers.'

'Hope you're better soon.'

'Here's to you.'

I smiled bravely. To drain the measure, I leaned back slowly and carefully, like a man with a glass broom handle up his arse.

Before we went into The Old Mill, Stan persuaded me to stick a lump of gauze on my forehead with a couple of pieces of plaster from the car's first aid box. I tried to point out the inconsistency of appearing in three different places with three distinct levels of injury, but Stan was on too much of a high to pay much notice. I only agreed to do it when he threatened to wrap his own head in bandages and declare he had lost his memory. We laughed again. By that time everything was funny. I hoped Macroom had decided to spend the night in front of his television set.

Stan greeted everyone loudly and cleared a passage for me to enter. The room was draped in flags and banners. Above the bar it said: 'Hail, Laddie, An' Feckle In The Nook'. Above the mantlepiece it said: 'Oot John Heddington! Oot Surly Andy!'. Nervously touching my head to check that the dressing was still in place, I sat down on a seat offered to me by an old gent twice my age:

'I heard about your mishap,' he croaked as we squeezed together on the bench. I smiled and nodded as far as the collar would allow. 'You'll have to look after yourself now.' He said this very loudly, as if the fictional bump on the head had damaged my hearing or turned me into a simpleton. 'We don't want to lose you just as soon as you've arrived.' His head shook loosely on his neck and he made a gurgling sound which might have been a laugh.

Stan came back without any drinks. He bent down to me and spoke quietly. 'Let's go.' I levered myself up on my walking stick and looked as far round the bar as I was able:

'Is Macroom here?'

'I'll tell you outside.'

'Bye bye.' The old boy weakly waved his hand towards me. I waved back. 'I hope you have a speedy recovery.' I limped after Stan, at each slow step feeling Macroom's hand on my shoulder.

'What the hell's going on?'

'It's Charlie Trummle.'

'Charlie Trummle? What's he got to do with…'

'Charlie could be in a bit of trouble. We've got to help him. Or, at least, I have to.'

'What's up?' I grunted. It is difficult getting into a car while wearing a surgical collar.

'He's been drinking all day and he got into a shouting match an hour or so ago in The Old Mill. Peter told me all about it. Apparently some of the younger lads were tormenting him about you know what and Charlie lost the head. You don't know what he's like when he gets going. He was cursing the town and the ring and everything he could think of. Then, to make matters worse, in come the Winkie Boys, demanding their free food and drink. Charlie starts shouting that he'll fix them, he'll spoil their fun; that this will be one Ring Day they won't forget in a hurry. Then he storms out of the pub.'

'Where did he go?'

'This is it. No one knows.'

'He'll probably be at home, sleeping it off.'

'Possibly. But you don't know how Charlie feels about all

this. Once a year he has to relive his misery all over again.'

'Why the hell doesn't he just bugger off out of it?'

'And go where? Charlie's a Bunter. There's no changing that.'

'So, what do you think he might do?'

'God knows. A few years back, he tried to set fire to Gourdie's timber yard where they build the ring.'

'You're joking. What happened.'

'A shower of rain put the fire out before it caught hold. The police found Charlie at home, lying drunk on the settee with an empty can of petrol in the cupboard and an economy-sized box of matches in his pocket. He's not cut out to be a master criminal. They gave him six months.'

'Jesus Christ.' We had reached the alley off which Charlie lived. We turned the corner, climbed the stairs, knocked on the heavy, black door. And waited. On the door there was a plastic button for a bell which didn't work, a peephole, and a plate which bore a name: C. Trummle. Sam knocked again, louder, and peered through the letterbox:

'Charlie!' There was no response. 'We'd better head on down to Gourdie's.'

'He surely wouldn't try it again.'

'As I've said, you don't know Charlie.'

Maybe I didn't know Charlie, but everyone else in Bannock seemed to have no problem in predicting his movements. There was a crowd of people outside of Gourdie's on Fogorig Row. They were noisy and they seemed very angry about something or someone. I could guess what it might be.

The faces of the crowd were tilted upwards towards the high wall which surrounded the timber yard. Spotlighted in the beams of two powerful lamps was a man entangled in the strands of barbed wire strung above the top line of bricks. It was Charlie Trummle, the Bunter arsonist.

In the lights, I could see that Charlie's hands and face were smeared with blood from wire cuts. The jacket of his suit was torn and the bright white of his shirt shone through. But he seemed calm as he looked down at us. I even thought he was smiling.

'What's happening? Has he done anything?' Stan had grabbed Malcolm Jeffrey by the lapels of his jacket but the

194

lorry driver could not remove his eyes from the man on the wall.

'Is that not enough? The old bastard should be locked up.'

'You know what I mean. Any fire?'

'Not as far as we can tell. There's some men in checking.' Stan released Jeffrey. I followed him as he went through the huge wooden doors which led into the yard.

I recognised some of the people conducting the search inside, but only after a second look. There was Roderick Macroom, dressed as the Sinning Wretch, his black, sackcloth suit topped by a floppy hat adorned with a feather. Derek from the bank was among a group of his fellow Winkie Boys, all of them dressed identically in lime green tunics and britches, red, knee length boots, white capes, and on their heads, small blue objects which looked like badly squashed top hats.

'Find anything?' An unfamiliar Winkie Boy looked at Stan then at me, then shook his head:

'Nothing. We seem to have got here just in time.' He pointed to the wall. 'Look, he had just put his ladder down the inside.'

'Well, how are you, Mr Weems?' A hand clapped on my shoulder. 'Recovering?'

'Coming along nicely, Derek, thank you very much.'

'A bit of excitement tonight, eh?'

'Certainly is, Derek. Certainly is. Is Charlie trapped in the wire up there?'

'No. He just refuses to budge.' Derek squeezed closer. 'Talking about things being trapped, Mr Weems, you won't have checked your mousetrap recently.' I pointed to my collar:

'My mind has been on other things.'

'You should check that trap, Mr Weems. Just as soon as you get back to work.' Derek attempted an innocent, yet concerned expression which merely succeeded in making him look like an imbecile.

'Has anyone tried to get him down?' Stan was looking up at Charlie's back. Winkie looked up too:

'The old bugger starts shaking the ladder every time anyone tries to climb up. Roddy says we'll have to get the police and the fire brigade.'

195

'You know what will happen then.'

'Well he deserves it, doesn't he? If we'd got here ten minutes later the whole place might have gone up in smoke.'

'I'll get him down.' Stan went over to the foot of the ladder. 'Charlie. Charlie, it's me, Stan.'

'Stan?' Charlie turned round and peered into the glare of the lights.

'I'm coming up, Charlie.' Stan climbed. The outside spectators came into the yard and we all watched the action together. Despite the new silence, we couldn't hear any of the words from the top of the wall. After about ten minutes, we saw the white of Stan's face. 'We're coming down.' The crowd began to rumble. Five minutes more, and the descent began, very slowly, Stan leading the way. The crowd got louder as the figures neared the ground. Stan's foot was at head height. 'Clear a space. Move back, please.' What did he expect? Congratulations and a pat on the back?

A jostle of Bunters and Winkie Boys formed at the foot of the ladder, their arms raised to receive their victims. Stan tried his best to protect himself and Charlie but some of the crowd shoved them against the wall. I saw a punch and heard it connect.

I squeezed my way in amongst the bodies with no clear idea of what I was trying to achieve. A blow struck me on the face and sent my head rocking back against the surgical collar. The dressing was torn from my forehead and dangled in front of my eyes, but I could not pull it free as my arms were under someone else's control. Suddenly, my feet lost contact with the ground and I half fell to my knees between a press of bodies. I freed one hand and grabbed on to a white cape but the seam ripped and I was on the cobbles of the yard. A heavy foot stamped on my back. I heard and felt my fingers crunch under a heel. Then, on the edge of unconsciousness, I felt myself being lifted away and upwards, into the fresh air.

I was in the arms of the Bannock police.

Half a dozen constables separated the bodies in the crowd. Taking account of my disability, they placed me gently on a pile of timber from where I could view things safely from a distance. A large sergeant spoke with the voice of the city:

'Quiet!... Quiet!...Will you be quiet or I'll arrest the

196

whole lot of you!' The confused struggle continued. 'Quiet!' To my satisfaction, I saw a punch land on Derek Winkie's ear. 'Quiet!' People began to listen. Heads turned. Slowly, the crowd fell silent. 'Right, I'm not even going to ask what's going on here. All I'm going to tell you is that if it doesn't stop you'll all find yourselves in court next Monday morning.'

'But sergeant...'

'Shut up.'

'But...'

'I told you to shut up, and I meant it.' The sergeant looked at Roderick Macroom as if he might strike him down. 'I don't know what's the matter with you lot. Every year it's the same: drunkenness, fighting, vandalism: all because of a bloody big hoop. Look at you.' He began to point to people in the crowd. 'There's an estate agent; there's a solicitor; there's a driving instructor; there's a dentist; there's a teacher. He concentrated on the latter. 'How are you going to explain that black eye to the pupils tomorrow?' There was no reply. The sergeant rubbed his face and pinched his nose between two fingers:

'Just what is the matter with you people? You nearly killed this man.' He was pointing towards me. 'Look at him.' Everyone looked. 'He's got a bloody big collar round his neck and there you were, kicking and punching him.' The sergeant paused for breath and gazed slowly at every face in the crowd. 'Now I'm warning you; once and once only. If there's any more trouble between now and Friday, whoever causes it will live to regret it. Understand?' There was only a sullen silence. 'Understand?' The crowd mumbled. The sergeant put a hand to his ear. 'I can't hear you. Understand?' People in the crowd shuffled their feet and looked at the ground. There was a disjointed muttering:

'Yes, sergeant.'

'Louder.'

'Yes, sergeant.'

'That's better. Now, clear off home to your wives and mothers before I change my mind.' The sergeant kicked a squashed topper from the cobbles high into the air. 'And take your funny hats with you.' A Winkie Boy pressed the battered cap on to his head. The sergeant turned to me as the disarmed mob drifted out of the yard. 'How did you get involved in all this? You're from civilisation. You ought to know better.'

I looked down at my swollen and skinned knuckles. My dressing hung from my forehead by a thread. It would take too long to explain. What could I say that would be of any use? I could only shrug my shoulders. As I did so, I felt a violent spasm in the muscles of my back, and an excruciating pain lanced my neck under its high collar.

Almost gone

The Bunter In Fact And Fic

The World According To Charlie Trummle

Charlie wouldn't stop talking in the car. He had obviously enjoyed all of the excitement. He sat beside Stan in the front seat. I lay stretched in the back, immobile, staring at the white cloth stretched over the roof. I felt pains all over. Serious pains. For the first time in my illness-dominated life.

'What a night, Stan, what a night.'

'Give it a rest, Charlie, would you?' I heard Charlie rub his hands together, as if he couldn't contain his emotions:

'All their faces, when that big sergeant was telling them off.'

'He was talking to us too, remember.'

'Did you see the Winkie Boys, Stan, did you? I sent one of their hats flying.'

'O.K., Charlie.'

'And young Macroom. Did you see him? Right on the nose I got him.'

'Charlie…'

'That'll make his head spin when he's in the hoop on Friday.'

'Charlie, will you shut up.'

'What a night.' I heard him rub his hands once more. 'And it can only get better.'

'What the hell are you babbling about?'

Charlie leaned over the back of the seat and looked at me. I swivelled my eyes towards him. 'Have you heard of our big celebration, George? Friday. The Rollin' O' The Ring.' I tried to nod but a pain in my neck warned me to remain still. 'It commemorates the biggest thing that ever happened in Bannock.'

'George knows all about it, Charlie. He doesn't want to hear any more.' But I had no choice. I was trapped.

'Just imagine. The highlight of the year. The whole town revolves round that day. Everyone turns out. And for why? I'll tell you.' Do you have to? I don't want to know. I'm not interested any more. I want to go away. 'I'll tell you for why. Because a wee Bunter whore screwed a high-up lord, and while they were at it her pimp, Winkie by name, stole his purse.' Charlie burst into a high-pitched laugh. 'How's that, George?'

I've told you. 'What do you think of that little story?' I don't care. 'Strachan's men caught the pair sneaking out of Fogorig House. They found the purse and Rankine's ring. So Heddington got his head chopped off. And so it all began. How's that?' Great, Charlie. Just great.

'Listen.' Stan was trying to concentrate on his driving. 'I think we've had just about enough for one night.'

'What's the matter with you? You used to enjoy my stories.'

'Used to. Past tense.'

'Pardon me for breathing.' Charlie sulked, hunched in his seat.

'I haven't got time any more for all your crap.'

'Crap? Who says? All the Bunters? You're a Bunter, Stan, aren't you?'

'And so are you, Charlie.'

'Well, who's to say my version isn't the truth, eh? Who's to say? What do you think, George.' At this point the car went over a bump and I let out a groan. 'You see: George thinks it could be true.'

'Jesus Christ, will you shut up. George has practically broken his neck because of you.' Charlie leaned back once more and patted me on the shoulder:

'Much appreciated, George. Much appreciated.'

'Now, I'm taking you home, Charlie, and you're not going to stick your nose out of the front door until after Friday. Is that clear? Not for anything: food, booze, fags: anything. I'll do your shopping tomorrow. Right? Stay out of trouble or I'll end up doing you in myself. Not one step out of the door.'

'Why do I have to go out again, Stan? My work's done.'

'What?' The car slowed and stopped. 'What are you talking about? Come on. Out with it. No more little hints.' We were parked in the alley near Charlie's flat. I was still groaning, only half listening. But I sensed a change in tone and was quiet.

'You should have helped me, Stan. I asked you.'

'You ask me every year, Charlie, and every year I say no. You don't seem to understand. I live here.'

'So do I, Stan. I've lived here for a long time. Remember?'

'How can I forget?'

'But I got a bit of help Stan. That wife of yours is a clever

201

woman.'

'Briony? What the hell do you mean? I'm warning you, Charlie.'

'I asked you, Stan. I asked you.' Stan grabbed a handful of Charlie's shirt. A button popped off and landed on my chest. 'Don't do that, Stan. You're my friend.'

'Listen, you old bastard. If you don't tell me what you've done, I'll throttle you myself.'

'I haven't done anything, Stan. You saw. I didn't even get in. No fire.' Charlie laughed as far as he was able. 'I didn't even have any matches, Stan. Look in my pockets.'

'Well, what the hell were you doing up on that wall?'

'I just wanted a look at the ring, Stan, for old time's sake. You don't know what it means to be chosen as the Wretch, Stan. They never gave you a chance, did they?' Stan threw Charlie back on to his seat:

'I was away for all those years, wasn't I.'

'That's right, Stan. You were away. I expect they would have picked you if you had been here.'

'And what's Briony got to do with it?'

'Nothing, Stan. Nothing.' Charlie laid a hand on Stan's arm. 'Just the drink talking. You know me. Can't stop talking rubbish. You know me.' I could hear only breathing. A door unlocked and Charlie got out of the car. 'So you'll be calling round tomorrow?'

'Uh.' Stan had already started the engine.

'Well, I'll be seeing you, Stan. Goodbye, George. And thanks.'

The car swept off before Charlie had a chance to remove his hand from the roof.

Stan was silent on the way back to the house. He didn't even ask how I was keeping. While I was lying there, feeling the pain shoot through my back and neck with every bump, every jolt, I wondered if he was thinking what I was thinking. That maybe Charlie Trummle had been caught on that wall on his way out, not on his way in.

Fire

As I lay in bed, in pain, I heard Sam and Briony argue through the night. It had begun as soon as we arrived back from Bannock when, having helped me out of the car, Sam had abandoned me on the doorstep and gone in search of his wife, whom he now imagined to be involved in some form of conspiracy with Charlie Trummle.

I couldn't sleep anyway. My neck and back throbbed; my right hand was skinned and swollen: I had lain down on the covers only with the greatest difficulty. Now, the room was bright with moonlight from the garden but I felt unable to rise and draw the curtains.

The words I heard through the closed door of my room were indistinct but the varying tones were unmistakable: interrogation; accusation; recrimination. The stamina required must have been enormous: hour after hour; astounding pace and intensity. Practice makes perfect.

The dualogue ended with a final, screaming climax in the entrance hall where the noise was amplified and hollowed out. Then there were the sounds of heavy footsteps over tiles, the slamming of a door, and a car escaping down the driveway. I tensed my body as if something was going to happen but there was only silence.

I tried to think things over but everything was too confused in my mind. Nothing ever worked out. I felt like running. It couldn't go on. There had to be an answer. Go where? I felt wet and uncomfortable, and the inside of my head seemed full of jelly.

I must have dozed off because I awoke with a jump when I heard the door of my bedroom creak open. A dim light shone in the hall, backlighting a shadow.

'Stan?'

'He's gone.' A whisper. It was Briony.

'Are you all right?'

'Just doing a bit of tidying up.' She came into the room, wheeling a large object before her.

'Can I help you?' With difficulty, I sat up and put on the bedside lamp. Briony was pushing a large, black, Edwardian perambulator.

'You go back to sleep. This won't take long.' She ran her arm along the shelves containing Stan's military collection, tipping the medal cases, the gasmasks, the old ration books, the helmets into the pram. Then she unhooked the prints and added them to the pile: carefully, one at a time. Finally, the flag was ripped from the wall and bundled on top. 'That's me finished in here. Sorry for disturbing you. Good night.' She left as quietly as she had come, closing the door gently behind her.

Later, I heard the pram squeaking outside in the garden. Every movement caused pain in my neck and upper back but I managed to squirm across the bed and swing my legs on to the floor. With the minimum of unneccesary movement, I got to my feet and took small steps towards the window, from where I could see Briony clearly lit by the full moon. She tipped the pram on its two front wheels and the load spilled on to the ground at the base of a pyramid of jumble on the lawn. The pile was over six feet high and from where I stood I could see books and magazines, maps and charts, uniforms and military hats, a large Zulu shield and a selection of spears, a fully rigged model of a sailing ship, a stuffed, crested penguin, and what must have been dozens of flags similar to the one which had just been removed from the wall of my room.

Briony stood back to admire her work then turned and disappeared from sight. She came back into view a few seconds later along with her two eldest sons, both of whom carried clear plastic containers. These boys sprinkled liquid around and over the pyramid then tossed the empties on top. They looked at their mother. I saw the flame jump from her hand to a stream on the ground, glide over the grass, and ignite with a whooshing flare through the pyre.

The three of them held hands and watched the bonfire burn. I could hear the crackling, I could smell the petrol in the smoke. Briony and Adam and Joseph stood back from the heat and I could see the flames light up their faces. There was now more than one incendiary in the borders town of Bannock.

Doctor Murgle Sees The Joke

Next morning, the smell of the fire was still in the air when Stan took me into town to see Dr Murgle. He didn't mention what had happened the previous night. I began to notice that there was a lot he didn't talk about.

Or rather, he would talk without feeling, like a bad actor reading for a part. He would enquire after someone's health, ask 'what sort of tricks' they were 'getting up to', but he would not listen to the answers, his mind being focused on more Stan Kowalik-related topics. It occurred to me that he had never asked about where I came from, or shown any interest in any of the factors which might have combined to produce my questionable mental state. This was not reticence, a product of his highly-developed, delicate sensibilities. I began to realise that it was because he didn't give a monkey's nuts about the answers. I wasn't hurt by this but it annoyed me slightly. (OK, I was hurt. I had imagined that he might be my friend. But then, I didn't know what friendship was. It had previously existed only inside my head.)

Why the hell had he taken me in? And Charlie? And all the other misfits and drunks his wife had told me about? He was only concerned with us in the most abstract of ways. Maybe he wanted to show he didn't care what the Bunters thought (but he did). Maybe he thought it would get him into heaven (but he didn't believe in god). Maybe he just needed people around who would love him uncritically (but in this, he failed).

'I went out late last night to find that little bastard Charlie.' When he said this, I didn't turn to look at him. I had woken up that morning to discover that my neck was locked in the forward position due to the punishment it had received at the timber yard.

'I heard you leave.'

'You probably heard all the shouting as well, eh? You must think we're a strange lot.' I tried to shrug my shoulders but retreated due to chronic upper back pain:

'What did you want Charlie for? You had just left him.'

'Old Charlie and Briony are up to something. I couldn't

get anything out of her so I decided to try Trummle again.'

'I thought he and Briony didn't get on.'

'They don't. But they would both forget about their differences if it meant settling with the common enemy.'

'You?'

'Not me. You don't know Charlie if you think that. No: Bannock. Briony wants to leave. She thinks then she'll be able to forget about what's happened if she can get away.'

'I could set her straight.'

'There's a lot of shit in Bannock but it's where I live.'

'And me.'

'It's not the same. Even Charlie could tell you that.' We reached the surgery and Stan helped me from the car.

'Did you find him?'

'He's gone. A couple of windows of his flat had been broken. He must have thought it was safer elsewhere. He has a couple of bolt holes for moments like this.'

'Well, if he's gone you've no worries.'

'No?'

In common with most of the other buildings in the town, the outside of the surgery was draped in flags and banners. 'Hail, laddie, an'...'. 'Oot, John Heddington...'. The receptionist wore a rosette in the colours of Bannock: black for the traitors, white for the Maid, gold for the ring. A child in the waiting room played with a model hoop while he sat with his mother. Two old women talked about the decline in the quality of modern baps.

Doctor Murgle laughed when he heard of my affliction. 'A spot of irony there, old boy.' His shoulders shook several times during his examination. This was the funniest thing that had happened to him in a long time. I had brightened up his whole day.

I left Murgle's office wearing a neck brace, holding an appointment for a precautionary X-ray in my freshly dressed hand. Stan had vanished from the waiting room. His car had gone from the car park. I took a taxi back to Eckford House and packed my bags before falling asleep on my unmade bed.

Stan Buys Me A Flag

Stan and Briony argued again that night. I also heard the two eldest boys shouting and the younger kids crying in their rooms. In the morning I asked Stan to drive me and my cases into town. I had never felt such an outsider.

Stan tried to persuade me to stay. Why? Maybe he felt safer with a stranger in the house. Maybe without me to divert him he would have to think about things he would rather leave buried. Before we left, I phoned round a few boarding houses. Most of them were full with visitors who had arrived to see the ring ceremony but eventually I found one with a vacancy. Stan said it was a decent place. The owner was a friend of his.

Stan carried my luggage to the car and as I followed I saw that his five children were lined up in the hallway like domestic servants ready for inspection. Each one shook my injured hand and said goodbye. First of all there was John, the youngest, dancing from foot to foot as if he was bursting for the toilet: ''Bye.' Ishbel, calm and serious: 'Goodbye, Mr Weems.' She almost curtsied. Then Heather, giggling at the sight of me in a neck brace: 'Cheeri..' Splutter. '..o.' Next to her, Joseph, embarrassed: 'Goodbye.' Finally, Adam, his nose broken in almost exactly the same way as his father, looking not at me but at some indistinct point over my right shoulder: 'I hope you enjoyed your stay. Please come again.' Stan stood in judgement, nodding his head in satisfaction, pretending the charade was for my benefit. In this carefully considered humiliation of his two eldest sons, he had shown both them and me the limits and consequences of our actions.

So, I left that house for the last time. Sitting in the car, I looked back through the glass of the front door and saw the children break ranks and gather round their mother. Stan appeared not to notice. His mind was already on other things. As we drove out of the main gate, I wondered if he, like me, had thought of the boy who had been missing from parade.

We parked on the edge of town as the centre was congested with people congregating for the big day. Stan carried my cases and broke a way through the crowd, nodding and exchanging greetings with every second person. He half turned and shouted to me over his shoulder:

'It's a great occasion, George. A bit silly, but worth seeing. You're surely going to stay to watch. This isn't a day for hiding away in a boarding house.'

'I don't think I'm fit to cope with crowds.'

'Don't worry. I'll find you a spot.' We were in the square. Spectators hung from every window and a few young lads sat astride the angle of the roofs fifty feet above the ground. The sun beat down from a pale blue sky, reddening necks, noses and seldom-bared arms.

Viewing stands had been erected along two sides of the square, one reserved for local and visiting dignitaries, the other occupied by those townspeople who had been alert enough to occupy or stake a claim to a seat around breakfast time that morning. From the side, these structures did not seem very solid, having apparently been constructed from scaffolding, thin wooden planks, and fresh air.

'Clear a space, clear a space.' Stan barged his way up the aisle of the nearest stand, climbing almost to the top, pulling me behind him, attached by an invisible chain. He stopped. 'Make way for this man. He's injured. Look at him: you're surely going to give him a seat.' Reluctantly, a family group squeezed closer together to make room for me and I sat down, thigh by thigh with a large grandmother dressed in the colours of Bannock. The noise of the crowd was loud and getting louder. A youthful marching band began to play a local tune. Majorettes strutted and preened to excited cheers. Stan had to shout above the din:

'You'll be okay here, George. I'll stick your cases at the top of the aisle, out of everyone's way.' I nodded. Once again I had voluntarily handed over control of my movements. People were shuffling past: spectators leaving or returning to their seats; a group of small boys playing 'tig'; out-of-towners selling ice-cream and souvenirs. Stan grabbed a vendor by the arm and fumbled for money. 'Here you go: we can't have you improperly dressed.' He pinned a ring rosette to the lapel of my jacket, and in my bandaged hand placed a cane which bore the black, white and gold flag of the Bunters of Bannock. I found I couldn't speak.

Stan laid a hand on my shoulder and bent towards my

ear. 'Listen, George, I've just spotted someone I've been meaning to speak to.' He patted me on the back and started back down the aisle. After a few slow steps he turned and shouted over the noise. 'I'll be back shortly.'

Of course, I knew he wouldn't. As I watched him barge through the crowd down to ground level, I knew that I was a closed episode in Stan's past. I had let him down, although he would never have told me so. I had not fulfilled my function. Stan only had room in his life for those who identified totally with his cause. I had deserted him in his hour of need. As far as Stan was concerned, I was history.

The Rollin' O' The Ring

I was alone in the stand overlooking the square, a speck in an inland sea of Bunters. If I could have left I would have done so, but the crush around me was intensifying. So I sat in my seat, my neck restrained in a surgical collar. The rosette on my jacket proclaimed my loyalties, as did the colours of Bannock I held in my bandaged hand.

The flag lay limp on its cane. Tiny letters were printed in one corner, as on the Russian Imperial banner which had hung on my temporary bedroom in Eckford House. I looked more closely: 'Made Under Licence In The Kingdom Of Malabbar'. A short breeze caught the colours and they fluttered gamely before collapsing once more on to my lap.

Running at a right angle from where I sat was the smaller of the two stands. This de-luxe accommodation was reserved for officials, guests of the Guild, and assorted bigwigs. In front was a raised apron decorated with bunting and multicoloured hoops, and there, a man in overalls made last minute adjustments to a microphone and a set of loudspeakers. Tap, tap, tap. 'Hello, hello, hello.' Some members of the crowd responded loudly:

'Hello! Hello!'

209

'Are you talking to me, Wullie Pumphry?'

The sound man ignored the hecklers and tried to maintain an air of dignity. 'One, two. Testing, testing.' Tap, tap, tap.

'Stop chapping that door and come in, Wullie!'

A rectangle with a statue in each corner had been cordoned off, and now the police were clearing the last, few, unauthorised strollers from the area. Behind barriers, spectators stood twenty or thirty deep across the road and the pavement, the last rows pressed close against walls and shopfronts. At the back, men and women stood on boxes or balanced on window ledges. Crammed in the middle, many had to rely on the view through one of the cardboard periscopes which were on sale all across the town. Some children had squeezed to the front from where they could better see the action, while others, braver or more athletic, had shinned up lamp-posts to swing and circle, one handed, like little apes.

From where I sat, I could see beyond the square and down Mill Street as it stretched towards the green banks of the River Irk. The roadway had been cleared of people and vehicles. Crowds lined the pavement on either side, hemmed in by steel barriers. Individuals merged as they receded, their colour and movement contrasting with the calm emptiness of the blue-black cobble stones. Further on, large numbers had gathered on the grassy banks of the Irk, looking expectantly back towards the town. Rising above them, dominating the scene, was the dark, pyramidal pyre which had been built to consume the ring.

The band stopped playing and they and the majorettes marched off to the heart beat of the bass drum. They disappeared beyond the celebrity stand, and as people stood back to let them past, I saw Briony Kowalik hemmed in by a column of silver bandsmen and junior tympanists. With hands and arms she clutched the three smallest children to her sides, restraining John as he tried to escape from her grasp. Joseph stood by one shoulder, pressed close. On the other, equally near, I saw Stan, but only for a moment. Son, not husband; boy not man: Adam: tall and protective; stroking his broken nose in imitation of his father.

A recorded fanfare blew from the loudspeakers and a

210

figure stepped from the front row of the small stand on to the staging. He paused before the microphone: silent, commanding; waiting for order. As the noise in the crowd died down, he adjusted the tricolour robe which draped loosely from his shoulders to the platform behind him. He raised a gloved hand and swept from his head the feathered, floppy hat which had concealed his features from my view from above. It was T.J. Macroom, Master of the Guild.

'Fellow Bunters!' The crowd roared. Macroom spoke in a voice I did not recognise. 'I welcome you here today in the company of the Ancient Guild to celebrate together in The Rollin' O' The Ring.' The crowd cheered again. Macroom paused then continued:

'People of many nations have joined us this afternoon to share in our celebration. Some may be standing next to you in the crowd, others may be seated in the stands. Let us show them this day the true meaning of friendship and hospitality.' The crowd nodded and clapped their hands, and at various points around the square I saw being waved the flags of Europe, the Old Commonwealth, and, borne I am sure by my shower-proofed fellow boarders from Mrs Tochle's, the United States of America.

'Let us also welcome our special guests here on this special day: people who have flown from the ends of the earth to enjoy with us the unique magic of the ring.' More applause. 'We have amongst us a man whose leadership of young Bannock men in both war and peace has led to him being awarded the status of honorary member of the Guild of Bunters and Broontailers: Field Marshall, Sir Arthur Draym, M.C.' Applause.

'From his home in New Mexico, we have the familiar face of a Bunter who often returns to God's Welk, a man who has brought fame and glory to the town of his birth, a man known to you all: Doctor Wallace Pumphry.' Applause.

'From the other side of the world we have the son of a great chum of ours, a young chap we are proud to call friend: Crown Prince Wan Do Lee of the Kingdom of Malabbar.' A small man of oriental appearance, dressed in military scarlet and black, stood up from the first row behind the stage and bowed deeply to the crowd. Applause. The Master of the

Guild held up a hand and was granted silence:

'But now, we come to the solemn and joyous part of the day: a ritual which has been celebrated in the town of Bannock since before our records began: The Rollin' O' The Ring.' There was a rumble from the spectators, the shuffling of thousands of feet, then: hush. 'And as we watch the unfolding of events, let us cast our minds back over seven hundred years to the events commemorated by the ceremony: the triumph of good over evil through the intercession of two young Bunters from The Maister's Ain Gairden. Macroom pulled himself up to his full height and spoke solemnly, as if he was closing a bad current account:

'As my last act as Master of the Guild of Bunters and Broontailers, I call upon The Fechtin' Lassie. Come forth, Mary Dunlin, and through the light of your virtue cast out the shadow of lust and betrayal.' The crowd went wild. The black and white and gold colours of Bannock were everywhere, obscuring everything. All around me, people got to their feet and cheered and waved flags. I stood up and, stiff-necked, looked over the heads of those in front.

A young, beautiful girl with dark, shining hair had appeared in the empty space before the stage. Dressed from head to foot in purest white, she ran gracefully from the centre of the square to each side in succession, approaching the crowds but not quite coming into contact with the arms which stretched out desperately towards her. The people chanted: 'Mary! Mary! Mary!', but fell silent as the girl came to rest, alone, distant from all of the faces, far from help. She fell to the ground and a thousand voices groaned in unison, a woman screamed.

Then, cheers swamped the despair. Appearing almost magically, the white caped Ring Bearer strode towards the Fechtin' Lassie and, to roars and exhortations, swept her up in his arms and carried her off out of sight behind the small stand. Everyone applauded. Flags flew and hats were thrown in the air. The band began to play off stage and the crowd sang:

'Once there was a Fair Maid, tillie-eyo,
Once there was a Fair Maid, tillie-eyo,
Once there was a Fair Maaaiiid......
Who came-to-Ba-nnock-town.'

The song repeated several times then ended, and slow drum beats sounded through the loudspeakers. To great applause, the Ring Bearer reappeared, this time carrying a flaming brand in his hand. He stood with his back to the dignitaries, removed his hat and bowed to the crowd. Then, turning a half circle, he spoke in a loud, clear voice: 'John Heddington! Andrew Rankine! Leave the free town of Bannock. Here, we have no room for slavery and treachery!' The drums sounded again and there was movement behind the small stand. Four Winkie Boys appeared, dressed identically to the Ring Bearer. They first pulled then rolled before them the Bannock ring, covered in opaque black cloth bearing the seal of Andrew Rankine.

It was seven feet in diameter and four feet across, looking in size and shape like a huge tractor tyre. When it had been manoeuvred into position, the Winkie Boys retreated and stood in line, sloping stout poles across their shoulders. Chanting broke out again: 'Mary! Mary! Mary!'. The Fechtin Lassie emerged from between the guard of honour and placed both hands on the ring. 'Mary! Mary! Mary!' She set it in motion. 'Mary! Mary! Mary!' It rolled slowly across the level flagstones of the square.

The Ring Bearer steadied the huge wheel and raised his torch in salute: 'Oot, John Heddington! Oot, Surly Andy!' The crowd took up the chant:

'Oot, John Heddington! Oot, Surly Andy! Oot John Heddington! Oot, Surly Andy!'

With his free hand, he reached for the cloth which covered the wheel, and with one sweeping movement ripped it from the frame and threw it spinning through the air. The crowd gasped. There, in the centre of the gold ring, braced, was the Sinning Wretch, dressed in black from head to toe. Roderick Macroom's legs and arms formed a saltire cross in the circle, and his head pointed towards the ground. His wrists and ankles were looped in leather straps, his feet and hands pressed close to solid wooden wedges.

The Winkie Boys ran forward and helped the Ring Bearer to turn the frame to face Mill Street and the River Irk, then they rolled the Wretch through one hundred and eighty degrees so that he could stand upright and rest before he began his journey. The chants grew louder:

'Oot, John Heddington! Oot, Surly Andy! Oot, John Heddington! Oot, Surly Andy!'

The Ring Bearer swept his brand through the air in response to the words, then pointed towards the Wretch. The crowd fell silent.

'Only fire shall burn the stain clean. Depart from this town, pursued by the smoke and flame of the Bannock men who fell at Slawning Mound.' The Ring Bearer touched each of the twelve, cylindrical torches which were attached to the rim of the wheel and they began to smoulder, sending wisps of blue smoke spiralling into the air. The Winkie Boys rolled the Wretch towards Mill Street and, with their poles, steadied him on the brink of the incline which led to the river. The crowd roared as the ring moved slowly on to the cobbles, stayed by the strength of its attendants:

'Oot, John Heddington! Oot, Surly Andy! Oot, John Heddington! Oot, Surly Andy!'

The wheel crunched forward, creaking when it rolled over an uneven part of the roadway. Roderick Macroom's body shook, his knees and elbows bent as he absorbed the shocks. Parts of the crowd began to move, filling Mill Street behind the ring as it passed slowly onwards. Spectators descended from the stands, crushing forward or running through backstreets to the river bank where the final, cleansing act would be played out.

'Oot, John Heddington! Oot, Surly Andy! Oot, John Heddington! Oot, Surly Andy!'

The wind picked up once more and blew smoke from the ring back over the heads of those who followed. At first, the strands were thin and pale blue, but when the ring had rolled twenty, slow yards down the incline, some oily, black puffs appeared, and from where I stood I heard the sound of coughing. The crowd seemed to slow and put more of a distance between itself and the Wretch. The chants continued but I could hear other voices too. Then a woman shrieked and a huge, dark mushroom cloud appeared above the ring. The spectators pressed back. The cloud dispersed high in the air and all the smoke cleared. Two of the Winkie Boys braced their poles in front while the others moved in closer to

214

investigate the dead brands. I could see them talking to Roderick Macroom, pat him on the shoulder and on his head which pointed back up towards the square. Down in the smaller stand, the Wretch's father looked on anxiously and exchanged words with some of his companions.

Suddenly, sparks appeared from one of the torches and the Winkie Boys jumped back. A gentle, golden fountain sprayed backwards and someone in the crowd cheered. Another torch burst forth, then another, green. Quickly, a red shower followed, then a second green. Then another gold, and more, until each of the torches was alight. But as the last one lit, the first was in decline, and as the sparks died down, the crowd moved cautiously back towards the ring. I saw that Macroom had left the stand and was squeezing his way forward in the company of several other men who were dressed in the same tricolour robes. Left behind was the Crown Prince of Malabbar, deep in conversation with an old, sun-browned man, shrivelled in a pale cream suit.

Macroom reached the ring in time to witness the first of the Roman candles. The multi-coloured, fiery balls shot from the torches into and over the crowd, or up in the air where they hung and dissolved or burst in a radiant scintillation. Some people screamed and ran for cover but others cheered, thinking this was part of the scheduled entertainment.

As the last shot fired, the crowd closed in once more, but almost immediately scattered back when golden sparks reappeared from each tube on the ring. Gentle at first, the flares quickly increased in intensity, spraying four feet, five feet, six feet, more, beginning with a soft sizzle, then a whoosh, then a roar which shook the whole structure of the wheel. In front, one of the Winkie Boys fell and scrambled to the side of the road. The pole of the other snapped and the ring containing the smouldering Wretch began to roll slowly, then more quickly, down the hill, gathering speed with each revolution, accelerating through gravity and the impulse from those rockets which had never burned more brightly, even during the darkest fifth of November nights before the eyes of six children in the wooded gardens of Eckford House.

On and on, faster and faster, the Bannock ring rolled. The crowds drew back and pressed to the sides of the buildings, and in the park below people scattered in every direction. On and on, faster and faster, a golden comet with a dark heart and a tail of fire. On and on, through the gate, towards the pyre. Hit and on, without pause, as if on a ramp, up and over and through the air like a new sun to shine for a second, hover on the river then sink in dousing waves, a meteor-splash and steaming sizzle.

Bannock, squealing, screeching, ran to the bank of the Irk. Behind, I was calmness in the middle of chaos. Standing high above the town in my surgical collar, I could see rescuers pull a wriggling Wretch from the river and pump water from his still functioning lungs.

As I watched the main scene, on the edge of my vision I saw the small, wizened man in the stands grasp the arm of the Crown Prince of Malabbar. He seemed excited and was grinning wildly. He patted the bemused boy on the shoulder and made extravagant, circular movements with his other hand. While Bunter teeth were being gnashed, while Bunter hands were being wrung, Wallace Pumphry, Bannock's favourite inventor, was reliving the glories of his past.

Goodbye

I carried the smaller of my two pieces of luggage with my good hand, and with the other pulled a strap attached to a case which ran on little wheels. The streets of Bannock were empty, as they had been on the night I had arrived in the town. Where was Stan, the Polish Bunter? Down on the river bank, advising on artificial respiration. Where was Briony, the amateur pyrotechnist? Back in Eckford, drinking tea with her children. Where was Charlie Trummle, failed Wretch? Hidden in a secret viewing room, savouring his triumph.

I passed by the street which led to the boarding house, walked on, further from the noise and the smell of smoke, towards the station on the edge of town from where there was a view through high sandstone walls to the open hills.

There were few passengers around. This was not a day for travelling. Most people had more important things to do.

A middle-aged backpacker studied the timetable on the wall of the padlocked waiting room. A solitary mother tucked her baby more closely into its pram. A red-bearded tramp with a string-tied coat sat on a bench, violently swinging the boot on the end of his tight-crossed leg.

Ten minutes after I arrived, the bus for the city, for home, pulled out of Bannock. I could hear its engine labour as it took the steep hill road which, once climbed, would lead gently down to the flat land and, two hours beyond, to the familiar haze produced by a million breathing lungs.

But the driver left without me. I caught a later bus, whose destination board I did not read.

As I sat on my seat, studying the unfamiliar scenery, I felt tired, but I willed my eyes to stay open. I looked at my fellow passengers and smiled, and determined to stay awake until I arrived.